Who Am I

Who Am I

DENITA CHRISTFUL

authorHOUSE®

AuthorHouse™
1663 Liberty Drive
Bloomington, IN 47403
www.authorhouse.com
Phone: 1-800-839-8640

Published by AuthorHouse 12/02/2014

ISBN: 978-1-4969-2805-4 (sc)
ISBN: 978-1-4969-2806-1 (e)

Library of Congress Control Number: 2014912952

Acknowledgments

My mother, Edna Thomas, and brother, Nathaniel Thomas Jr.,
you are always loved and never forgotten.

My loving husband, Leroy Christful, thanks for not
complaining too much about all the long days and
nights of writing and for making this possible.

My daughter, Brandy Seabrooks, thanks for always having
an open ear and for all your encouraging words.

A special thanks to my granddaughter, Nyah Seabrooks,
for all the trips into the woods for the posies.

I love you all with all my heart.

Chapter 1

I woke up alone in a dark, cold place, with no memory of how I even got there. I could not remember anything about myself, and I had no idea who my family was or where they were. I was a little girl who could not remember anything. Who was I? Where was I? How had I gotten here, cold, hungry, and alone in this dark place with no memory, no parents, and no nothing, only me? Where was my family? Those questions haunted me.

As I stood up, I started to move around in the dark, looking around, calling out to my mom, dad, or anyone who would hear me. Only one voice echoed in the darkness—mine. What was going on? I was here alone with so many questions and no memories that could provide answers. I began to cry. I was afraid of the dark and even more so because I was outside in the dark with nowhere to hide. As I cried alone in the dark, my mind started to wonder if anything was out here that might harm me. My mind was full of what-ifs. It was so dark I could not see anything.

I kept moving on my knees until I felt a tree. I sat next to the tree, staying put, listening to everything and anything that sounded like something. Some of what I was listening to was in my mind—scary thoughts—and I heard the sounds of my own crying. As I listened, I drifted off to sleep.

The sun awoke me early that morning. At first, I thought the darkness of the night before was a dream. But before long, I realized it wasn't. I began to look around, still having no clue as to who I was or even how I'd gotten here. I was in the middle of woods that led out to a park or something.

Shortly after I awoke, I began to hear something. I followed the sound, and it led me to a woman sitting on a bench talking. I looked around to see whom she was talking to, but I did not see anyone else. She was alone. She looked scary; her clothes were dirty and torn. Her hair hung long from underneath a covering on her head. She looked up and saw me, and I saw sadness in her eyes. She kept talking to whoever she was talking to. I wasn't ready to move from the tree I was still standing by. I wanted to know if this woman was a good scary woman or a mean scary woman. She looked up at me once again, still saying nothing. She looked at me with a blank stare. Something in her eyes told me she was not that mean scary woman. She had a wagon that was full of bags, which made me think she might have food, and I was hungry.

As I stared a little longer, she stood up, took hold of her wagon, and began to walk away. I didn't know what to do. Should I stay put or follow her? But my feet were moving in the same direction she was going. I didn't want her to see me following her, so I stayed a little ways behind her, watching her closely all the while. I didn't take my eyes off her. She came to a big can and began going through it. She took something out of it and then bowed her head, closed her eyes, and began to eat. As I watched her eat, my stomach let me knew I wanted some of what she was eating.

I began to walk closer until I was finally behind her wagon. She took something else out of what I knew then was a trash can. She handed it to me. I took it and, not thinking about where it had come from or whether it might even be nasty, put the food to my mouth. But she stopped me before I could eat. She showed me how to bow my head, close my eyes, and then begin to eat. To me, nothing had ever tasted so good. I didn't know what I was eating. All I knew was that I was hungry and whatever I was eating was good.

Every time the old woman would move, I followed her. She went from can to can looking for more food. She shared some food with me and placed some into her bags.

She never said a word to me, but I knew she could talk, even though she remained quiet as if she couldn't. I broke the silence by saying, "Thank you."

She nodded her head as she continued to pull her wagon, leading us out of the park to a wooded area under a bridge. She knew I was behind her. She kept walking; never once did she try to stop me from following her. We finally made it to the bridge; she had so many things under it, as if she was living here. I was wondering if this was her place away from home, like kids have their tree houses. She had blankets and crates under the bridge. On the far side of the bridge was a small tent she fixed up like a little camp. She walked to the other side of the bridge and opened a crate. She pulled a large jug out of the crate and picked up an old can. She poured something into the can and stretched it out towards me. I came closer to her so I could reach the can. I began to drink from the can, realizing I was drinking water. I was thirsty. I drank every drop and handed the can to her saying, "Thank you."

She still did not say anything, only giving a nod.

She then went to retire on a blanket she laid out. She laid one out for me, and I went over and sat beside her on the blanket. I wanted to ask her so many questions. But she sat in silence, and so I did the same. I felt cold, and as I lay down, she wrapped the blanket around me. For once, I felt a little safe, not so afraid. I was with someone and not alone. Was she my mother? Was this our home?

I had so many questions for her, for anyone, but for now, I decided to keep the silence and fell into a peaceful sleep.

I didn't know how long I'd been asleep. But when I woke, I realized the woman was not there. I jumped up and looked around; yes, she was gone and the sun was going down. Her bags were still here; only her wagon was gone. Had she left to return to her home and left me here?

As a grip of fear began to come over me, she appeared, pulling her wagon. I felt a sigh of relief, glad to see her. She came and sat down beside me, handing me food. I ate, thanked her as I began to eat my food, and thanked her when I was finished. She still only nodded, not speaking a word.

She was as nice as a mom to me. Was she my mother? I really wanted to know, so I broke the silence with the question. "Are you my mom?"

She looked at me with a look of love in her eyes; yet the look also contained great hurt and pain. She never answered yes or no; nor did she even nod. She just offered a smile. I smiled back as she turned and looked away. We sat there in silence again.

I had to try again, even though I knew my efforts might lead to no response from her. Therefore, I asked, "Do you know me? Am I your daughter? If so, what is my name?"

I began to tell her that I did not have any memory of anything. I went on to ask, "Is this home? Why are we here?"

I also asked about my dad. Still she said nothing.

Then I asked, "Do I have any brothers or sisters?"

That final question seemed to bring sadness—her eyes filled with pain—but still no answers. She stood up and walked away. I felt bad, since I seemed to have made her feel and look so sad.

She soon came back to where I was; her face was still full of sadness and pain. I told her I was sorry for making her so sad. She smiled and patted me on the head. I was relieved and assumed everything was all right again.

As it began to get dark, somehow being with her, I did not feel so afraid. I felt the woman would protect me from anything. Her smile reassured me. She began to gather different things to take to the backside of the bridge, where she had a small tent. As she began to walk toward the tent, I jumped up to follow her. There was no way was I staying out here alone in the dark again. She went in the tent with me right on her heals.

She took the blankets out and laid them on the floor of the tent. I was so excited; it felt like we were on a camping trip. She had a big flashlight she would turn upside down for light. She zipped us up in the tent, closing us out from anything on the outside. I felt safe inside. In that quiet moment as I lay there, many questions and thoughts raced through my mind. There were so many unanswered questions that I wanted to know the answers to.

I knew I was not going to get any answers tonight, so I closed my eyes and fell asleep. As I slept, I began to dream I was lost, alone, and running. I could not find my mother anywhere. I saw many children with their mothers, but I could not find mine. I was all alone in my dream crying. I must have awoken the woman crying in my sleep. When I woke, she had her arms around me just as a mother would. Even if she was not my mom, I clung on to her that moment as if she were. I was so afraid, and to have someone with me at that moment made a big difference. She laid me back on the blanket, covered me once again, and kept her arm around me. She began humming a little tune to comfort me. It was the most beautiful sound my ears ever heard. She continued humming it in a low tone; it was beautiful. She never once looked down at me. I tried my hardest not to move, thinking if I moved she would stop humming. I lay as still as I could and listened to the beautiful sound coming from her voice. My eyes began to get heavy, even as I tried with all my might to keep them open. Sometime, while listening to the beautiful sound of her soothing voice, I drifted off to a peaceful sleep.

Chapter 2

*M*y eyes opened early that morning. The old woman was not in the tent. She left it open, so I was able to look out and see her. I could see her from a distance in the woods. I walked toward her and noticed a small stream of running water. She was filling her jug with the water. It was beautiful back here in the woods, away from everyone. The only sounds were the chirping of the birds. For once, I did feel like a family with her.

I went to offer her a hand; she showed me how to fill the jug up without getting dirt in it. As we walked back to the bridge, she placed the jug back into her crate.

She had some more food for me; again, I took the food, bowed my head, and closed my eyes, never saying anything. This ritual before eating became an everyday routine. She always bowed her head and closed her eyes before eating. Therefore, I did so too. As I sat there eating the food, I did not think once about where it had come from. I was only thankful and ate.

My mind constantly wondered why she was out here and not at home. I had no memory, but I somehow knew people lived in houses, not in a tent in the woods. Then I thought about how, if she wasn't out here, I would be out here alone with no one and nowhere to stay. I was so grateful to be out here with her in her tent. I didn't know her name. I didn't even know my name. As I looked at her, I could feel sadness for the both of us. Maybe something happened to us, leaving her like she was and me with no memory. Was that why she looked at me with so much love but sadness in her eyes?

When I finished eating, she came over to me with clothes in her hands. She handed them to me. They were not the best of clothes, but they looked much better and warmer than the ones I had on. I felt like a child in a store getting new toys. I was happy to get the clothes, which were new to me. I put on the first item. The sweater was a little too big on me, but it didn't matter. It was the perfect size in my eyes. I slipped on the jeans. They dragged on the ground, so she folded the bottoms until they were the perfect length. I hadn't had any socks on, so when I saw the socks, I was all smiles. I looked up at her and said, "Thank you." She nodded her head and smiled.

I was a child with many unanswered questions, living with a woman in a tent in the woods, a woman who talked to herself but not to me. I still didn't know whether or not she was my mom, but she was all I had. She had so little, but she showed me so much love. I knew I was going to stay out here with her, whether she was my mom or not.

I looked around for the bathroom. I did not know where it was, so I asked the woman. She still did not answer me; she just took my hand and led me a little ways off in the woods. We came across a board lying on the ground, she pushed the board aside, and there was a hole in the ground with a toilet seat covering it. She turned the opposite way to give me privacy. I sat on the toilet seat, used the bathroom, and then I thought to myself, *I don't have any tissue.* She must have read my mind. Just then, she pulled some paper out of her pocket and handed it to me. It was not soft, but it did the job. I stood up, pulled the board back over the toilet seat, and walked back with her she. She showed me where to wash my hands. *How long has she been out here?* I wondered.

Maybe I'd been here with her all along, and that was why she was keeping me here with her. She taught me that, even though living the way we were was, there were many ways to survive. She took me to different places to get food, mostly trashcans behind grocery stores. We would only go at night when crowds of people weren't around. She never took me out where there were people. I often wondered why. I learned quickly, though, not to ask any questions, since no answers would follow them.

Many mornings, she would wake up early and leave. If she did not want me to go with her, she would put her hand out signaling me to stay. I felt sad when she wouldn't take me. But I always obeyed and stayed behind, waiting for her return. I could always tell when she was going by herself. She would wake me early, give me something to eat, and then set my food aside for later that day. When she would do this, I knew she was going to be gone for a while. When she did return, she would have many good things, even fruits at times.

For once in my life with her, I was starting to be happy. I only wished she would talk to me. I would listen to her talking to someone, but she was always alone. I could never understand what she was saying, but I really wanted her to talk to me like that. I constantly wondered why she chose to talk to no one when I was here with her and she could talk to me.

After staying with her awhile, I had gotten used to her not talking and just learned to accept the smiles and nods she gave me. Even though we did not have much, I learned to love and be thankful for what we did have. Whenever she would leave and return each day, she always tried to bring me something special, which may not have meant much to others, but to me, it meant a lot and was always special to me.

I never knew what to call her, so I did not call her anything. When I wanted something, I would just ask. We both enjoyed each other's company. Maybe that's why I never tried to leave and she never tried to push me away. Neither one of us wanted to be alone.

Whether or not she was my mom, she taught me to do many things. She taught me how to take a bath from a bucket. She brought soap, but I did not have a washcloth. So I used an old sock that was too large for me to wear. Once I was finished bathing, she taught me how to wash the sock out. She brought me a toothbrush and toothpaste and showed me how to brush my teeth morning and night. She would not do my hair often, so she brought me a brush. That way, I could keep my hair brushed daily. She gave me a hat to wear in the winter, and when summer came, she brushed my hair at times and would tie a scarf around my head in a bow. I learned the basics to living in the woods. We were surviving off little to nothing, but somehow we always got by.

During the winter, it was cold, sometimes unbearable. We would stay inside the tent most of the time during the day, until the sun came out, warming up the outside. She had plenty of blankets that kept us warm while we slept during the long, cold nights. I did not have a coat, only the sweater she gave me along with a poncho she'd made me out of one of the blankets; that kept me warm during the day. It was extra wide and long, so I could wrap it around me to stay extra warm.

Over the years we lived in that spot, no one ever came around. It was extra dark during the night, and sometimes, her flashlight would go out and she wouldn't have batteries. We would go into the tent to get everything just right before dark. When the darkness fell, we would already be in bed and ready to go to sleep. It was scary without any light, but I felt safe knowing we were in the tent together.

Early one morning, something was strange about the woman. She was not out of bed like usual. I had never before woken up and found her still in the tent, let alone in bed. I got up, trying to be as quiet as I could. She turned over and looked at me with a smile. I unzipped the tent and went outside. It was a beautiful day; I began to walk around, thinking she would be out soon.

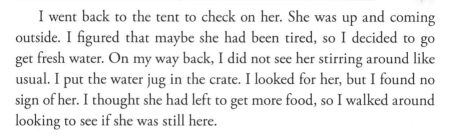

I went back to the tent to check on her. She was up and coming outside. I figured that maybe she had been tired, so I decided to go get fresh water. On my way back, I did not see her stirring around like usual. I put the water jug in the crate. I looked for her, but I found no sign of her. I thought she had left to get more food, so I walked around looking to see if she was still here.

As I walked back toward the side of the tent, my heart seemed to stop beating. There she was, lying face down on the ground. I ran to her and rolled her on her back. She still did not move, and her eyes were not open, so I started to shake her. I wanted to call out her name, but I did not know it. As long as we'd been here together, we'd never known each other's names.

I began to cry, pleading with her, "Please wake up." I continued shaking her and begging her to wake up. She still made no response.

I was terrified, and I didn't know what to do. I didn't know anyone to ask for help. All we had was each other. I knew something was badly wrong with her. I didn't want anything to happen to her – not to the only person I had in this world. I bent down and kissed her as tears rolled down my face. I told her I was leaving to get help. I promised her I would be back with help.

I stood there for a moment, not knowing which way to run or to whom to go. I started running from the woods with tears falling. This was like my dream. I was running and crying, not knowing where to go. I just knew I was with someone I had grown to love who needed help. It was up to me to go find help.

I went back to the place where I had first found her. I figured that, if food was in the cans, someone had to be putting the food in there. When I arrived at the area where the cans were, I did not see anyone. It felt as if I had been running for days, although it had only been minutes.

I kept running, with tears flowing. I knew I could not stop; all I could see was the image of her in mind, lying helplessly on the ground.

When I finally stopped running, I was out of the woods. I heard some voices but did not see anyone at first. From over the hill came a man and woman running at a slow pace. I ran toward them, almost out of breath and still crying. They finally saw me and stopped in their tracks as if they had seen a ghost. I kept running toward them but looked back to see if something was behind me that had made them stop so quickly. They both started running again, moving toward me. I was scared, but I wanted them to help the woman.

They both asked many questions at the same time. The woman asked, "Where are your parents?" The man asked, "Are they okay?"

I answered, "No," to both of them.

The man had something in his hand he was talking into. He was telling someone where we were and telling him or her to hurry.

The woman asked, "Could you take us to your parents?"

I finally caught my breath and said, "She will not wake up."

The man started talking to the thing he had in his hand again, asking someone to come with a wagon. I told him we had a wagon. I did not know he was referring to an ambulance. I said, "Please help her, please."

We hurried back to the bridge. They both came to a halt when we'd finally arrived. They just looked around for a second. I waved for them to come toward me. The woman was still lying on the ground. They ran toward her and began trying to help her. The man lifted up her head and started pushing on her chest. I broke loose from the woman, trying to stop him. I did not want him to hurt her.

The woman grabbed me and told me he was only trying to help her breathe. "That is how you help her to breathe," she explained.

I looked on, not trying to stop them. I had to trust them; they were all the help we had at the time.

Suddenly, I heard all kinds of noises. Soon people were running from every direction. The man was able to gather up many more people to help. The people were doing all sorts of things trying to help the woman. I had never been more afraid in my entire life. Someone took me to the side to see if anything was wrong with me. Everybody kept asking question after question. The one question they kept asking me was my name. I didn't know my name, so I didn't answer that question. I didn't want to seem rude, but I didn't know the answers to any of their questions.

One question the man asked was, "Is she your mom?"

Tears started rolling down my face once again. All the love the woman had shown me through her caring eyes, her smiles, and even her head nods poured out of me and straight back to her. Even though I didn't know whether she was my mother, I felt the same love a child has for a mother. So out of all the questions he asked, this one made me open my mouth and answer. "Yes," I said.

The man who was helping me smiled. "Everything's going to be all right," he told me.

Deep down within, somehow, I knew that not everything was going to be all right. As I watched the people I didn't know put the woman I now called my mom on a stretcher, I was terrified. The man assured me she was going to the hospital so she could get more help.

The people who were taking me also wanted me to go, but I wanted to know why.

The man responded, "They want to make sure you are all right."

In my mind, I wondered if they could help me remember, so I went along without putting up a fight. They put me in the ambulance with her. They kept doing things to help her all the way to the hospital.

Chapter 3

Once we'd arrived at the hospital, the nurses took the woman from the ambulance and ran in with her. Someone picked me up and laid me on a stretcher. People were coming from everywhere. I was looking for the woman; they had her in a room. People were standing around crying. I was taken into another room.

The nurse told me she wanted to check to make sure I was okay. First, she looked into my ears and then my mouth. She examined me from head to toe, and as she did so, she asked many questions. I did know the answers to them, but I did not answer. I had learned by staying with the woman that, sometimes, keeping quiet was best.

The nurse said she was going to give me a bath, wash my hair, and give me a clean gown to put on. She helped me take off my dirty clothes. I didn't want to give them to her. I couldn't let them out of my sight; they were all I had. She said she would place them in a bag for me. I let the clothes go, and she got the water ready for my shower.

This was the best feeling, being in a shower with running water. I did not want to get out of the warm water. I took a long shower and washed my hair. When I got out, I put on the gown the nurse gave me. The nurse told me to get in bed after I took my shower. Soon someone came in with a tray of food. The food smelled so good. I was hoping it was for me. I ate it as if it were my last meal. I could not believe how warm and good the food tasted. I finally had a drink that was not water.

When I did stop eating, I looked up, and all eyes were on me. Then I thought that maybe not all that food was for me. Maybe some was for the woman. I stopped eating and pushed the tray away. I felt really badly that I had eaten most of the food so quickly.

The nurse told me to eat the rest of my food; she assured me that it was all right. She must have been reading my mind because I really wanted to eat the rest of my food. I gobbled it down quickly, not stopping until ever bite was gone. The woman was writing down everything I did. I wanted to ask why, but I didn't ask questions. When I was through eating, I lay back on my pillow. I had never known how it felt to be full. It was a good feeling. As I lay back, I closed my eyes and drifted off to sleep.

When my eyes opened, several people were in the room. There was a woman with papers and books in her hand. She told me her name was Mrs. Williams and that she was there to help me. She started by asking my name, my age, my parents' names, and my phone number. She asked me if I knew my address. The last thing she asked was why I had been with Miss Robinson. She had many questions that came with so little answers. *Who is Miss Robinson?* I wondered.

The woman said she was from family services and that she would help me. She was going to take me to a nice home. She said the family would take care of me and promised me I would have my own bed, plenty of food, and more children to play with. It did all sound good, but the woman and I had a home. It was not much, but it was our home.

Mrs. Williams then told me someone wanted to talk to me. It looked like one of the women I had seen crying as we'd come into the hospital. She sat beside my bed, tears rolling down her face and began to talk. "Hello," she said, "my name is Emma Robinson. I know you have not said much, but please talk. We really need answers."

She needs answers. I was thinking to myself. I needed answers to many of my own questions.

Emma started telling me who she was. When I understood that she was saying she was the woman's daughter, I felt as though I could not breathe. Maybe Emma was my sister, I thought. She asked me my name, but by that time, I could not have answered the questions even if I'd wanted to. I knew then this woman was not my sister and that the woman I had been living with all these years was not my mom. I was in shock, so I just listened to what she had to say.

"The doctor told me you said the woman you were with was your mom," Emma said. "I know she's not your mom. Who are your parents? Tell us and we can help you find them."

Tears rolled down my face. I was finally getting answers to some of my questions, only the answers came with great pain. Hearing her say the woman I had been with was not my mother was especially painful. Who was my mother and where was she?

She asked, "How did you get together?"

I could not talk about it; it hurt too badly.

She told me, her mother's name was Isabella, "but everyone calls her Bella," she added. She told me how her mother had disappeared after her sister's death. She went on to tell me the story.

Emma was nine years old when her little sister, Cassie, who was two years old at the time, got ill with a fever and died. She said it was as if part of her mother died with her little sister. From that day on, her mother stopped talking to anyone. One day, Emma had come home from school, but her mother hadn't been there. She had never seen her again, until she'd showed up here. She told me that her aunt worked at the hospital and that she'd called to tell her an ambulance had brought her mother in as soon as she'd recognized Bella. Emma said she could not believe that, after all these many years, her mother was still alive.

Emma asked me if I'd been staying in the woods with her mother all this time. She told me she had a little girl named Sadie. She also let me know her mother was in stable condition and doing well. She said she knew I cared about Isabella and reassured me that Isabella would be all right. She said she was leaving so I could get some rest and that she would come by and check on me later and maybe even bring her daughter, Sadie, with her. She then stood and walked out.

She'd had tears running down her face the entire time she was in my room. She looked just like the woman in the woods when she was sad. I was glad that she had her mother back but sad at the same time. I realized that Isabella was not going to be with me anymore. I began to feel all alone again. I was going to have to start talking to someone to get some answers.

The woman from social services said I had to go with her to a new home. I did not want to go with her to a new home. I wanted to stay with the woman I had been with, the one who had showed me so much love. I wanted to go to her room so I could be near her. Her daughter had said she was coming back, so I sat back and waited. I wanted to know how Isabella was doing.

Food came again, and I sat back and ate it all again. I even had a bathroom to use. The nurse came in. I pointed to the bathroom, and she helped me with my IV pole and into the bathroom. It was nice to have the bathroom so close. I could stay here maybe, I thought, as long as the woman from the woods was here. Everyone was nice here—if only they wouldn't ask so many questions. I looked out the window. It was raining I was glad to be in here where it was warm. I lay back, thinking of Isabella, and soon fell asleep.

The sunshine woke me early that morning. The woman's daughter Emma was sitting in the chair next to me. She looked so much like her mother as she smiled at me. "Good morning," she said. "Do you have anything you would like to ask me? I know I asked questions yesterday, even though you did not feel like talking. Now it's your turn to ask. I will answer all your questions if I can, okay.

"But first," she added, "I have someone who would like to meet you, and she has something to give you."

Her daughter, Sadie, walked in with a gift. She stood by her mom and held her hand out to me, offering me the gift. Her mom picked her up sat her on the bed beside me. I reached for the box and started to open it. It was the most beautiful doll I had ever seen. A big smile came over my face. I'd had one gift in my life—the clothes the woman in the woods had given me. This gift was almost as good as that. I had never had a doll before. We both looked at each other; she smiled, and I smiled back.

I looked at Sadie and said, "Thank you."

When I looked up at Sadie's mom, I saw tears rolling down her face. I did not know why she was sad all the time and crying. I was happy as I tore into the box to remove the doll. She was beautiful. I hugged the doll tightly. I knew I would never let the doll out of my sight.

Sadie said she would come back later and bring her doll and they could have tea together. I smiled and said, "Okay."

Sadie mother stood and said, "I will come back and you can ask your questions. Now I will let you enjoy your doll."

They both left, and I played the rest of the day with my doll.

More people came in asking questions, but I wasn't listening. My mind was on my doll and waiting for Sadie to return with her doll.

The nurse came in to give me more medicine asked if I wanted to "watch TV." I did not know what she was referring. She turned on the TV and turned to a channel showing cartoons. Between my doll and the cartoons, I never wanted to sleep. But sometime, while holding on tightly to my doll and laughing from the cartoons, I drifted off to sleep.

The nurse woke me and gave me medicine again. She said I had a little fever. I felt good, just sleepy. I woke in the middle of the night not feeling good. I was thirsty and sweating. The nurse took my temperature and gave me more medicines. I finally began to feel better that night.

The nurse came back later that night and took my temperature again. "Your temperature is back to normal," she told me.

I pointed to the TV.

"It's three in the morning," she said. But she turned on the TV, and I watched it a little while and soon fell back asleep.

The nurse with breakfast and the announcement, "Good news," awaked me. You are well enough to leave today."

Leave today. I thought. Where I would go?

The same woman who'd said I would go to a good home came in. She was all smiles. "Hello," she said. "I'm Mrs. Williams. Do you remember we talked about helping you find a home until we can locate your parents?" She said she was with social service and that she was going to be taking me to that home today. She told me there would be other children there for me to play with.

I held on to my doll tightly. I was sad that I would be leaving the woman who'd kept me all this time. Isabella—I could not get use to her name. I just mostly referred to her as the woman from the woods. I wanted to see her before I left. I wanted to talk to her and see if she was doing okay. When Mrs. Williams left, I decided to go find the woman,

Isabella, and have a see for myself that she was doing okay. I really just wanted to see her.

As I was getting out of bed, her daughter Emma was walking in. She had a smile on her face and sat down in the chair next to the bed. "I heard the good news," she said. "You will be going home today."

Home, I thought. Where was my home? I knew I was going to someone else's home. I kept quiet and listened.

Emma kept talking. "I came back to give you your turn to ask me questions. You didn't get to do that last time. Do you have anything you want to ask me?"

I looked at her. I knew this might be my last chance to ask her anything about her mom. My mouth opened, and I asked, "How is she, Isabella? Could I see her?"

Emma looked at me with tears rolling down her cheeks and a big smile on her face. "Yes you could see her," she said. She helped me out of bed, took my hand, and led me to Isabella's room.

There Isabella lay in the bed with her eyes opened just staring, not saying a word. I stood next to her bed, and tears formed into my eyes. I wanted so much to stay with her; it hurt to think about being without her. How was I going to live without her in my life? I knew Isabella was going to be staying with her daughter Emma and not in the woods anymore. I was going to a home. I should have been happy for the both of us. Only I wasn't. That sadness and pain I used to see in her eyes—I was feeling it now in my heart.

Emma stopped by the door so I could be alone with her mother. I knew I could talk to her, even though she did not talk back. I always knew she was listening to every word that came out of my mouth. Her smiles reassured me. I walked over. Tears flowed as soon as I saw her lying there. But through all the tears, I said, "Hello. I miss you. I am sorry for all that has happen, but I'm glad you're better. They are taking me away today. I don't know where. They said it would be a nice home for me until they found my parents. I am going to miss you so much. Thanks for letting me stay with you and taking good care of me. I will never forget you and all the love you showed me. How am I going to live without you?" I took hold of her hand said, "I know you are not my mother. Your daughter told me. But to me, you will always be my special mom." I threw my arms around her and said, "I love you and always will. You will always be special to me, and I will never forget you and never stop loving you. And I promise I will be there for you like you've always been there for me."

As I turned to walk away, I felt her grip on my hand tighten. A smile came over my face. I looked back at her, and she smiled as we looked at each other. She looked sad, and tears rolled down her face. I wiped her tears and she reached her hand and tried to wipe mine. She then gave me a pat on the head.

By that time, her daughter Emma was standing closer to us. I told Isabella I was glad she had her family. I turned and walked away, but I stopped at the door and looked back. We held each other's gaze, and I saw the same sadness in her eyes that I knew she saw in mine. But her smile gave me hope that everything would be okay.

Her daughter took my hand walked me back to my room. I sat down, waiting on Mrs. Williams. Emma said that was the first time her mom had responded to any one since she'd been here at the hospital. I began to tell her how I'd met her mom and how I couldn't remember anything about my family or myself. As we talked, she looked at me with the face of her mom. With much love but sadness, she reassured me that I was going to be in good care and that she would stay in touch. She said, "Good-bye." She was going to talk to Mrs. Williams. She left, promising I would see them again.

Mrs. Williams came in with clothes—nice, clean clothes. I removed the gown and put on the clothes with a smile. She said, "I know it will be hard at first, but I promise you will be just fine."

As we walked out of the hospital, my heart was very heavy and sad. I knew I was leaving the one and only woman I cared for deeply. That one woman who I'd started to love was all I had. I was leaving my only family behind.

Mrs. Williams saw my tears and told me it was going to be okay—that they were working on finding my family. "We're going to need all the help you can give us," she said.

I wondered what kind of help I could give them. I couldn't even remember my name.

Chapter 4

*M*rs. Williams said, "You will be staying with the Daniel family. They have two children staying with them—two girls around your age. They are all waiting on you."

I was happy that there would be girls there.

I held my doll as I climbed into the car. We traveled for what seemed to be all day. Then we came to a dirt road that led to a big country house with a fence around it. I could see the children outside playing and many toys. As we came to a stop, the children ran to the car and a tall woman came from the house. She had an apron on, and she was removing it as she hurried to the car. A man followed behind her.

Mrs. Williams began to introduce them all to me saying, "This is Mrs. Clara and her husband Richard Daniels."

They both shook my hand and told me they were glad to have me stay with them. Then Mrs. Williams introduced the girls. "This is Sara and Kaylin."

They were both smiling. The two girls looked the same age as me. They each grabbed one of my hands, and Sara said, "Let us show you our room. You'll be sharing a room with us."

That was when I knew I would be okay living here with them and that they were glad to have me.

Mrs. Williams looked and me with a smile and said, "You go ahead. Have fun. We will get you settled in later."

I ran off with the girls. The room was big. It had three twin beds in it. The girls could not wait to show me around. The first stop was the playroom. It was huge and filled with every toy you could imagine playing with. I smiled and knew I would love living here. Sara and Kaylin showed me around the rest of the house. Then it was off to outside. The yard was big. In it were swings, slides, and a pool. I could not believe I was going to be living here.

Mrs. Daniels caught up with us and told us to wash up; it was time to eat. I had smelled something good as we were going through the house. We all sat down at this big table, and Mr. Daniels said grace. The food was good and there was so much of it. I had started to feel right at home.

After we ate, we all went outside to play. We played with all the toys out there for a long time. When it was getting late, Mrs. Daniels called us in to take baths and put on pajamas. I ran in with the girls. Then I realized that I didn't have any pajamas. In fact, I didn't have any clothes at all, other than what I had on.

That's when Mrs. Daniels called me into the room and showed me a drawer full of clothes. She said, "This is your dresser. All the drawers have clothes in them, and they are all yours. Whatever you need, it will be in one of these drawers. Take your pick. They are all yours," she said again.

I could not believe what I was hearing or seeing. "Thank you," I said, a giant smile crossing my face.

She then showed me shoes and coats and gave me my own toothbrush. I was so happy at that moment. The girls were both waiting with smiles on their faces as big as mine was.

Mrs. Daniels said, "Off you go. Get your baths. And make sure you all brush your teeth well."

After our baths, we watched one TV show, and then it was off to bed.

Sarah and Kaylin were like sisters to me. We all got along so well. They said they would teach me to swim, since they had a pool. We all lay in our beds and talked about our families. Neither of the girls remembered their parents, both was killed in a car crash when they were smaller. They had been staying with Mr. and Mrs. Daniels ever since. Kaylin said she would never want to leave the Daniels family. To her and Sarah, the Danielses were their family.

Kaylin asked, "Do you remember anything about your parents?"

"No," I said, "not anything." I explained that I didn't even know if my parents were still living and told them about the only person I knew of as my family. "I used to stay with her," I said after I'd described the woman. "She took care of me. We didn't have a home like this. We lived in the woods in a tent."

They thought living in a tent in the woods sounded cool. I told them it was like camping, but things were bad at times, especially when it rained or was cold or the times when we didn't have food to eat. "The old woman always made sure I had food, even if she didn't eat," I recalled. "I love her and miss her so."

Sara and Kaylin were laying there listening to me talk, as if I was reading them a story. We talked until we were all sleepy. I was tired. As I lay in the nice, warm bed, I thought how being here was a dream come true. I was happy yet so sad. My heart was still with the woman from the woods. I thought about how she was doing at home with her family. I was glad she didn't have to stay in the woods anymore. But I wished she were still able to live with me. I missed her and wanted to be with her. I loved staying here with the Daniels family. Everyone was nice and treated me well. But it was not the same as staying with the old woman. The more I thought of her, tears ran down my face. And I fell to sleep thinking of her.

The next morning after breakfast, a woman came from social services asking all kind of questions. I tried my best to answer. However, I didn't know any of the answers. The questions were all about my family and me—the simple questions that everyone should know but I did not. I did hear someone say I was Jane Doe. I figured they knew more than I did, so I start telling everyone who asked that my name was Jane.

I started school, and Jane was the name I used. I loved going to school and learning, but playing was my favorite part of the day besides lunch. I never knew you had to stay in school so long. I had to learn everything. I didn't know anything that I should have known. Everything was new to me—I didn't even know or understand the little, simple things. But over time, I finally started to fit in and things became much easier for me.

Somehow, at the end of the school year, I passed. I had studied extra hard, and it had paid off for me.

Summer came and then winter again. Time had gone by so quickly for me. I was doing great in school and living with a great family. As the years went by, no one ever had any information on my family. People would still come and ask me questions, the answers to which I didn't know, but not as often now. I had been living with the Daniels's for a long time, and I enjoyed staying with them. However, I could never feel the closeness and love for them that I'd felt with the woman from the woods. I missed her so much. A day never went by that I did not think of her in some way.

One night when we were all in bed, I felt somehow strange. I thought it was because of all the extra running I'd done that day. I lay there not thinking too much, about what the feeling could mean and soon drifted off to sleep.

I dreamed of a woman who said her name was Natasha Summers. She said she was my mother. In the dream, I said she could not be my mother. She was different from me. She had skin that glowed like a light. "No," I told her, "I am not your daughter."

She went on to tell me there were things I need to know about myself. She said I was different from others—that I was special. She said she could only talk to me through dreams until I learned how to communicate to her through my mind. She told me no harm could come to me while I was here and said how much she missed me and my father and that she loved us so much.

When I woke, I could not put the dream out of my mind. Was it just a dream and no more, like a nightmare? I knew I was supposed to report all dreams with information about my family so the social workers could help. However, I decided not to say anything about this one.

All I could think about was the dream. I tried to push it out of my mind, but somehow it would pop back up and I found myself replaying it repeatedly throughout the day. I got through the day without saying anything about my dream.

The next morning, I woke up to Mrs. Daniels on the phone crying. She was very upset after the phone call. She and Mr. Daniels went outside, and they talked for a long while. When they came in, they told us all they wanted to talk to us.

"I'm going to have to go away for a while," Mrs. Daniels told us. She explained that her mother had taken ill and needed surgery and that she was going to have to stay with her for a while. "That means you all will be moving to stay with another family," she added. She assured us the change would be temporary and concluded, "I don't know how long I'll have to be with my mother." She looked sad as she was talking to us. And she said that she hated all this but her mom needed her. She would be leaving in three days.

I started to feel bad because I loved living with the Daniels. Mrs. Daniels said all three of us girls would be together. I hoped that the family would be as nice as Mr. and Mrs. Daniels and that they would have cool things too. I hoped Mrs. Daniels would not be gone long, so we could come back here to live.

The next day, another couple came to the house. Mrs. Daniels called all of us in to meet the couple, Mrs. Mary and Mr. Jake Fuels. She told us we would be staying with them until she returned. They had a son, Teddy, who was ten. Mrs. Daniels said, "Mr. and Mrs. Fuels will pick you up tomorrow morning." The Fuelses told us all they were looking forward to us staying a while with them.

We were all sad as we packed our clothes that day, and it was very quiet around the dinner table that night. Mrs. Daniels said, "I will call you often. Cheer up; you are going to enjoy the stay with the Fuels."

We were up early the next morning, all packed, ready, and waiting. Although I was heartbroken, I tried not to show it. Mrs. Daniels was already sad about her mom. I had heard her crying throughout the night. We hugged Mrs. Daniels good-bye, and she told us she would call us to check on us. I thought *that's what Emma Robinson said*. I had not heard from her but once.

Chapter 5

*M*r. and Mrs. Fuels arrived early that morning. We all got into the Fuels car teary eyed, not talking at all. The Fuelses told us they lived on a farm and we were going to have lots of fun during our stay. We listened to Mrs. Fuels talk, but none of us said a word.

We arrived at the Fuelses' home in the country. It was nice and large, and they had many animals. They did have a swing and a trampoline too. They showed us around the house and the room us girls would share. It had a big bunk bed. Mrs. Fuels told us that two of us would sleep on the bottom and one on the top. She left it up to us to decide who would sleep where. I ended up on the top bunk, which I thought was cool.

Later that day, we met Teddy. Mrs. Fuels told him to show us the animals. He smiled and told us we would love all the animals. They had chickens, ducks, and an animal that had beautiful feathers. Teddy said it was a peacock. They even had horses. He told us we could help feed them during feeding time so they would get to know us. He also took us to a place that led to a pond where the ducks were swimming. It was quite and beautiful and Teddy explained that the family fished here. He told us he would teach us how to fish but only if we weren't afraid of worms. I started to have a good feeling about this place. They didn't have a pool and things like the Daniels had, but all the animals made up for it.

Teddy said, "You'll be busy every day keeping up with everything. You'll see."

That evening, we all had dinner. Life here was different than it was with the Daniels. I wanted to watch TV, but the Fuels family went to bed early.

We girls lay in the bed that night and talked about the animals. We couldn't wait to see them again. We talked about Mrs. Daniels. We were all missing her. I thought about the woman from the woods. I'd always end up thinking about her. It had been a very long time since I'd seen here, and I still thought of her often and found myself missing her. I finally drifted off to sleep.

It felt as if I had just closed my eyes when I was awakened by loud noises and talking coming from downstairs. Teddy and his father were planning their day.

I could smell food cooking. I got up and went downstairs. When I peeked around the stairs, I saw that Mrs. Fuels was fixing lunches. I looked out the window. It was still dark. Teddy couldn't be going to school. It was summer.

Mrs. Fuels was up and had already cooked them breakfast this early. I watched her as she placed their breakfast on the table and then said, "Your breakfast is ready." After Teddy and his dad had eaten breakfast, Mr. Fuels, said, "Off to the fields."

I wondered *what are they going to be doing in the fields. It's still dark.*

After they left, I walked into the kitchen. "Good morning," Mrs. Fuels said. "Did we wake you with all the noise? Are you ready for breakfast?"

"No," I replied. "I never ate breakfast this early. It's still dark."

"You'll get used to the noise every morning," she told me. "You'll be up eating breakfast with us after a while.

"We get up early to feed the animals, water the gardens, and take care of all the farm work," she explained. "It takes a while to get it all done. That's why we get an early start."

I was sleepy but stayed up with her. "Are you sure you don't want join me for breakfast?" she asked.

"Okay," I said, "let me wash my face and brush my teeth."

When I came out of the bathroom and went into the bedroom, Sara and Kaylin were waking up. When they looked at me, I told them, "Get up and wash up. Breakfast is going to be served."

They both looked at me with questioning eyes. "This early?" Sara asked.

I smiled and said, "Yes."

Mrs. Fuels smiled as we walked into the kitchen and said, "You all are up early."

We had pancakes, eggs, and sausage. "After breakfast, you girls can help me collect the eggs," Mrs. Fuels said.

I asked, "Do we get them from the store this early?"

She laughed and said, "No. We have chickens. They lay eggs. You ate some with your breakfast."

I had to say the eggs were good.

After breakfast, we all went out to the big coop. It was absolutely filled with chickens. Mrs. Fuels showed us how to feed the chickens by throwing corn on the ground. The chickens came running from everywhere. Sara, Kaylin, and I ran, thinking the chickens were after us. Mrs. Fuels laughed and told us to come back. They were only running for the corn. They wouldn't harm us. While the chickens were eating, she showed us how to look in the hen boxes for the eggs. All of the boxes had eggs in them. Mrs. Fuels had a bowl into which she put the eggs.

After we were done with the chickens, she said, "Off to feeding the cows." She showed us how to put water in the long water bucket and how to throw the hay the cows ate. She said, "We do have to clean out the stalls when they are dirty."

They were clean today, and I was glad about that.

"We're going to pick figs and other fruits today," Mrs. Fuels told us. "With some of the fruit, we'll be making jelly."

I saw why the Fuels family got up early. There was a lot of work to do.

We girls enjoyed helping Mrs. Fuels do it all. Soon it was hot, and she said, "It's time to go fix lunch. Mr. Jake and Teddy will be back soon."

I commented that they'd taken their lunch with them that morning.

She smiled. "No. That was more like a snack for them," she explained. "They're replacing the old fence poles. They will be hungry."

We went back to the house to make lunch. Mrs. Fuels said she was going to fix club sandwiches. She even let us help put different pieces of meat on the toasted bread. She made a pitcher of fresh lemonade. She had some long pickles that she said were good on the side with the sandwiches.

Mr. Fuels and Teddy arrived, and we sat down to eat lunch. The sandwiches were good with the pickles, which were somewhat sweet.

Mrs. Fuels smiled as we asked for more pickles and said she would show us how to make the pickles one day.

After lunch, Mr. Fuels and Teddy left on the tractor with their wagon full of posts. Riding on the wagon looked like fun. We stayed to help Mrs. Fuels with the rest of the work. It was a lot of work. After we finished with the animals, we went straight to the garden. The Fuels family grew many vegetables—greens, corn, cabbage, and some kind of peas. We even picked figs and apples after we were done in the garden.

Finally, Mrs. Fuels said it was getting late and we had better call it quits for the day so we could get dinner started. It was late. The time had gone by quickly. We had spent all day working on the farm. We helped with dinner also. There was always something to do here.

After we'd finished dinner, we all sat and talked about our day. I was tired, and I understood why they all went to bed early. I was not up for any TV. After our baths, I wanted to lie down and sleep. I knew we would be up early tomorrow doing it all over again.

We girls finally got used to getting up early, and soon we were all in the kitchen together eating and talking about our day and what all we had to do. I had to say, living on a farm with animals was fun but a lot of work.

When finally Saturday came around, we were still up early. Mrs. Fuels said, "All we do today is collect eggs and feed animals." She asked if any of us had ever ridden a horse.

"No," we all answered.

"Then we will have lessons starting today," she announced.

We couldn't wait.

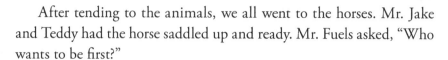

After tending to the animals, we all went to the horses. Mr. Jake and Teddy had the horse saddled up and ready. Mr. Fuels asked, "Who wants to be first?"

No one volunteered. We were all scared. Then Mr. Fuels picked me. I was scared at first, but after the horse had walked around a bit, I was all smiles. He handed me the ropes and told me how to pull them when I wanted the horse to go in a different direction. It was fun, and I was catching on well. When I asked Sara and Kaylin if they were ready to ride, they both said, "No." I was getting used to the horse, so I kept riding since Sara and Kaylin were too afraid.

After a while, we stopped. Teddy said he would show me how to brush the horse. "She likes a good brushing after a ride," he explained.

Sarah and Kaylin kept their distance. Teddy showed me how to brush the horse and told me I could give her a treat after a brush. She loved treats like apples and even a lump of sugar.

"What's her name?" I asked Teddy.

"We call her Daisy," he replied, pointing to a white spot on her side. "It looked like a daisy when she was born."

I loved that name. I brushed her and then fed her the apple. Teddy said he thought she liked me a lot. He said he do not get to spend much time with Daisy because he was busy helping his dad with the work around the farm. He said, "Daisy loves company."

I wasn't ready to leave, so I stayed a little longer, just brushing and talking to her. I found myself going to the stall with Daisy often. Soon she was used to me. She would walk up when I came, knowing I would brush her, and she was always ready for a treat.

Teddy taught me how to ride Daisy the correct way and all there was to know about riding.

One day, Teddy and his dad were going to take the horses out. They both had their own horse. However, Daisy didn't have anyone to ride her. Mrs. Fuels was busy that day and couldn't join them. They asked me to join them, saying that I could ride Daisy. I was all smiles and hurried out to help Teddy saddle Daisy up for the ride. During the ride, I was able to do all the things I'd learned really well. Mr. Fuels also commented on how well I rode. It was late in the evening when we headed back.

Once back home, I helped Teddy brush, feed, and water all the horses.

We returned to the house to a nice dinner. That night, it was hard for me to fall asleep; all the excitement of the day had me revved up. Still, I soon drifted off and fell into a dream that seem very real.

The same woman from the dream I'd while I was still living with the Daniels family was there again. She was happy to see me and again she told me she was my mother. Then she started telling there was something she needed me to know. She told me I couldn't remember things for a reason and that I would remember everything again when the time was right. She said she needed me to learn to communicate with her. "You will be able to talk to me through your mind," she told me. "You have to learn how to focus on me, but you have to believe in what you are focusing on. You have to believe I am your family. You have to believe in you. You have to accept who you are. Get a picture of me in your mind and focus only on me and nothing else. It is best to be alone when you do this. You have to pull me into your mind. You will know when I am there. You will be able to feel me there, and you will be able to see me. Then you can talk to me. Do not be afraid when this happens. It is the beginning of the door being open to what you can do. You will be surprised at what you can do through your mind. You will be able to see others even though you are not with them. You will not be able to communicate with them, only me. You will be able to help others and move things that will cause harm—all through your mind.

You will be able to do many things when you learn how. First, learn to focus and to communicate with me. Then I can talk to you anywhere and not just through your dreams. Practice using your mind and you will be surprised at what you'll discover about yourself.

"Sleep now," she concluded. "I will visit later, unless you break though and visit me. I love you."

I woke up soaked with sweat. The dreams were so real. Why was I was dreaming the same dream? I didn't know what to think. It was as if I could hear her voice telling me to focus and believe. I was beginning to think something was wrong with me. I had begun to accept that I was never going to remember who I was and had learned to adjust to living the way I was. Everyone I'd interacted with had helped me become the person I had become, yet I knew I was not the person everyone had shaped me to be. I didn't know anything about this person, Jane, who I suppose to be. Who am I? That would always be my question. Would I ever know who I was?

In my dream, the woman had said I was her daughter. Was she telling me the truth? Could all that she'd said be true? I looked nothing like the woman. I did not shine at all. My mind was all twisted. I closed my eyes and then opened them again, afraid to go to sleep, afraid of dreaming. Somehow, I drifted off to sleep even while I was trying with all my might not to sleep.

The next morning, all I could think of was my dream. I helped with all the chores. Mrs. Fuels kept asking if I was okay. I said yes and told her I was only thinking of Mrs. Daniels. I hated lying to her. But I could not come out and tell her about my crazy dreams. I had enough going on. I could not have the Fuels family, Sara, and Kaylin thinking I was crazy too. Mrs. Fuels told me she was sure we would hear from Mrs. Daniels soon.

In truth, my mind was far from Mrs. Daniels. That dream was all I could think of. I had made up my mind to try to do what the woman in the dream said—focus so I could talk to her. She had been doing all the talking in my dreams. I wanted to talk and ask her questions. I needed answers from someone; maybe I could get some from her. She said I was her daughter; if that was true, she should have the answers to all my questions. I thought hard that day and decided to try it. I had some hard thinking to do. I had to find a place where I could be alone.

"Jane! Jane?" I realized that Sarah had been calling me repeatedly.

When I looked up at her, she asked if I was okay. "You have been staring at the ground for a while," she said. "Is something there?"

"No," I said.

That day, I couldn't really get into doing anything. My mind kept going back to the dream. I could hear the woman's voice telling me to focus and believe. "You have to believe," she'd said. What did she mean by believe? Did I have to believe I was like her—that she was part of my missing family?

It sounded crazy, but I was willing to try. She had told me more about myself than anyone here had. My mind was thinking too much. I had forgotten where I was. When I looked up and saw Sara and Kaylin staring at me, I said, "No more talking right now. I needed a break."

Sara said, "No one is talking. All you were doing is staring at the ground."

They both raced off to look at the little chicks that had hatched.

I decided to visit Daisy. I visited her often, and I knew I could talk about anything with her. She wouldn't think I was crazy. I took her a treat, and I talked and talked. She listened very well. She made me think of the woman in the woods, who had never talked back but was always listening. Like the woman from the woods, Daisy always made me feel good about talking to her. I always felt better when I left from visiting Daisy.

Mrs. Fuels called everyone in for dinner. My mind was racing in many directions. I didn't know what to do. I couldn't eat; I had no appetite for food. Too much was on my mind.

Mrs. Fuels asked if I was feeling okay. I said yes, explained I wasn't hungry, and was excused. In our room, I lay across the bed and tried to clear my mind. It was no use. All I could think about was my dream. I began to cry. I thought about how my life had been and how I could not do anything to turn it around. I felt bad and could only hold my doll and cry more. I really needed my mother at that moment. I knew I was too big for dolls, but somehow the doll gave me comfort, so I held her tightly as I cried. I closed my eyes and fell asleep.

That night, I dreamed of the woman in the woods. Isabella was back in the hospital, and she wasn't doing well. I woke with tears in my eyes. I asked Mrs. Fuels that morning if she could get Emma's number so I could call her. She said she would.

The day went on as usual. Teddy and his dad left to do work around the farm. Mrs. Fuels and we girls kept busy with the animals. The day was fun as usual.

Mrs. Fuels called me into the house and told me she had Emma's number. When she pointed to the phone, I ran to it and dialed the number.

A voice on the other end said, "Hello."

I recognized Emma's voice. I said, "Hello," and told her who I was.

After a pause, she greeted me. She sounded grateful to hear my voice. She told me the caseworkers had told her not to contact me but to wait until I wanted to talk. She said they had been waiting. I told her that was crazy. I gave her the phone numbers at both the Daniels and the Fuels households and told her to keep in touch with me.

When I asked about Isabella, she paused and then said softly, "Mom's in the hospital again." I could hear in her voice that she was worried.

"Can I visit her?" I asked.

"Sure," she said, "but Mom doesn't respond to anyone."

I got the address for the hospital and said I would talk to Mrs. Fuels about going to see Isabella.

I asked about Sadie, and Emma said she was growing like a weed. Then I told her I would call her back soon and said good-bye.

I talked to Mrs. Fuels. She said she had already spoken with Emma and told me that it was okay if I wanted to spend the day at the hospital; she would pick me up later.

Chapter 6

*M*rs. Fuels and I stopped by the gift shop, and she let me pick out a bouquet of flowers for the woman in the woods. I could not wait to see Isabella.

Emma met us in the lobby. She and Mrs. Fuels talked. Mrs. Fuels told me Emma would call when I was ready to leave.

I followed Emma to Isabella's room. She was asleep. I put her flowers on the table. Emma said, "You could sit next to her on the bed."

I didn't sit but stood beside her bed. I felt sad all of a sudden—sad that she was sick again. I turned and asked Emma, "What's wrong with her?"

She told me the doctors were waiting on more test results but that they thought she might need to have surgery. Emma said she was going to step out for coffee and asked if I wanted anything.

"No thank you," I said.

I moved closer to Isabella's bed. I held her hand and began to talk to her. "Isabella, it has been hard living without you," I said. "It has been a long time since I last talked to you, and I am sorry. I wish that things were different. Sometimes, I wish it were just you and me still at your place in the woods. I miss you so much. I never wanted to leave you and stay with someone else, but I had no choice in the matter. I thank you again for taking care of me when I had no one. I had a dream of you last night." As hard as I tried, I couldn't hold back the tears, and they began to fall.

"I love you no matter who I am with and no matter how far apart we are from each other," I told her. "I will always love you." I stretched my arms across her, cried, and told her I wished she were well. At that moment, I didn't care who saw me lying over her and crying; all that was on my mind was her getting better and not having to have surgery.

This warm, tingling feeling came over my hands. I did not think much of it. I was worried about Isabella. Then I felt her squeeze my hand. I looked up. Her eyes were open, and she had a smile on her face. She picked up her hand and patted my head. A big smile crossed my face as I looked at the smile on her face.

Just then, Emma walked in. She was shocked to see her mother awake, and she ran and called the doctor.

The doctor came in and checked her, saying, "That she is awake and alert again is a good sign." The doctor ordered more tests and wanted them done right away.

I stepped aside and let the doctor and nurse do their work. Watching them working on her brought back so many memories. The people in the ambulance had said they were there to help her; only that had led to us going in different directions.

Emma was crying. She took me to the waiting room outside the room. She said, "Mom has been in a coma for a month. She hasn't responded to anything the doctors tried. You come to visit and Mom is responding, smiling, and patting you on the head. I think you have a connection between you two. You bring the best out in Mom."

I didn't know what Emma was talking about, but I was glad to see Isabella smiling and looking at me with the love in her eyes once again. I somehow felt and knew she was better. The nurses stayed with her for a while—until it was getting late. They did make it out so I could see her again before Mrs. Fuels came to pick me up.

I sat and talked with Isabella. She smiled and never said a word back, but the love coming from her weak eyes and the smile across her face was enough for me. I said I was with a new nice family and told her about all the animals the Fuelses had. I told her about the horses and how I'd learned to ride. I told her that I still had no memory of my family or myself but that I was happy to see her and see her feeling better. I said that I would have to leave soon.

In truth, I wanted to stay with Isabella. I never wanted to leave her—not now and not ever. But I told her I would keep in touch and call her. I stood up and bent over to kiss her cheek. She raised her hand and wiped my tears away.

I never wanted to say good-bye, so I told her I would see her later and that she was going to be okay.

She gave me a nod and a smile as Emma and I walked out of the room.

Emma had called Mrs. Fuels. I told Emma to keep in touch and let me know how Isabella was doing. She gave me a big hug and told me she would keep me informed and that I could call or visit anytime. Mrs. Fuels was waiting, and smiling, she told me Emma had told her the good news. "Emma will call and let you know how Isabella is doing after all her test results come back," she assured me.

I was happy that Isabella was better.

The next day, Emma called and told us that her mom was doing great. The doctors had said she wouldn't need to have surgery after all. Relief washed over me. Emma told me that I could visit any time; Mrs. Fuels had the address. I was glad to hear that I could go spend time with Emma and her mom. I cared for Isabella as if she was my own mom.

Teddy and his dad were going horseback riding and invited me to come along. They didn't have to ask twice. I was ready to go quickly. We saddled the horses and were off for the day.

That evening when we returned, Teddy and I watered and brushed the horses.

Mr. Fuels asked me if I was okay. "You were quiet during the ride," he said.

"I was thinking of Isabella," I told him.

I wanted so much to live with Isabella. She was more family to me than anyone else was. I felt different with her. I loved her and wanted her to be with me. I wanted her to be my mom. Or maybe I just wanted a mom of my own. I knew Isabella couldn't take care of me, as her daughter was taking care of her. I was glad I could go visit her.

That night, the woman of my dreams came to me in a dream again. Who was this woman? Was she real? All the things she was telling me. I didn't know for sure, but I was going to test it out and see. I would have to be by myself. I did not want anyone to see me and think I was suffering from more craziness than just memory loss.

That next day, I headed out alone after we were done with all the chores. I told Mrs. Fuels I was going for a walk so she would not miss me and think something was wrong. I walked to the pond. No one ever came here, and it was quiet and beautiful. I found a nice spot and sat down. I started by trying to focus. I thought of the woman in my dream, and I tried believing. Nothing happened. I tried again, thinking and focusing harder. Nothing happen. *Of course nothing is going to happen*, I thought. *It was only a dream.*

I stopped, got up, and walked around, looking at the squirrels as they ran from tree to tree and listening to the baby birds. I kept hearing a chirping sound that stood out among the others. Following it, I found a baby bird lying on the ground. I walked over to the bird and picked it up. Its wings were broken. I looked up in the tree. I could see the nest and hear the other baby birds chirping. I held the bird in the palm of my hand, rubbing its head. All I wanted was for the little bird to be better. I held the little bird close to me, closing my hands around it and wishing it were better so that it could be back with its family.

A warm, tingling feeling came over my hands as I held the bird up to rub it. When I opened my hands, the bird moved. Then it was out of my hand and on the ground. I leaned over, and when I tried to pick it up again, it flew up into the tree. I could not believe the baby bird could fly. How had it flown off with its wing hurt the way it was? Maybe the bird was not hurt as badly as I had thought. I could not figure out what had happened, but I was happy the bird was okay and back with its family.

I decided to give up on the focus thing, thinking it had all been just a dream. I went back to the house to find Sara and Kaylin on the swings laughing and talking. Mrs. Fuels came out of the house calling me. She said I had a phone call. It was Emma.

I ran to the phone, thinking something was wrong with Isabella. Instead, she had good news. She told me Isabella's doctors were releasing her. She was doing great and could go home with Emma. She said again that I was welcome any time.

I told her to tell her mom hello and I expressed how happy I was to hear she was better and going home. I thanked her for calling, and after I hung up the phone, I sat still for a moment, enjoying the feeling of relief.

Mr. Fuels came inside and asked us if we wanted to go with him to pick up supplies for the farm. We were all ready to go. We hardly ever went to the city with him. We all loaded up in the truck, and off we went to the city. The city was large and had so many stores that it took a while to get all the supplies and food for the animals. Going from store to store was fun. After Mr. Fuels had purchased all the supplies, we went to the candy store. We kids could pick some of our favorite pieces of candy. While traveling back home, we ate our candy and played games with each other.

When we arrived home, Mr. Fuels asked if I could help Teddy with the horses while he put away all the supplies. I really did not mind. It gave me a chance to see Daisy after we'd finished up with the chores. Teddy and his dad went to the house, and I stayed a little longer with Daisy.

Before long, I was getting hungry, and I knew Mrs. Fuels had cooked by now. "Good night, Daisy," I said.

When I walked into the house, I found a crowd of people. I was shocked because I hadn't seen any cars in the front. Everyone shouted, "Surprise."

I wondered whom they were talking to. I knew it couldn't be me. I didn't even know when my birthday was.

Mrs. Fuels walked over and stood in front of me. "Jane," she said. "This is your birthday party.

"We know you don't know when your official birthday is," she added before I could say anything. "But it has to be one day out the year, which means it could be any day. We know you've never had a birthday party, so this one is for you."

Tears began to fall—not sad ones but happy ones. So many people were here—even Emma and Sadie. I felt special as they all sang "Happy Birthday" and gave me hugs.

Mrs. Fuels said, "You run upstairs and clean up and change. Hurry."

I ran up to the room I shared with Sara and Kaylin. Mrs. Fuels had laid a new dress out on my bed. Next to it was a note that read, "I know you will look beautiful in this at your party."

She was right. The dress was beautiful, and I loved it. I hurried back to my party.

The party was great. I saw lots of food and a big, long cake that said, "Happy birthday, Jane." I was the happiest girl in the world at that moment. I never had a party and had no idea how much fun it was, especially at your own party. We played games, danced to music, ate food, and then enjoyed cake and ice cream. Then it was time to open my presents. Everyone had given me nice things. We all laughed, danced, and ate until it was getting late and the party ended.

Emma gave me a big hug and said she was glad to share my birthday with me. Sadie did not want to leave we were having so much fun. Her mom told her there would be other times. I told Emma to tell her mom hello for me.

When everyone had left, I told Mrs. Fuels, "Thank you for the party. It was the best day ever."

I helped clean up everything and then went upstairs. I was tired. It had been a long day, and had I enjoyed every moment of it. Sara and Kaylin were already fast asleep. I lay in my bed and thought of all the fun I'd had today. In my thoughts somewhere, I drifted off to sleep.

By the time I woke up the next morning, everyone else was already up, had eaten breakfast, and had gone outside somewhere. I dressed and walked into the kitchen. Mrs. Fuels was on the phone. She pointed to eggs and sausage for breakfast. I shook my head no and pointed at the juice. She smiled and poured me a glass of juice.

Once I'd finished drinking my juice, I walked into the yard. I didn't see Sara and Kaylin in the yard, so I decided to walk to the pond. I loved it there; it was my little spot where I could be alone, as no one else went to the pond. I lay on the grass, looking up at the beautiful blue sky with all the white clouds moving across it. I sat up. Looking around, I saw that a tree had fallen. I got up and walked over to the tree. I jumped on top of it, thinking I could walk across it. As I started to walk, I lost my footing and fell. My arm hit a sharp part of the branch that cut into it. I didn't feel any pain, but my arm was bleeding. The cut was deep; I could see inside it. I placed my hand on it, and holding it, I started to run toward the house. As I was running, I felt a warm feeling coming from the hand that I'd placed over the cut. I knew it was bad, and as I ran, I took my hand off the cut to check on it.

When I looked down, I stopped cold in my tracks I looked again. My cut was not there. In fact, I saw no sign of a cut ever having been there. I knew I wasn't crazy. I knew there had been a deep cut in my arm, but it was gone. Not a trace of the cut remained, only blood from the cut had been.

I knew I could not go to the house and tell Mrs. Fuels what had happen. The family would really start thinking I was crazy. I had enough going on in my life without adding this. I walked back to the pond. I didn't know what to think or do next. I thought I was crazy now myself. I knew something was different about me. What was wrong with me? I knew what had happened to me was real. But who would believe me if I told anyone? How had the cut gone away? Was I seeing things? No. I knew what I'd seen. I wasn't crazy. This had happened to me.

My mind went back to the woman in my dream. She had told me I was different from others. Maybe I was who she said; maybe I was her daughter even though I didn't look like her. My mind was going crazy. I needed answers. I decided to close my eyes as the woman in my dream had suggested. I would focus and try to talk with her. I needed to talk to someone. I could not talk to Mrs. Fuels or anyone else, I needed to talk to the woman in my dream. Maybe she could tell me what was going on with me. I had no other choice but to try to focus.

Nothing happened. What was I doing wrong? I was focusing just as she'd told me in my dream. I kept trying. Tears were starting to fall from my eyes. I had nothing else to do but cry. My mind was so confused. I had no one. I was still alone in so many ways. I lay there and cried and cried. I didn't know what to do. *Who am I? What am I?* I thought.

At that moment, I had no choice but to accept that I was different from others. I did not know how, but I knew I was different. I knew what had happen to me did not happen to normal people. I needed to know about myself. I just sat there for a moment longer in silence and cried.

I finally got up started walking back toward the house. I stayed outside, though, as I knew Mrs. Fuels would notice something was wrong. I could not bring myself to try to explain what had happen to me. I did not understand what had happened enough to explain it to someone else.

Mrs. Fuels called for me, and I went inside. She asked me to sit down, saying that she wanted to talk to me. She said she had been on the phone with my social worker and that they'd found a doctor who wanted to see me and who might be able to help with my memory. I thought that would be great. Then I would know who I was. I would know my family, and I could go home. I was excited over the good news, so much so that I forgot about what had happened to me at the pond.

Mrs. Fuels said, "The doctor is not here. You will have to take a trip in order to go and see him. One of the social workers will go with you and be with you every moment you are there. You will not be alone during any part of your stay."

I smiled when she told me I'd be flying on a plane. I had never flown, but I'd always watched the planes in the air and had always wanted to fly in one. "I can't believe I'm going to fly in an airplane," I exclaimed. I was thrilled.

But then I stopped and asked, "Will I be able to come back? Or am I going to stay there?"

She smiled. "No. You will only be there for treatment. Then you will be returning," she assured me.

I felt relieved. I did not want to have to move and leave everyone here behind for good.

She did tell me she wasn't sure how long I was going to have to stay there. She asked if I had any questions.

I had many but asked only one. "When will I be leaving?"

She smiled and said, "In two days. We have to get all your clothes packed and ready by tomorrow. You will be leaving early the next morning."

I thought this was good. I could get some answers finally. I felt good about this trip.

Mrs. Fuels told me to pick out outfits I would like to take and lay them on my bed. She would come later and help me pack everything. I ran out to the swings to tell Sarah and Kaylin about the trip to the doctor. They looked sad; they thought I was going for good. I told them I was coming back and added that I would be flying on a plane. They were excited about that. Neither of them had flown before. The rest of the talk was about flying on the plane and how much fun it was going to be.

The next day, Mrs. Fuels packed all my things to take with me. I also took my doll along. I couldn't wait until the next morning. I was actually going to fly on a plane. The plane ride kept my mind off all the crazy things that were going on with me. That night, I went to bed early, but I couldn't close my eyes and sleep with all the excitement of flying.

Mrs. Fuels woke me early the next morning. "You do not want to be late and miss your flight," she said. She told me to get dressed while she fixed me breakfast. Mrs. Suzan Winters, who would be traveling with me, would be here in an hour to pick me up.

I was happy Mrs. Winters was going with me. I knew her very well. I got dressed and went down for breakfast—my favorite, pancakes and sausage. Mrs. Fuels smiled and said, "Now eat up."

Mrs. Winters arrived just as I was finishing my breakfast. "Don't rush," she said. She was early. Mrs. Fuels offered her breakfast, but she politely declined, as she had already eaten breakfast.

Sara and Kaylin walked into the kitchen. "Sorry we woke you two," Mrs. Fuels.

"No," said Sara.

"We wanted to say good-bye to Jane," Kaylin added.

They both gave me a hug, and Sara said, "Remember everything about flying on the plane so you can tell us all about it."

Mrs. Winters said it was time to go. Mrs. Fuels gave me a big hug, and Mrs. Winters promised to call and keep her informed on everything that happened.

We left for the airport, and she told me she was happy to be going on this trip with me. I told her I was glad to be going with someone I knew.

Chapter 7

I was so excited when we arrived at the airport, which was huge. So many people were busy, going in all directions around the airport.

Mrs. Winters said, "We have our tickets. We just have to check our bags."

We walked in the direction of the counter where attendants were checking bags. You had to go through so much to ride on a plane; the whole process took what seemed like forever. Finally, we were done and waiting to board the plane. I stood in front of the big window looking at the big planes. They were much bigger here than in the sky in fact, they were huge. I was excited but a little scared at the same time. I had a funny feeling in my stomach. I went to sit by Mrs. Suzan, and she told me I could have the window seat; she said I would enjoy the view more than she would.

It seemed like forever before they called for us to board, but finally we were standing in line and ready to board. My heart beat rapidly as we walked through this thing like a tunnel, which led to the plane. It was huge inside. We found our seats. My eyes stayed glued to the world outside the plane's window while the flight attendant told us all about safety. I paid no attention; I was ready to fly high. A voice on the intercom told us to put our seat belts, stay in our seats, and get ready for takeoff. The plane finally started to move but very slowly. I could tell by watching how slowly things were moving outside the window.

Then the plane started to move faster and faster, and my eyes could not keep up with the things outside. When we were going really fast, we started to go up. The things on the ground grew smaller and then started to look like little ants. Then they were gone. We were high in the sky. The view outside my window looked different than anything I'd seen before, but it was beautiful and so peaceful. We could remove our seat belts. I tried to take notice of everything so I could tell Sara and Kaylin all about the plane ride. I could really see the clouds. They were so close, as if I could reach out my window and touch them. I couldn't believe how beautiful it was up here in the sky, and I wanted to capture every moment. I didn't want to miss anything.

After a while, the flight attendant came with snack and drinks. After the snack, Mrs. Suzan said I could lay back and take a nap. She explained that the flight was long and it would be a while before we landed. I lay back and tried to sleep, but it was hard. I didn't want to miss anything. I kept my eyes focused out the window. But they grew tired, and I was soon fast asleep.

Mrs. Suzan woke me, saying, "We have to put on our seat belts."

I asked, "Are we landing?"

She said, "We are going through some bad turbulence, and the flight attendants asked us to put on our seat belts."

I thought maybe we were going through bad weather. I looked out my window. It didn't look like bad weather; it was too beautiful for bad weather. I looked at Mrs. Suzan, and I saw in her eyes that she was afraid. The plane was shaking badly. Mrs. Suzan took my hand and looked at me with much fear in her eyes. I could also tell she was frightened by how tightly she held onto my hand.

I looked at her and told her, "It's going to be okay."

The plane's shaking grew worse I had never been on a plane, so I thought this was normal. I wasn't afraid at all. The same voice from earlier came back on the intercom to tell us we were going to have to make an emergency landing. The voice explained that the plane was having some problems that would force us to land but assured us everything was under control. We had to put our heads down and keep them down. The flight attendant was going over safety again.

I looked at Mrs. Suzan. She was crying. She kept telling me to keep my head down, and she was holding on tightly to my hand. I looked out the window before putting my head down. I could see we were going down fast. I put my head down and kept it down. I could hear people screaming and crying. That was all I remembered before everything went blank.

I must have been dreaming because the woman in my dream was there. She said, "Now is the time. You have the ability to do things. You have to learn to use your abilities to help everyone on the plane who is hurt. I will tell you how, but you will have to do it yourself. You will have to focus on what you want to happen in order for it happen. You have helped others, not realizing it. Yes, you healed your arm. Yes, it was you who helped your friend the old woman in the hospital, get better. Listen to me. You have to work with me, but you have to do it on your own. I need you to focus so you can be able to talk back to me. You can do it. You will be able to see and talk to me through your mind and not only in your dreams. Now focus. Picture yourself talking to me. Focus hard on talking to me through your mind."

I did try to focus on what she was saying, but nothing happened. I was trying. I could still hear her voice telling me to focus on who I was. She said, "You are of us. You can talk to me. Focus hard."

At that moment, I made up my mind. I was part of her; she was my mother. In my heart, I accepted that I was on this earth but not from this earth. I had to be part of her and the others she referred to as *us*.

That's why I was different. That's why I'd healed as I did. I accepted who I really was. I was part of her, the woman in my dreams. She was my lost family.

I opened my mouth and said, "Mother," focusing on her.

Only this time, she answered. "Yes, my child," she said. "You are of me, and you are my child."

I could not believe I could talk to her, like two people having a conversation. I asked, "Am I dreaming?"

"No," she answered. "You are talking to me through your mind. You have connected with me."

She went on, explaining gradually what I needed to do. "You now have to focus on where you are at this time," she told me. "You will be able to see your immediate surroundings and get an overall picture of how things are by focusing on a certain place. Focus on where you are on the plane. Look at your surroundings. Take in how things look, and understand what has happened."

I started to do what she told me. I focused hard, pushing everything out of my mind until I saw only myself on the plane. I did it. I could see the plane. It was down; we had crashed. I looked to where I was sitting, and what I saw sent chills through me. Mrs. Suzan was sitting there next to me, but I was not the girl I was used to seeing. I was one of them. I looked like the woman in my dream. I had a glow just like her. I saw myself for who I was at that moment.

I looked at all the people on the plane. Some was still in their seat belts, and some were crumpled over on the floor. But most were unconscious. Then I saw a little girl. She was hurt. Her leg was stuck under something, and she was crying. I could see everyone on the plane.

I focused on the woman in my dream, or my mother, and asked, "Is this a dream?"

She said, "Your dreams are always real. You are able to see things in your dream that are happening now, and you can even see things *before* they happen. You can also see things while you are awake and not through a dream. Don't be afraid when this happens to you. It's how I see you there. When you come out of this dream, you will see things just as they were in your dream. You must help the little girl and the others who are hurt. Lay your hands on their bodies and focus on making them better. You can do it. I love you and am proud so proud of you." She was gone as I began to wake up.

My eyes opened slowly. I could not believe what I was seeing. Everything in the plane was just as I had seen in the dream. The plane had crashed, and people were lying everywhere. I looked at Mrs. Suzan. She was out cold. I started to shake her, and she slowly opened her eyes. Good. She was not hurt. She threw her arm around me and started to cry. "Are you okay," she asked. She took her seat belt off and began to look around. Still crying, she said, "We have to start helping everyone."

I remembered the girl and ran in that direction.

Mrs. Suzan called out to me, "Be careful." She started helping everyone she came to.

I wanted to get to the little girl. I heard her crying and followed the sound. When I got to her, she said, "My leg hurts." She was only about two years old. Her mom was next to her; she was unconscious, but she was breathing.

I asked the little girl's name. Between her cries, she said, "Sammie."

I told her that was a pretty name and said, "I am going to pick this seat up off your leg. It will hurt some, but it will make it better."

She was still crying but said, "Okay."

I lifted the seat off her leg and saw the deep cut it had made. Her leg was swollen. I didn't know if it was broken or not. I didn't try to move her. I was scared and sad to see her in so much pain. I put my hand over the little girl's leg. I told her to close her eyes, and I began to focus as the woman in my dream had told me to do. I really wanted Sammie to be better. I kept focusing on her leg being better, and then I felt the warm feeling that was becoming familiar going through my hand.

When the feeling of warmth stopped, I took my hand from her wound. The cut was gone; her leg looked as though it had never been cut at all. "See, you're all better," I told her.

The little girl stopped crying. She didn't ask how I'd done it. She just said, "Thank you."

I helped her to her feet and said, "Now we can help your mom."

The little girl started calling her mom. I shook her, trying to wake her. Soon her eyes opened. I asked her if she was hurt.

She shook her head no, but I could see she was in shock as she looked around. She saw her daughter, grabbed her and started crying.

"She's fine," I told her.

The woman looked around, and I told her I was going to see if anyone else needed help.

I walked to the next person that needed help and helped each injured person as I came to him or her. A lot of those I helped were unconscious and never knew they'd been hurt.

Mrs. Suzan had found the flight attendant, and together they were helping people. They had the first aid kit bandaging up everyone who needed it.

I heard a voice from the back of the plane calling for help. I ran, following the sound of the voice and found an elderly man. He looked up at me and said, "My back is hurt. I can't move. Can you get me help please?"

I looked at him and could see he was hurting badly.

"I'll get help," I told him. I knew I had to try to help him and make him better but without him knowing. I saw a pillow and a blanket. I got the pillow to put under his head I could see the pain in his eyes as I tried to lift his head. I told him to lie still. I would put the blanket over him. Help was coming, I told him. I would stay with him until they came. I really hadn't gone for help when I'd left briefly; I just wanted him to think I had. I stayed with him, knowing I had to help him. I laid my hand on his stomach, closed my eyes, and started to focus on him being better.

"Thank you for staying with me," he said.

I had stopped focusing and was listening to him. When he was quiet again, I started to focus again on him getting better and not being in so much pain. I started to feel the warmth in my hand, and I knew he was going to be better.

After the warmth stopped, I knew he was better. He looked up at me and smiled said, "You know, baby, I think I feel better. I don't have any pain now at all."

I looked back at him and smiled. I was so glad he was better and not in pain.

He said, "Let me try to get up."

I removed the blanket and helped him as he tried to stand up. I noticed blood on the side of his head but saw no cut. He was able to stand up. He looked at me. "I haven't felt this good or been without pain in years," he said.

I told him about the blood on his face, knowing there was no cut and only blood, and pointed him in the directions of the first aid crew, where he could get it cleaned up. He walked toward Mrs. Susan and the flight attendant. I watched him go. He was walking well, clearly free of pain, and even stopped to help someone.

I couldn't believe the plane had crashed and what was happening here. With all the hurt people, I didn't have time to think of the changes taking place in me. I was trying to make sure everyone was okay, and what was happening with me hadn't really hit me.

I caught up with Mrs. Suzan. She said that everyone on her side of the plane was okay and taken care of. I told her the same was for everyone in the back of the plane.

"The pilot is trying to get help and give the rescue team our location," she told me. Someone else was outside, making sure we were in no danger by remaining in the plane.

The pilot came out. "Everyone will need to stay together on one part of the plane," he announced. "It's going to get dark soon, and the lights on the plane aren't working." He assured everyone that someone was working on the lighting situation, noting that two mechanics were on the flight. "We are working to get contact, and we will get help as soon as possible," he added. He then instructed everyone to start picking up things from the aisle. "We have to make it clear before dark," he explained. "We don't need anyone else getting hurt. Gather all the blankets and pillows and make sure everyone has one." He asked if two people would be willing to help the flight attendants, and two women volunteered. "Please stay together for your safety," the pilot concluded.

"We are sorry this has happened and are doing everything we can to get help here. The flight attendants will help with everyone's needs."

The flight attendants showed the two women who'd volunteered to help out where the food and drinks were and asked them to set themselves up in that area.

The man who was outside checking the plane and its surroundings said it would be safe for us to get off the plane but added that it would be important that we stay together. He said, "We have to account for everyone on this plane, and we need to be sure we know where everyone is."

The door opened, and the steps were lowered. Everyone got off the plane. We'd landed in a large open space. The plane had imbedded itself into the dirt from the landing. However, it appeared to be in good shape. At least we had shelter. Everywhere I looked, I saw woods. It brought back so many memories of the woman and me and how we'd lived in the woods. I knew that, if there were no lights, there would not be a bathroom on the plane. I thought of the woman in the woods and how she'd made one. I went back to the plane and found the flight attendant. I told her what I was planning on doing and what I needed. She gave me a shovel and a board. I asked if I could even get the seat from the toilet.

She smiled and said, "Yes, but we have an extra one in the storage room."

She even asked a man from the plane if he would help me. He thought it was a great idea. He helped from start to finish. We even used some stuff we'd found on the plane to build a structure around our homemade toilet for privacy. All we needed was some tissue from the plane. We even had a bucket so people could wash their hands.

Soon, we had our first passenger to test the bathroom. A girl named Noah had to go, and her mother asked if they could try it. We showed them how it worked, and they went in to test it. We waited.

"Good job," Noah's mom said when they came out. "It's the next best thing to the real deal."

More and more people began making use of our bathroom. Everyone told me that it was a good idea. I smiled and thought of the woman from the woods. I was glad she'd taught me so much while I was living in the woods with her.

Everyone outside was back on the plane. Someone took a head count to make sure everyone was on the plane. The flight attendants were bringing the food on the carts to us. We found a seat. Everyone was in the first-class section. The seats were still together and in place there. It was a lot nicer here. After we ate, we started to prepare for a night without lights. We had some flashlights.

It was good that we were getting started before dark, ensuring we had everything we would need. The flight attendant went over everything. She told us two buckets had been placed in the bathroom; we could use these as a toilet for the night so no one would have to go outside. A flashlight on the table in front of the bathroom door was for our use while we were inside. She reminded us to leave the flashlight for the next person. We got the sleeping arrangements in order.

Soon the night had come, and as the pilot had predicted, it was dark on the plane. The pilot said the doors would be locked so everyone could feel and be safe. Everyone was in his or her seats with a pillow and blanket.

Mrs. Suzan kept trying to get a signal on her phone but was unable to do so. I knew Mrs. Fuels would be wondering about us and trying to call. I thought about Sara and Kaylin wanting to know everything about the plane ride. They were in for the story of a lifetime. Mrs. Suzan said we would have made it to where we were going by now, which meant she was sure someone would be out looking for us, as it would be clear that something had happened.

Mrs. Suzan said we would be okay. Then she got out of her seat, knelt down on her knees, and started to pray. I listened to her, as she prayed aloud. Her voice wasn't very loud, but I heard her say, "Jesus, I am so thankful for your mercury and love. I'm grateful that you kept your hands upon us though this whole ordeal and that you guided us down safely without anyone losing their lives. Thank you for your protection. I know you have watched over each one of us here. Cover us with your blood. Lead someone in this direction. But until then, make a way for us. In Jesus name, amen."

She stood, laid our seats all the way back, laid down again, and said, "Sleep now."

For some reason, despite the fact that there was nothing but darkness, I wasn't afraid. I closed my eyes and slept.

I woke early. The sun was just starting to come through the plane's windows to give us light. I could tell that everyone was up by all the voices. I knew breakfast was being served. I could hear the attendants as they placed food on the cart. I thought that, even though the plane had gone down, this was still kind of fun. No one was stressing out, and we had a place to sleep, food, and water. I only hoped someone would rescue us before the food and water ran out.

Mrs. Suzan was up, but she seemed to be just sitting there in a daze. I asked her if she was all right. She said she was but that she had a lot on her mind. I knew what she was talking about I always had a lot on my mind. I realized that, in my excitement about flying, I had never asked where we were going. So I decided to ask now.

She looked at me and said, "You didn't know where you were flying?"

"No," I admitted. "I forgot to ask. I was just happy to be flying."

She looked at me with sadness in her eyes and said, "California."

I smiled and said, "Oh."

"Someone will find us," she said. I could tell by the look in her eyes that she was worried. But I somehow knew that it was going to be okay.

I had bigger problems going on with me than sitting here in the middle of nowhere in the woods waiting on someone to come find us.

I decided to get up and find the little girl, Sammie, to see how she was. I walked around and soon found her playing with some toys. She looked up, smiled, and held a doll out for me to play with her. "Hello, Sammie," I said. "How are you?"

"Good," she replied. "Want to play?"

Her mom smiled and asked if I could stay with Sammie until she got a drink so she could take her medicine.

"Sure," I said.

When she was gone, I asked Sammie how her leg was.

"Okay," she replied.

I asked, "Does it hurt any?"

"No," she said. "You made it all better."

I smiled and said, "No, we made it better."

Her mom came back, and I got up. I told Sammie I had to go but that I'd be back to play with her later. I wanted to check on the older man whose back had been hurt. I soon found him laughing and talking to another man. He saw me and said, "Hello there."

He told the other man how I'd stayed with him while he was hurt. He talked about how he'd been on the floor in great pain and unable to move and how he'd had to use a cane to walk. He told the man he didn't know what had happened to him but that something had happened. He'd felt a warm feeling go over his body, and all the pain had disappeared. Now he could walk straight as anyone, with no cane and no pain anywhere. "Thanks again for being there with me," he said, smiling at me.

I told him I was glad he was better, returned the smile, and moved on.

The flight attendant was coming with breakfast, so everyone found his or her seat. After breakfast, the plane's door was opened. It remained open throughout the day so that everyone could come and go as they pleased.

I went outside to walk around. I was careful not to go too far, but I wanted to be alone. I wanted to try to talk to the woman from my dreams. I started to focus, even though it was hard to say *Mother* to someone I didn't know. To me, the glowing woman was a stranger. Still, I called out in a quiet voice, "Mother."

She answered, saying simply, "I am here." She was standing in front of me. It was like looking in front of you and seeing an image of a person that glowed. That is how this woman who said she was my mother looked. She wasn't scary looking at all but sweet. She had a smile on her face, and somehow, she looked caring. She told me she was proud of me.

I told her I needed to talk to her. I needed some answers to many questions.

"In time, I will tell you everything you want to know," she assured me.

I asked her my name and then how old I was. Then I asked, "If you are my mother, why am I here alone?" I started asking questions, one after another, not waiting for her to answer one before going onto the next.

She stopped me. "We will talk later," she said quickly. "You're about to have company."

I looked up, and she was gone.

From behind me, I heard someone walk up and ask, "You okay?"

"Yes," I replied, without turning to see who was there.

"I heard you talking," the person said. "You sounded upset."

"I'm okay," I said. "I was just thinking aloud, wishing things were better."

"I know what you mean," he said softly. "Someone will come for us. The pilot and the others are working to get the radio going so they can let someone know where we are."

"Good," I said. "I'm going back to the plane." I turned and walked back to the plane.

I was still upset because I hadn't gotten any answers. I knew I had to be alone with the woman from my dreams for that. I settled for getting answers later.

Back on the plane, everyone was happy and shouting. I saw Mrs. Suzan. "I was looking for you," she called enthusiastically. "We have good news. The radio is working and the pilot has contacted the airport. They have our location, and help is on the way."

I was happy to hear the news. I was ready to get out of here. I needed to be alone to talk to the woman (or my mother). I needed answers. I asked Mrs. Suzan, "Are we still going to see the doctor?"

"I'll make some calls when we get out of here," she said.

I was happy and couldn't wait until help arrived. I knew Sara and Kaylin were going to be excited to hear about this plane ride—and crash. I couldn't wait to get back and tell them everything that had happen. Everyone else was happy too. The rescue team was looking in the right direction.

***

Then days went by and the rescues people hadn't found us.

"I have an announcement," one of the flight attendants said one afternoon. "The food and water is getting low," she told everyone. "We're going to have to drink only when we're thirsty to try to make the water supply last."

That was not easy. It seemed that, when the flight attendant told everyone the water was low, everyone was thirstier than ever. Soon, we were drinking only when we ate, unless you had a prescription that required water.

It was getting harder and harder for people to deal with not being able to get a drink when they wanted. Everyone started to get mad and fuss over food and water. I hoped the rescue people would come soon.

Chapter 8

*T*he pilot called everyone together to share more news. He told us the rescue people could not get a plane here because of all the woods. They said they didn't see how we had landed as safely as we did with all the woods surrounding us. They would have buses waiting on us in a certain area. A rescue team would be here to lead us to the bus. We would have to walk. He said he needed us to gather whatever we were going to carry in our hands and told us to make it light. He said not to worry about our luggage. Someone would pick our suitcases and bags up along with everything else on the plane. We were to take only our personal belongings. He concluded by saying he didn't know how long our walk would take and reminding us that the rescue team would be arriving soon.

Everyone was excited, and soon all the passengers were gathering the things they planned to take with them. Mrs. Suzan and I had only one small bag and her purse, so our load would be light. I noticed that some of the others had large items to carry. The flight attendants told them to lighten their loads. That night, everyone was happy. Knowing we would be leaving soon was a terrific feeling. All the passengers were thanking other passengers for the help they'd received from one another.

As much as I loved planes, I was also glad to be leaving this one. Mrs. Suzan asked me, "Will you be okay with flying again?"

I answered, "Yes."

"We have to get on another plane to go where we are going," she said.

I told her I was okay with planes, adding, "I loved this trip, even going down."

She looked at me and smiled.

I started thinking about everything that happened on this trip and what I had learned about myself. I knew I would never be the same. In a way, I was still learning more about myself and how I was different from others. I knew there was more about myself that I had to know, and I was ready to learn it all. I felt good knowing that I could help people who really needed help and keep them from hurting. I couldn't wait to talk to the woman in my dreams; I had to adjust to thinking of her as my mom. I had accepted her as my mother. I had realized I was one of her people, whoever that was.

I wanted to know why I had been left here alone and she was there, wherever there was. I closed my eyes, hoping to see her in my dreams and get answers, but it didn't.

I woke early the next morning to the sound of many voices. The pilot had called everyone together again and was going over all that we needed to know and do before leaving. He wanted to be sure that everyone would be ready. That night before, after everyone was lying down, Mrs. Suzan had gotten on her knees and prayed again. I'd listened to her pray for everyone's safety, and a good feeling had come over me as I listened to the calmness and sincerity in her prayer. Who was she speaking to with so much love in her words? After she'd finished, she had stood up and laid next to me. I didn't ask any questions. I closed my eyes and slept.

The rescue people had arrived early that morning, and everyone was happy to be leaving. A man from the rescue men was telling everyone what to expect. It would be a long journey through the woods. "I hope everyone's baggage is light," he said, stressing the point. He told us to each find a partner and to stick with him of her at all times; we were each to be sure and keep track of our partner. The man said we needed to leave as soon as possible if we were going to make it the buses before night.

The rescue team went over the plan again and then grouped everyone in twos. The flight attendants handed out sandwiches for breakfast and gave everyone food for later. Then we left, walking behind the rescue team. Mrs. Suzan and I were partners. We all walked in pairs in two double lines. I looked back; it was a long line. We were behind the old man who'd had pain in his back and leg. He was walking with no signs of pain. I hoped he would be okay during the long walk. No was talking much; everyone was busy walking to keep up.

After we'd been walking for a while, the rescue men stopped to let everyone take a break. Sammie and her mom were behind us. Sammie was beginning to get tired; she had been doing good walking. The men offered to take turns carrying Sammie when she got tired.

During our break as we were sitting down, Sammie said, "This is like camping." She said she was going to see her grandma and papa.

I told her I knew they were waiting to see her.

We started the walk again. Soon, we had been walking for hours, taking breaks only to rest. Many of the passengers were beginning to get tired, but the rescuers kept encouraging everyone; they reminded us that, if we just kept walking, we would reach the bus before night and pointed out that it would be much harder to walk in the dark. No one wanted to be walking through these woods in the dark, so no one asked for breaks any more. We just kept walking.

Finally, one of the rescue team said, "We don't have much longer. We'll be there soon."

The weather was good. It wasn't too hot or too cold. But I could tell everyone was tired, and our walking pace had slowed down. I was tired of walking. Many people complained of aches and pains they were experiencing.

Before long, it was late in the evening, and the sun had started to go down. Many of us were getting scared at the thought of being stuck in the woods after darkness had fallen. I thought about all the wild animals that might be in the woods and that might come out at night. I hoped we were getting close to the bus.

Finally, a rescuer announced, "The bus is just over that hill." He told us that, if we could make it over that hill, we would all be able to rest on the bus.

That gave everyone a boost of energy, and we started walking fast. Soon we had arrived at a long line of buses. I couldn't see the end of them there were so many. Ambulances were there for those who needed medical treatment.

We all climbed onto one of the buses. It was so good to be able to sit. No one talked; everyone was too tired. Those who stayed awake sat in silence, and others went to sleep. The entire duration of the long ride home passed very quietly, and I soon went to sleep.

When we made it to the airport, I saw reporters everywhere. Here too ambulances were waiting to provide assistance. A man from the airline came on the bus and told us about the reporters. We could talk to them or not; it was our choice. He told us that everyone would get a hotel room to rest in and assured us the airline had everyone's name and that someone would be contacting us. "There are ambulances if anyone needs to go to the hospital or a doctor," he added. Before leaving the bus, he told everyone how sorry he was.

I don't know what everyone else did. Mrs. Suzan and I could not wait to get to the hotel room. We were both tired and wanted a bath and to sleep.

When we walked off the bus, reporters came at us from every direction. We talked and answered some of their questions as we walked. A reporter asked me how I was doing and if I could tell them what had happened. I told them some of what the past few days had been like for me. Mrs. Suzan told them we were tired and needed to rest.

We climbed into a cab, and Mrs. Suzan asked the driver to stop at a store and wait on us.

He agreed and assured us we didn't have to worry about the fare, as it was taken care of.

"Thank you," she replied.

We stopped at a store and picked out some clothes and other items we needed. We returned to the cab, and the driver drove us to the hotel.

After we'd checked in, the clerk at the reception desk told us that the bill would be paid and that room service was included in the bill.

After Mrs. Suzan had expressed our thanks, we went to our room. The room was big and beautiful. It had two bedrooms, each with a large TV and its own bathroom. Mrs. Suzan made some phone calls and talked to many different people. She told me she was calling Mrs. Fuels to let her know we were okay and that she would let me talk. Mrs. Suzan passed me the phone.

Mrs. Fuels was crying as she spoke with me. She told me how thankful they all were that we were okay. "Hold on," she said. "Sara and Kaylin want to talk."

"We saw you on TV," Sara said as soon as she got on.

"Really?" I asked.

"Yes," she told me, "at the airport talking to the reporters." Then she said, "Hold on. Kaylin wants to say hello."

Kaylin's voice sounded excited. "You are having so much fun," she said. "I wish we were there."

"Maybe next time," I told her.

Next on the line was Teddy. He said he was glad we were okay and told me he'd been brushing Daisy for me. "She missed you," he said. And before saying good-bye, he added, "Hurry home in one piece."

Then Mrs. Fuels was back. "You take care, and we will be waiting on your return," she told me.

I gave the phone back to Mrs. Suzan. I heard her say that we would keep in touch, and then she hung up the phone. She said she was going for a bath in her room. She gave me the things she had purchased for me, and I went to my room to take a bath.

I stayed in the water for over an hour; it was so relaxing. Then I put on my pajamas and went to the living room. Mrs. Suzan was looking at the menu. She asked me to look over it and order anything I would like to eat. She smiled and said, "Anything."

I did order what I wanted—a big, juicy burger and fries. I even ordered desert.

The food was delicious, and once we'd eaten, we were both tired. Mrs. Suzan said she was going to bed. I went to bed and turned on the TV. I fell asleep watching it, and I slept so well that I didn't wake up even once.

When I got up, Mrs. Suzan said she had checked on a flight, and we could leave today on the late flight. I didn't think she was in a hurry to fly again, but I was ready. We ordered breakfast, ate, and got dressed.

Then she made more phone calls while I watched TV. Someone from the airport came and wanted to talk with Mrs. Suzan. He asked questions and took down a lot of information about her and me.

After he left, she said, "We have to get dressed and get to the airport."

The cab took us to the airport. After we'd gotten our tickets and gone through all the security checks, we sat waiting to be called to board our plane. Mrs. Suzan asked me again if I was okay with flying.

Smiling, I said, "Yes."

She was not smiling. I think she was a little scared. I told her it would be okay.

She smiled and said, "You're right."

We boarded the plane and found our seats. I asked her if she wanted the window seat since I'd had it last time.

She smiled and said, "No. You are welcome to the window seat."

I was glad because I wanted to look out the window. After all the safety talks, we buckled our seat belts, and the plane started to move. I looked at Mrs. Suzan. She looked scared. I took her by the hand and smiled. She smiled back, only she didn't look happy. We were up in the air, and I could see the clouds again.

Mrs. Suzan didn't say much the entire trip. She turned down the food and only took the drink. The trip didn't take long before we were there. I could tell Mrs. Suzan was happy to be on the ground again by the smile she had on her face when we landed. We got off and claimed our bags, and were off to the hotel. The hotel was nice here also. We went down to the restaurant, ordered dinner, and ate there. It was very nice, and the food was good.

Mrs. Suzan told me she had made an appointment for me to see the doctor tomorrow morning. I was happy in a way, but I wondered whether the doctor would be able to help me now that I knew I was different now.

We finished our dinner, walked around the hotel, and sat at the pool watching the children swim and play in the pool. We went back to the room, watched TV, and went to bed soon.

I was up early the next morning. When Mrs. Suzan came to wake me, I was up and ready. She smiled and said she would be ready soon. We could eat breakfast before we left. After breakfast, we were in the cab and heading to the doctor's office. When we got there, we had many papers to fill out.

I told Mrs. Suzan that I didn't have answers for most of these questions.

"That's okay," she said. "Answer the ones you know."

The doctor called me in. I wanted Mrs. Suzan to come in with me, and he said she could. He started telling me about himself and explained what he was going to do. He told me I would have to stay here for three days while the hospital ran tests. The tests were going to be running at night. "Mrs. Suzan is welcome to stay with you," he assured me.

I looked at her, hoping she would.

He said he wanted me to start by telling him everything I could remember as a child, about my family, or any dreams I might have had. *This is going to be quick*, I thought. I didn't remember my childhood or my family, and I knew I wasn't going to tell him about the dreams or me being different. I couldn't let anyone know about that. I started telling him the story of my life from the time I did remember.

He looked at me, smiled, and said he and his team would do all they could to help me.

"Thank you," I said.

He told us to come back the next day at 5:00 p.m. and explained that they'd start the first test, which would run through the night, then. A nurse would come in and go over what would happen. Then he stood, shook my hand, and told me I would be fine.

When the nurse came in, she explained that I would be in bed with tubes attached to me. She said it wouldn't hurt and would only give information from my body when I slept about how I reacted when I was sleeping and dreaming. She told me that I should just be myself and that I would have to stay in bed unless I was going to the restroom. "Do you have any questions?" she asked.

I asked how long the test would last.

"Over night," she said. "You'll be done by breakfast."

After the nurse finished going over everything about the test, we left and went back to the hotel room. Mrs. Suzan said she would be there with me through it all. We called Mrs. Fuels, and she told me she had good news. Mrs. Daniels had returned home and said I should call her. She was worried and wanted to talk to me.

After I hung up with Mrs. Fuels, I called Mrs. Daniels. When she answered, as soon as I said, "Hello," she was crying and saying how glad she was to hear that I was okay and how worried she'd been. She said I could come home when I was all done with the doctor and told me Sara and Kaylin would already be there when I returned.

I said that was great.

She asked how it had gone with the doctor. I told her what I had to do. She said everything would be fine and that I would be back home soon. I told her we would talk later and hung up.

I was somewhat sad that I had to leave the Fuels family and Daisy, but I was glad to be going back with the Danielses. I hoped the Fuels would let me visit Daisy. I was going to miss them all; being on a farm with so many animals had been fun. As for tomorrow, I was excited even though I was scared. Mrs. Suzan said she was going to go to bed; tomorrow was going to a long day.

When I woke the next morning, Mrs. Suzan was still asleep. I didn't want to wake her, so I stayed in bed and watched TV. I soon heard her up and moving around. She saw my TV on, came to the door, and asked, "Are you ready for breakfast?"

"I'm not hungry," I told her.

"Try to eat something," she said.

"Okay," I agreed. "Cereal will be fine with some fruit."

After breakfast, she asked what I wanted to do.

"Nothing," I said. "Could we stay in and watch TV?"

She smiled. "Sure," she agreed. "There's nothing wrong with staying in, relaxing, and watching TV."

We watched movie after movie, and then it was getting time to get dressed to leave. We packed my bag, dressed, and headed out the door to the hospital.

Soon, a nurse led us to the room where I would be staying the next three days while the tests were running. The room was large and very nice. A nice, large recliner chair sat next to my bed. The nurse told us she would be our nurse for the day, and then someone else would be here for the night. She went over what was going to happen during the night. I would be free most of the days while we were here. She said we could explore the hospital during the day; we just couldn't leave the hospital. She showed some gowns I could use if I did not have a special gown to wear.

"I brought my own," I told her.

"We want you to be comfortable as possible," she replied.

She showed me a sheet with food options for dinner and breakfast. *That's cool*, I thought.

"After dinner, we'll start getting you hooked up to the machine for the test," she said.

Mrs. Suzan said she was going down to the cafeteria to get her dinner and that she would be back. She asked, "Are you okay here until I get back?"

I said, "Yes," and turned on the TV and started watching.

Mrs. Suzan was back quickly, and my food had arrived. We watched TV while we ate.

Then the nurse came in and said, "It's time to start getting you ready." She told me to change into my gown and get in bed. She would be ready for me in ten minutes. I got up and changed into my pajamas. The nurse was in the room when I came out of the bathroom. The machine, which had a bunch of tubes coming from it, was ready. She looked at me, smiled, and said, "I know it looks scary, but it's nothing to be scared of. It's like putting stickers on your skin. You won't feel a thing." She hooked me up to all the sticky patches and tubes, and it didn't hurt.

"Are you comfortable?" she asked.

I said I was.

She told me the doctor would be in to talk to me and start the machine. "Once the machine has started," she reminded me, "no getting up—only for bathroom breaks."

"Okay," I said.

The doctor came in asked how I was feeling.

"Fine so far," I told him.

He smiled. "It will be as easy as eating a piece of cake," he said. "Do you have any questions before we start?"

When I said I didn't, he turned on the machine. I didn't feel any different. I couldn't even tell the machine was on, except that I could see all the lines it was making. He pointed to the papers coming from the machine. "This is charting everything that is going on in your body— your heartbeat, your blood pressure, and all that good stuff," he explained. "You'll be fine," he added. "I'll see you first thing in the morning."

Mrs. Suzan and I watched movies and talked about each one. She lay back in her recliner with a blanket trying to stay awake, but sleep overtook her as soon as her eyes closed. I watched TV a little longer before I went to sleep. I slept well through the night. The nurse kept coming in and charting things from the monitor. I didn't ask any questions. I just watched and went back to sleep.

That morning, the doctor came in and turned off the machine. "Everything went well," he told me. "You have the rest of the day off, and we'll start up again at seven o'clock."

We did the same routine for the next two days. After the third night, I was glad it was the last one. I was ready to go. I was tired of this hospital.

That morning, the doctor came in and went over the results with Mrs. Suzan and me. He told us everything looked great and that the test didn't show any problems. He went on to tell us that some people went through this, and soon their memory came back as if nothing had happened at all. He told us that he didn't see a problem—that this was something that was going to have to work itself out on its on time. We both thanked him. I felt bad I was leaving the same—not knowing anything new about myself from the test. He gave us a copy of the report, and we left.

I was quiet all the way back to the motel. Mrs. Suzan kept telling me how sorry she was about the test and saying that my memory would come back, just like the doctor had said. She tried her best to cheer me up and told me how blessed I was, saying it could have been a lot worse than it was. She went on to tell me how many children there had much worse going on in their lives. She said that some were blind, and some couldn't walk, and many children were there fighting for their lives, to get a chance to just live a little longer.

I'd never looked at it that way. She must have done a lot of walking while I was sleep. I hadn't seen or noticed any of that. I started to be thankful and was feeling a lot better.

"Are you ready for the plane ride back home tomorrow?" she asked.

"Yes," I said. I was ready to get back home. I couldn't wait to tell everyone about the trip and everything. I knew Mrs. Suzan was not too thrilled to get on the plan again. She had told me she was going to take a break from planes after this one.

I had a lot going on in my life. I needed to get answers. The doctors couldn't give me any answers. I knew who had my answers—the woman in my dreams, or my mother as she said. I was ready to find out who I was and what I was. I had accepted myself for what I was as far as I knew. But I needed to know who I was in terms of the totally different person I was learning more about. I had so many questions, and most of them started with why. I wanted to know why I was here if I did not belong here. It made me angry and sad at the same time. I was sad that I didn't even know my name or my birthday. There was so much hurt within me; all I could ask was why.

Mrs. Suzan interrupted my thoughts by calling my name. "Are you okay?" she asked. "You've been in that daze a while. You didn't even hear me calling you."

I looked at her, trying to make out what she was saying. "Sorry," I said. "I was thinking about a lot of things."

She asked if I wanted to talk about it.

As much as I needed to talk to someone, I said, "No, it's not important." Only it was more important to me than anything.

We arrived to the motel, and she said we could pack now so we could have the rest of the day to do something. We packed and were off to do whatever there was that was exciting to do.

A fair was going on, and we decided to go there. We had lots of fun riding the rides, playing games, and eating all the different foods. I'd never been to a fair before. This was the only trip I had ever been on, and I was having a lot of fun, despite the plane crash and the not-so-good news from the doctor. In fact, I was having the best time of my life.

Mrs. Suzan had a way of making me feel better when I was feeling down. As we sat eating a funnel cake and taking a break, I told her, "Thank you for everything; you have been here with me through some rough times, and you never gave up. When we were on the plane, and it was looking bad at times, you would say a prayer. That always made me feel so much better. Thank you, Mrs. Suzan. I mean it from my heart. You have done so much for me, trying to help me get help. Even after you almost lost your life on the plane crash, you never stopped. You got back on the plane with me. I will never forget what you've done."

She looked up, and tears were forming in her eyes. She told me that she and her husband had wanted to have children but that the doctor had told them they weren't able. "If we were able to have children," she said, the tears now rolling down her cheeks, "I would want a child just like you, Jane." She put her arms around me, hugged me tightly, and said, "You are welcome. I am glad that I could be here for you."

It hurt me to hear that she wanted children and couldn't have any. She was a good person and would be a great mother. Looking at her and seeing how happy she seemed, you would think she was happy and had everything she wanted out of life. Then a thought occurred to me; everyone carries around hurt in his or her life somehow, even though it doesn't always show. If you could talk to every person who looked happy in this world, you would find hurt somewhere in all of their lives. I knew how she felt when it came to hurting. Why did things turn out bad for such good-hearted people?

We got up and rode some more rides. We were having so much fun. The rest of that evening at the fair, I felt sad for her. It was as though I could feel the hurt she carried. I wished things were different for her. Then it occurred to me that maybe I could help her. I had helped others. Maybe I could help her. It was all I thought about the rest of the day. I didn't know if I could help, but I was surely going to try.

Soon it was getting late, and we decided to leave. Mrs. Suzan was having just as much fun as I was. I was sure she would love to be with a child and her husband having fun like tonight.

We got back to the hotel. I was tired and wanted to get a shower and watch TV for a while. I thought Mrs. Suzan wanted the same thing. We turned down dinner, took our showers, and lay back to watch a movie. The movie we picked was sad, and I could see Mrs. Suzan was teary-eyed. She had her Kleenex ready. "I love this movie," she said, "but it always makes me cry."

"Would you want to watch something else?" I asked.

She said no quickly.

I wasn't into the movie. All I was thinking about was how I could help Mrs. Suzan. She has been through so much to help me, even a plane crash I had to try to help her. How could I help? I wondered. I noticed she was crying her eyes out through the movie.

This is a good time to try, I thought. I could lay my hand on her leg to comfort her through this movie. At the same time, I could try to focus and help her.

I moved beside her, gave her another Kleenex, and put my hand on her leg. She had stretched out on the couch. "Thank you," she said as she took the Kleenex and blew her nose. I kept my hand on her leg and focused hard on her having a child to complete her family.

At first, nothing happened. I held on and focused harder. I wanted this so much for her. The warmth started to come into my hand, and I knew it was happening. I held on, focusing until tingling warmth stopped, and then reached for another tissue. As I handed it to her, I said, "It will be all right."

"Jane, you are a special girl," she said. "I know you will find your family. They are lucky to have a daughter like you."

I wiped her tears and said, "I am sure we will find each other."

She told me I had so much love in my heart. Then she smiled and said, "Thank you."

After the movie, she went to bed. I went to bed happy, knowing her life was about to change.

Chapter 9

*T*he next morning, Mrs. Suzan was up early. I got up, dressed, and joined her.

"We have four hours before the flight," she said. "Do you want breakfast?"

"Yes," I told her, "pancakes and sausage."

She ordered just for me. She said she wasn't feeling too good from all the junk food she had eaten. She smiled and added, "It was so much fun."

I ate breakfast. Then we watched TV until it was time for us to leave. She lay on the couch, saying her stomach wasn't feeling any better. "I am not eating anything today," she said. Then she jumped up and ran off to the bathroom; all the junk food from last night came up. She came back saying she should feel better after all that was off her stomach.

I said, "I hope you do feel better. Are you going to be okay flying back home today?"

She said she'd be fine.

We got our things together, checked out at the front desk, and thanked the motel clerk for everything. Then we were off to the airport.

We arrived an hour early. It always took a while to go through all the checks. Mrs. Suzan had to stop a lot to go to the bathroom. She said she still wasn't feeling well. We finally arrived at the area where we could sit and wait to start boarding. Mrs. Suzan was sitting quietly. I thought she was a little scared of getting back on the plane after the crash. I broke the silence and asked her, "Do you miss your husband?" I'd never heard her mention him once on the trip.

She looked at me, and when I saw shock and sadness in her eyes, I knew I'd asked the wrong question. "I'm sorry," I said.

"No," she replied. "It's ok." She went on and started to talk to me about him. "The night before we left to come here, we had the biggest argument and he moved out," she told me. "I haven't talked to him since. He hasn't tried to call me once. He doesn't know I left to come with you or about the crash. I haven't tried to call him. I care so much for him, but there's a lot that has to change on both of our parts. I told him we should go our separate ways. We both wanted children so badly. The stress of trying and not being able has taken a toll on both of us, causing us to make each other's lives hell."

"Do you love him?" I asked.

She looked at me for a moment and then said, "For a young girl, you have a way of talking in such a caring manner and showing so much love." Then she added, "Yes, I do love him—enough to let him go and live his life. Maybe he can find a wife who can give him what he wants—a child—something I will never be able to give him. I don't want him to go through life with me having to give up something so important to him."

"What about adopting?" I asked.

"No," she replied, "we always said we wanted our own."

"You never give up on the things that mean so much to you," I told her. "Don't give up on either your husband or your child. Always believe, even when everything's at its worst. You have to hold on that much stronger and believe even more for what is so dear to you."

She looked at me. "It's easy talking to you. Something about you is different from anyone I've ever meet. You don't find too many people like you in a lifetime," she said.

"Thanks," I told her. "Keep holding on. Never let your dream go."

It was time to board our plane. She wiped away the tears and said, "Never change who you are." She kissed me on the forehead and asked, "Are you ready for this last trip?"

On the plane, she said, "The window is yours. Enjoy it."

Mrs. Suzan said her prayer as usual, and the flight was pleasant all the way home. We landed, and I could tell she loved being on the ground much more than she did being in the air. We got our bags. In the cab, she told me she was going to take me to the Danielses' home. I thought it was nice to go back to the Daniels family.

"I really wanted to say good-bye to the Fuels," I told her.

"I am sure you will get a chance to see them," she assured me.

When we arrived at the Danielses' house, Sara and Kaylin were the first ones out the door. They showered me with hugs. The Daniels ran out, and more hugs were exchanged, these between tears. I could see they were all glad to see me.

Mrs. Suzan hugged me. "Thanks for the talk," she said. She told me she was going to give her husband a call when she got home.

I smiled. "That's good," I said. I told her to call me sometime, and she promised she would.

We said our good-byes, and she headed home.

That night, I called Mr. and Mrs. Fuels and told them I had made it home safely. I thanked them for everything, especially the party. Mrs. Fuels told me to come to visit anytime and added that they would all miss us. She said they had enjoyed having us girls stay with them. After I'd assured her I would come and visit, we said good-bye.

I was glad to be back here—back home—with everyone. Mr. and Mrs. Daniels and Sara and Kaylin were all waiting to hear about everything that had happened on my trip, and I couldn't wait to tell them every detail. We stayed up later than normal that night. The others asked me all kinds of questions, and I had an answer to them all. Even though it was late by the time we went to bed, we girls still talked until we all fell asleep.

The next morning, I woke to the delicious smells of sausage and pancakes. I jumped up and joined everyone in the kitchen. Mrs. Daniels told us that today would be a fun day. We had to go school shopping, as school was going to start in two weeks. I was ready to go back to school. I would be in high school, and I was sure high school was going to be more exciting than ever.

After breakfast, we all loaded into the van and were off to shop. It was an all-day thing, and we still didn't get everything we needed. We had lunch together while we were out. It was fun to see what we each picked out for school. We bought a lot to get us started, including all that was on our list of supplies. Even though we still had a few more things to get, Mrs. Daniels said we would bring the shopping to an end for the day. She wanted to get back to start dinner. She said we could come another day to finish all the shopping.

We girls were happy. We had brought many cool outfits. When we were home, we tried them on and modeled them for each other. After putting away all our clothes, we went outside. It was good to be home.

Sarah said she missed the little chicks. I missed Daisy, and Kaylin missed the rabbits. We all said we'd rather be here, though. This was home. Here, we were a family.

I had lived most of my life not knowing the truth about myself. I had always just gone along with how my life was supposed to be. I knew it was time to find out the truth and get the answers to my many questions. I would have to talk to the woman in my dreams to get the answers, and to do that, I would have to be alone. Getting away from Sara and Kaylin wasn't going to be easy. I decided my answers would have to wait a little longer.

We were outside for the rest of the day until it was time for dinner. All we talked about was the plane ride. After hearing about the crash, Sara and Kaylin still wanted very much to fly. They loved the idea of being high in the sky on a plane; the next best thing to them was to talk to me about my experience. They did a good job of that. They had so many questions; I never knew what they'd come up with next. I always put smiles on their faces by talking with them about how it was to be flying high in the clouds. We ate dinner that night, went to bed, and talked more about planes.

The next week, we finished our school shopping. We were ready and waiting for school to start.

The morning of the first day of school, we were up early, dressed, and eating breakfast well before it was time to leave. Then we were off to the bus stop. School was the same. All my same friends were there.

One day after school, I told myself it was time to find a way get away; I was determined that, somehow, I would get some answers about myself that evening after school. I did all my homework as soon as I got home. I knew Sara and Kaylin always started late. Finishing early would give me a change to get away by myself.

It worked. I was all done before they'd even started. I headed out the house for a walk. I loved it here. During my walks through the woods, I'd watch squirrels running through the trees and stop to see the beautiful wildflowers that grew everywhere here. I decided to take a long walk through the woods so I could get as far away from the house as possible. Sara and Kaylin never came out this far looking for me. I went to my own little spot where I loved to go when I wanted to be alone. It had flowers and plenty of trees for shade.

When I reached my spot, I lay down on the ground by a big tree and started to focus, hoping I could talk to the woman in my dreams who said she was my mother I was ready to find out more about me. I focused harder, trying to bring us together.

It worked! She was there. I could feel her in my mind. I opened my eyes, and there she was standing in front of me with a smile. "Hello," she said warmly.

"Hello," I replied.

I told her it was time. I needed to know who I was.

She agreed.

I started by asking her what my real name was.

She spoke softly. "Please keep an open mind about all this."

"Please tell me my name," I asked again.

"Nyah," she said.

I smiled. "Nyah is my name."

"Yes."

"What about my last name?"

"Tompkins," she replied.

"How old am I?"

"Fifteen," she answered.

"When's my birthday?" I wanted to know.

"April 20, 1998," she told me.

My next question was a little more difficult. "You said we are a family," I said softly. "Why am I the only one here? Why did you leave me here?"

"You are part of that world," she told me. "You were born in that world. Your farther is of that world. I was born in my world, but I was able to come there."

"My father is here?" I asked.

"Yes," she told me. "When I was there, I fell in love with your dad, and we had you. He named you Nyah. He called you Sunshine. He always said you brightened his days like the sunshine. Your father knows nothing of our kind. I told him nothing of me and never involved him in anything to do with this world. I tried to close the door to my past life."

I could not believe what I was hearing. I had a father who had been here all this time. I asked her to tell me his name.

"Nathan Tompkins," she told me. "He doesn't know you are there. He thinks you are with me, but he doesn't know where I am. I haven't had a chance to talk to him since the day I left." She told me that she'd wished many times that she had told him everything.

I listened as she talked. "I was at the park with you when the door to my world opened. I was bringing you with me. We walked through together, and somehow you ran back through. I couldn't get to you. The door closed right as you walked out."

"Why didn't you come back for me?" I asked.

"I couldn't come back," she told me, her voice full of emotion. "If I could, I would be there with you and your father, not here. The door to my world hasn't opened since the day I left. It will open again one day." She told me how sorry she was and explained there was nothing she could do. She had no way to get in contact with my father and tell him about me. "Find your father," she told me. "He is a good man who loves you very much."

I knew she was hurting. I could feel the hurt, and it came through her voice as she talked. Tears fell from my eyes, and all the anger I'd bottled u went away. I felt for her. I knew she hadn't left me here on purpose; it was my fault. "I'm sorry," I told her.

"We will all be together again one day, as a family," she told me.

"Yes," I said, "one day. I have to go."

"Take care until next time," she said. "I love you."

I closed my eyes, stopped focusing, and she was gone just like that.

I lay there for a little while longer thinking of my father. I had to find a way to find him. Could I tell everyone my real name now? Should I tell Mrs. Daniels, Sara, and Kaylin about my dad? Should I say that I'd remembered and give Mrs. Daniel's my dad's name? Maybe she could find my dad.

I got up and started walking to the house. I could see Sara and Kaylin were outside swinging; they must have finished their homework. When I walked over to the swings, Sara said, "We were looking for you."

"I took a walk," I replied.

"You had a phone call from the woman you were with on the plane," Kaylin told me. "She wants you to call. Mrs. Daniels took the message."

I ran into the house. Mrs. Daniel told me about the call from Mrs. Suzan. "She said she wanted to tell you something."

I called, and when Mrs. Suzan answered, I said, "Hi. This is Jane."

"Hello, Jane. How are you?" she asked.

I said I was doing great and asked if she was feeling better.

She told me that her stomach problem hadn't gone away so she'd gone to see a doctor, where she'd learned that her "problem" was that she was pregnant with not one but two babies. "I cannot believe it," she told me, gushing with happiness. "We are going to have twins. The doctor detected two heartbeats during the ultrasound. My husband and I are doing well and working things out between us," she concluded. "I wanted to give you the good news."

After I told her how I was happy for them, she said she won't keep me any longer but said that I should take care.

I told her good-bye and hung up. I was happy for her.

Chapter 10

*A*ll I could think about was my father and finding him. I would love to live with him. I loved staying here with the Daniels. Only I knew it was time that I found my father; it was time for me to be with him. *What if he is married and has other children?* I wondered. After all he'd been through, maybe it would be best for me to let him go on with his life and not put him through any more difficult times.

But as much as I wanted to leave him alone, I had to find him. He was my father; I wanted to be in his life. The next day when I got to school, I was with my friends. They were all talking about their weekends and their dates with their boyfriends. I had a friend named Teddy, not the same Teddy from the Fuelses' farm. I didn't look at Teddy as a boyfriend, even though I liked him a lot. We were good friends, and I enjoyed talking and hanging out with him. Teddy knew about my life all the struggles I'd been through. I could talk to him about anything. He was always willing to go the extra mile to help me. All my friends teased me about him. They knew I liked him more than I let on.

I talked to Teddy that day at school. He asked a lot of questions and finally just came out asked me what was going on. I decided to tell him about my dream, only I'd put it in a different way. I told him I'd had a dream of a man who I thought was my dad. I told him I kept dreaming of this man and the house we'd lived in. Teddy said it was good that I'd started to dream about those things. When the bell rang, he said he would call me and we could talk more.

I left school that day still thinking of my dad. I had to reach out to Teddy I needed someone to talk to, someone to help me find my dad. I knew I could trust Teddy. What we talked about was always kept between the two of us. I got home that day and went straight for the phone book. I looked up my dad's name, and sure enough, there it was—Nathan Tompkins. To my surprise, the address was also included. I took a piece of paper and wrote all the information down. My heart was beating like crazy, and I was truly shaking as I looked at his name and address on the paper. For once in my life, I felt full of hope. I wanted so much to dial the number, but I was too afraid to touch the phone to call him. I couldn't move. I just stared at the information that told me who and where my dad was.

I needed to talk to Teddy. I couldn't tell Mr. and Mrs. Daniels or anyone else. There would be too many questions. I wasn't ready to share the information I had and how I'd gotten it. I wanted to find out more about the situation for myself before I brought it out in the open.

I called Teddy and told him I'd found my dad's number and address.

"Did you call him?" Teddy asked.

"No," was all I could say.

"You should make sure he is your father first," he suggested.

I knew for sure, but since Teddy didn't know what I knew, I went along with what he was saying.

Teddy said, "You have the address. Drive by the house and check things out first on the down low."

I agreed that was a good idea. Teddy could drive, but he didn't have his own car. He used his dad's car when we wanted to go out. "Maybe I should find out where the place is, and we can go from there," Teddy offered.

I gave him the address, and he said he'd check it out and let me know.

I had no idea where this address was. Mr. and Mrs. Daniels knew Teddy. They let him come over for dinner and let us go out at times. They were good at letting us have some time out. They had their rules, and we girls always followed them. Mrs. Daniels had the "big girls' talk" with me the first time I talked about going out. I knew what and what not to do. Mrs. Daniels also told me what to do when I thought it was time to do the "not to do" on a date. She told me all about the not to do. And she gave me the information I would need if I decided to do it. I was covered on all bases when it came to information. Teddy and I had never looked at each other in that way; we both just enjoyed each other's company and acted like kids having fun.

After I'd finished my homework and eaten dinner, Teddy called. He told me he'd found out that the address I'd given him was on the south side of town, which was a nicer part of town. Hearing that made me feel good. Teddy suggested that he could ask his dad if he could use the car and maybe on Saturday we could ride over there and check the place out. I said that would be fine and told him I'd check with Mrs. Daniels and let him know.

We talked for about twenty minutes and then got off the phone.

By the time Friday rolled around, I couldn't wait until Saturday. I was happy and scared at the same time. Teddy and I both had the okay on going out. We told his parents, Mr. and Mrs. Daniels we were going to a movie and dinner, which we were, after we checked out the house.

Finally, Saturday came. I couldn't wait until it was time to go. Teddy could not get here fast enough. Finally, he arrived and we left. Teddy smiled. He was just as thrilled as I was and glad to be helping. I was happy. I could not wait to see where my father was living—and him too hopefully.

I told Teddy I hoped my father would be out in the yard so I could see him. The closer we got, the faster my heartbeat. All the houses were huge and beautiful. "Look for the address," Teddy said. "It should be one of these houses."

Finally, we saw the address. No one was outside. The home was big and beautiful, and a truck with a boat hooked to it was parked outside. I wanted so much to go in.

Teddy shocked me when he pulled up in the driveway. "What you are doing?" I asked.

"Turning around," he said. "What better way to get a good look."

As Teddy was getting ready to back up, a man stepped from around the house. He was tall and handsome. He threw up his hand and headed to the car. My heart went from beating fast to pounding like a hammer in my chest. "Do you need any help?" the man asked.

"No," Teddy said. "We were only turning around."

The man smiled and asked if we were lost.

"No," Teddy told him. "We missed our turn."

The man smiled again. "You have a nice day," he said then turned and walked to his boat.

I felt something in my heart when I looked at him. He was my dad. A strange feeling came over me. "Yes," I told Teddy, "he is my father."

Teddy asked how I could be sure just from looking at him.

"Somehow, I felt it," I told him. I wanted to go back, but I knew there would be other times and soon.

We went to get something to eat and then went to the movies. I had fun but could not keep my mind off my dad. I wanted so much to be in his life.

Teddy and I talked before he took me home. I told him I was ready to make a change in my life. I was ready to add my dad into my life. I had a father here; he was my family, and I wanted so much to have a family of my own. I had been through a lot, and I knew my dad had been through a lot, losing two people he loved so much. My dad still had me, and it was time to let him know I was here. "I don't know how, but I will find a way to let him know I am his daughter," I told Teddy.

How could I find anything out about my dad if I didn't talk to him? I didn't want to bring anyone else in just yet; I want this to be between my dad and me. I had to find a way to make it happen.

Teddy took me home. I thanked him and told him to put on his thinking cap.

He smiled and said, "Always."

We said good-bye, and he drove off.

I wanted to talk to Mrs. Daniels and tell her what was going on. But I knew I couldn't tell her everything, so I decided not to say anything. I had to do this on my own. The next few days were hard. I couldn't concentrate on my schoolwork; all I could think of was my dad. I had to talk to him. I couldn't go on like this much longer. My mind was a wreck. I was ready to find out about my dad; I was ready to move in with him and for us to be a family.

I called Teddy and told him I'd decided to go to my dad's house, sit down, and just tell him who I was, and we'd go from there. I asked Teddy if he could drive me back there when it was the right time. I first wanted to find out if my dad had another family of his own. I suggested that we might drive by his house a few times to see if we saw any children or a woman.

"That might not be a good idea," Teddy said. "Someone could notice us driving by and maybe call the cops. Then what would we tell the cops?"

I told Teddy I just had to go over and talk to him. "Maybe I could call him and tell him I need to talk to him. Then we could set up a good time for both of us," I said, thinking aloud. I told Teddy I'd think about it some more and let him know what I decided.

Just then, Sara came in all excited about a boy she had started talking to at school. As she talked about him, I was listening, but I was a little lost in my own thoughts.

"Please, enough with the boy talk," Kaylin said. "I am reading."

We looked at each other and laughed, and Sara and I said we would keep it down. Kaylin smiled at us both and then went back to reading.

I thought long and hard about the situation and what I was going to do about it. Finally, I determined that I would call my dad, not tell him who; I would just tell him I needed to talk to him about something. If he asked what I needed to talk about, I would simply tell him that I'd rather talk to him in person, if he didn't mind.

The next day at school, I told Teddy my plan and asked what he thought. He said it sounded good and then asked when I was going to do all this. I asked him to let me know when he could get the car again; I would make the call then.

"Do you at least want to find out if he is your dad first?" he asked.

"He's my dad," I told me. "When I talk to him, the truth will come out."

The rest of the week, Teddy's dad was busy and using the car a lot. He told Teddy he could use it Saturday after twelve. I said that would be fine.

Today was Wednesday. I had three days to build up my nerves and make the call. My heart pounded faster every time I thought about it. I knew I had to make the call before Friday to make sure Saturday would be a good time for my dad and get the okay to meet him. I practiced what I would say often. I even wrote it down.

Friday came too quickly. I still hadn't built up the nerves to call my dad. I was a walking zombie at school. I was there, but my mind was so far away from school it hardly mattered. I had been waiting for this day my entire childhood. Now that it was here, I was both very ready and scared at the same time.

All day, I talked to Teddy about my plan.

"You'll be okay," he said. "I'll be there with you. And we can leave anytime you're ready once we're at his house."

I was thankful to have someone like Teddy in my life. He had listened to many stories and wiped away many falling tears. Teddy was the type of person you could call a true friend. He was a good person, with a loving and caring heart. I was thankful to have him as a close friend.

After school, I found myself in the house alone. I knew I had to make the call now. I picked up the phone and put it down a number of times before I worked up the nerve to dial the number. And when I finally dialed all the numbers, the last number was hard for me to hit. I finally did it.

The phone rang. I really hoped he was home. I couldn't go through leaving a message or calling back. Then a voice on the other end said, "Hello." It was a man.

I couldn't talk. I couldn't remember anything I had practiced to say. I went blank.

The voice on the other end said, "Hello," again.

I still couldn't say anything. Just hearing his voice sent a funny feeling down my spine. I finally spoke up. "Hello," I said. "Could I please speak to Mr. Nathan Tompkins?"

"Speaking," the voice on the other end, replied.

"Hello, Mr. Tompkins," I managed. "You may not know me, but I really need to talk to you about a matter."

He asked what the matter was about.

"I would not like to discuss it over the phone," I said. "It has to be in person. Believe me, it's nothing bad; in fact, it's good. Would you be free any time after twelve tomorrow?"

"Well," he said after a moment's pause, "I think I will have some free time around one thirty. We could meet at about two o'clock."

"That will be perfect," I said. "I have your address. Thanks. I'll see you tomorrow. Bye." I let out a loud sigh of relief after I hung up the phone.

I called Teddy and told him what had happened. I asked if two o'clock would work for him.

After assuring me the time would work, he asked, "How'd it go?"

"I was scared," I told him. "At first, I couldn't think of anything I had practiced. But think it went well. He sounded like a nice person." I told Teddy how scared I was going to be. I knew there was a chance my dad might have another family, but I had to talk to him alone. It had to be him and me only. I explained this to Teddy and told him not to feel bad that I didn't want him there during the conversation.

Teddy said he understood and that he hoped Mr. Tompkins was my father and that everything would work out as I'd planned.

I was tired and wanted to lie down. I said good-bye to Teddy and hung up.

Mrs. Daniels asked me during dinner if I was okay. "You barely touched your food," she said.

I told her I wasn't very hungry. I'd had a long day. I asked to be excused and went to bed. My mind was on meeting my dad the next day. I felt bad about not telling Mrs. Daniels what was going on, but I had to talk to my dad first—before everyone else got involved.

It was late, and I was still awake. I had tried everything I could think of to go to sleep. Sara and Kaylin were in bed sleeping peacefully, but I couldn't sleep at all. I lay there all night thinking of tomorrow. Finally, somewhere in my thoughts, I drifted off to sleep.

When I awoke the next morning, it was early, and everyone was asleep. I made my bed, got dressed, and went downstairs, trying not to wake anyone. I went outside. It was daytime but still early. I went to the swings and sat in one, thinking about everything. I could very well be leaving here soon, I realized. I felt a sadness come over me; I knew it was going to be hard to leave everyone here. It was just that I wanted to be with my father.

Then I thought, *What if he's married and has more children? What if he doesn't want me there with them?* That would hurt even more than the not knowing had hurt. *What am I doing?* I asked myself. To have found him after all these years just to have him turn me away would be a lot harder than I'd realized. I didn't think I could take that.

I knew I had to go through with my plans no matter what the outcome was. I hoped my dad still loved me now as much as my mom had said he loved me then. I'd known I loved him when I saw him the first time. Still, I couldn't remember anything about him or us as a family. I sure hoped he would believe me when I told him I didn't remember anything about my childhood. I only knew what my mother had told me. How was I going to tell him about me and her being different? I wouldn't bring that up during the first meeting.

The day was already going by too quickly. It was time for breakfast, and I wasn't hungry. But I made myself eat something so Mrs. Daniels wouldn't think I was feeling bad. I didn't want anything to spoil my plans for today.

It was soon twelve o'clock. Teddy called. "Are your plans still on?" he asked.

"Yes," I said. "Can you get the car?"

He said his dad was out and had promised to be back by one o'clock.

"Okay," I said and hung up.

I went upstairs to decide what I was going to wear. I wanted to look good but simple. I picked out a pair of jeans and a nice shirt and fixed my hair. I stood in front of the mirror and took a good look at myself. I wondered if I would change like my mother. I remembered her talking to me about that, but I couldn't remember everything. I would have to ask about that again. I needed to know.

It was one o'clock when I looked at the clock. At one fifteen, Teddy called and said he was on his way. I felt a sick kind of feeling in my stomach. The day had come; I would finally meet and talk to my dad.

Teddy arrived, and Mrs. Daniels told us to have fun and be careful.

We both said okay and left.

I was quiet at first. Then I told Teddy that I was scared to do this. He pulled over to the side of the road asked, "Do you want to cancel your plans? We still can if you want to."

"No. I have to do this," I told him.

We drove on to my dad's house and pulled up into the driveway. We didn't get out immediately. As before, I didn't see any children or any toys in the yard that would indicate their presence.

"I'll walk you to the door," Teddy said.

"That would be great," I told him.

We both got out the car and walked to the front door; it was quiet inside.

"Are you ready?" Teddy asked.

I shrugged and took in a deep breath. "No but yes."

"I'll stay until he comes to the door," Teddy said.

"You can come in with me to meet him first," I said.

Teddy said, "Okay," and rang the bell.

The same man who we'd seen in the yard a few Saturdays back answered the door and said, "Hello."

"Hello," I replied. "I'm the one who called you for this meeting."

Mr. Tompkins smiled. "Okay," he said. "Come inside."

"Hi," Teddy said, adding that he'd wait for me in the car.

I walked inside, and Mr. Tompkins said, "I remember you two from the other day. You turned around in my driveway."

I said, "Yes."

He smiled. "Have a seat," he said, gesturing to the couch. "Do you want something to drink?"

"No thank you," I replied. I was so nervous I was shaking. I held my hands together so he wouldn't notice.

"Are you selling something for school?" he asked.

"No," I answered.

"Oh, many children around here are," he replied. He sat down across from me. "So, what can I help you with, young woman?"

I told him I needed to talk with him alone and asked, "Is your family home?"

"You don't know me, or you would know that I'm not married and my daughter isn't with me." He had a funny look on his face as he asked, "How can I help you?"

I told him that what I had to say was about his daughter.

He looked at me with a mixture of shock and concern on his face. "My daughter?" he repeated.

"Yes," I told him. And without waiting for him to say anything else, I started asking him questions about his daughter.

He asked me why I wanted to know about his daughter.

"Please tell me about her," I said gently. "Then I will tell you everything."

He looked very puzzled, but he started to tell me about his daughter and her childhood days.

"Where is she now?" I asked.

With a sad expression on his face, he told me the story of her and her mother disappearing.

After he talked about his little girl for a while, I asked, him her name.

"Nyah," he said.

I was waiting for him to say Sunshine, but he didn't say anything at all about the nickname my mother had mentioned. He continued talking about his little girl, and during the entire time, love and joy shined on his face. The joy changed to sadness when he told me Nyah was four when he'd last seen her and her mother. I knew in my heart he was talking about me. He told me she would be fifteen now. While he was telling the story, he kept looking at me. At one point, he stopped talking and asked, "Do I know you from somewhere? You look so familiar."

He had tears in his eyes. I could see how much love he had. But I could also see that pain and hurt resided in him. He didn't say much about the girl's mother, but talking about his little girl clearly brought him much joy. He finally said, "I have been going on talking, and you haven't been able to get in too many words. It's your turn now." Then he asked me my name.

I knew it was time to tell him everything. I started to say Jane, but I could not see him hurt another moment. I opened my mouth and said, "My name is Nyah."

He looked at me with his mouth open for a moment. He couldn't move or say anything. He only stared at me in shock. He finally moved from his chair, came over, and sat next to me. He looked at me hard, like he was looking through me. I started to feel afraid.

He then told me that his Nyah had a scar on the inside of her knee. He asked me to pull my pants leg up and let him look. He said she'd had to get stitches that had left a scar.

I felt every kind of joy leave me. I hadn't seen a scar on my leg. I pulled my pants leg up anyway, even though I knew nothing was there. He asked if he could turn my leg, explaining that the scar was on the inside, just above the knee. He took my leg and turned it over. And sure enough, I had a scar there that I had never seen before.

"It is you," he said. Tears were falling from his eyes. Through the tears, he showed me the stitch marks. He hugged me tightly and said he never wanted to turn me loose. "Please let this not be another dream," he said.

He kept saying, "It's you; after all these years, you are here."

We held each other tightly and cried together, never wanting to let each other go. This was my father. I had found him after all these years. This was the happiest moment of our lives.

Through his tears, he told me how much he loved me. He said he'd never given up on me and that he'd known that one day we would be back together. And here we are.

He asked about my mother. I told him she wasn't with me. I was sorry.

He told me how my mother and I had disappeared one day and that he'd heard and seen nothing of us until this day.

I told him my story—everything I remembered—and how I'd woken up in the woods with no memory alone. I told him I was staying with Mr. and Mrs. Daniels, a foster family, and assured him that they had been very good to me over the years I'd been with them. We held on to each other, and I told him how much I loved him. I added that, as much as I wanted to, I couldn't remember anything about us. "I don't even remember you as my dad," I concluded softly.

He held me, with sadness on his face, that he knew I was his daughter. "One day, you will get your memory back," he assured me. "But until then, I will take care of you and be there for you."

I told him I needed to talk to the Daniels and tell them about him. I explained that no one knew I had found him. He said he understood but that he was going to start today to straighten all this out so we could be a family. He knew he would have to go through changes to get me back with him where I belong. He asked if I needed him to talk to Mr. and Mrs. Daniels.

I said that I wanted to talk to them myself and assured him, when he asked, that I'd be okay talking to them alone. "This is something I have to do," I said. "And I am sure that they will be happy for me." I told him that as much as I hated to leave, I had to go. I gave him the Daniels phone number and address.

He told me he would give them a call after I talked to them. I cried as I got up; having to leave my dad was difficult. As we hugged each other, tears streamed from our eyes. He walked me to the door and told me this was my home.

I promised to call him once I'd talked to Mr. and Mrs. Daniels.

He kissed my forehead and told me how much he loved me. I turned and walked toward Teddy, who was standing beside the car.

We both got in the car, and Teddy backed out of the driveway. I waved to my dad as he stood in the door until we were out of his sight.

I looked at Teddy. Tears were still rolling down my face. I told him that Mr. Tompkins was definitely my dad and about the scar on my leg that I'd never seen before.

Teddy was happy for me. He asked if we could get something to eat while I told him all about it.

"Yes," I said, smiling. "I'm sorry that took so long."

Teddy took us to a hamburger place that had the best burgers. We ordered and drove to the park, where we sat and ate. Teddy listened as I did all the talking, telling him how my life was about to change and that I would be staying with my father. "I'm so happy," I told him.

Teddy finally got a word in. He said it was time to go home, and we talked more as he drove me home. I told him I didn't know how to tell Mr. and Mrs. Daniels about my dad, but I had to. I was ready to move in with my dad; he was my family.

Teddy walked me to the door. I didn't see anyone in the front, and it was quiet. I thanked Teddy for being there for me, and he said he would always be here for me. I smiled and told him I would call him later.

Chapter 11

*W*hen I walked in the house, everyone was watching something on TV. I didn't want to interrupt their TV show, so I decided to wait to share my news.

Mrs. Daniels asked me how my evening had been, and I said it was great and that I would love to talk about it with her after the show.

She smiled and told me the show was almost over. I went into the kitchen to get a drink. My heart was beating fast. I'd talked to Mrs. Daniels many times, and I'd never felt like this before. I knew this talk would be different. It would end with me moving out of her place and in with my dad. I felt happy but sad too. I was happy that I had someone to call mine. But I was sad that I was going to have to leave the only family that I'd accepted as mine, even though they were not.

I went to my room and thought about how I was going to break the news to my family here. I hadn't been in there long before Mrs. Daniels came into the room. "Tell me about your evening," she said with a smile.

I smiled and told her it had been a very good day. I asked Mrs. Daniels if I could talk to the whole family and tell everyone at the same time.

"Sure," she said with a smile. "You must have had a wonderful time."

She agreed to gather everyone downstairs.

I let out a big breath and said to myself, *this is it.*

I left the room and started down the stairs. Mr. and Mrs. Daniels and Sara and Kaylin were sitting there waiting. I looked at everyone's faces. They all had smiles on their faces and were waiting to hear my news. Mrs. Daniels was smiling but had a puzzled look on her face as well.

I sat in the chair across from them all. "I don't know where to start," I said. "Someone told me once when you don't know where to start, just start talking."

Everyone was quiet and waiting. I cleared my throat. "I have been staying with you for many years," I began. "You are the only family I have known. I love you all dearly, as if you were my own family. Mr. and Mrs. Daniels, you are the best. You have so much love in your hearts that you share so widely with not only me but with others. You have taken me into your home and treated me with so much love. And you've truly made me feel like I was one of your own. Thank you so much for showing me so much love. When I did not have anyone, you gave me the closest thing there was to a mother and a dad—and that was the two of you."

I looked at them. They both had tears in their eyes. Mr. Daniels said, "Thank you so much for thinking all this and feeling so close to us."

"You are a sweet, loving young woman," Mrs. Daniels added. "From your childhood to now, we have always enjoyed you being here with us."

"Sara and Kaylin," I said, "you are the sisters I never had and always wanted. I have a family somewhere but had no memory of them. I had no idea where they were. But I was placed with another family, one who loves me as much as any family could truly love each other, and that is you all."

I told Mr. and Mrs. Daniels that I had something else I wanted to tell them. I knew I couldn't tell them my real dreams, so instead, I said, "I started having dreams—not of a whole family but of a man with me. We were always in the front yard of a house playing. I had that dream repeatedly. I was a little girl, and we were happy playing together. He always would say I was his little sunshine. But in the dream, I would say, 'No. I am Nyah.' Then he would say, 'Yes, that's your name. But you are my sunshine.'

"I didn't want to say anything to you all because it was just a dream."

Everyone's eyes were on me, and they were all listening quietly, waiting to hear what I was going to say next.

"In my dreams, we were always playing games. The man would ask me what his name was and then would say different names. I would always pick the name Nathan Tompkins. He would hug and tickle me and say, 'You are right, Sunshine.' I never said anything to anyone here, but I always talk to Teddy about my dreams. I am sorry that I didn't come to you all and tell you my dreams. It was just that I wanted to come to you with good news and not just to find out that it was only a dream. I wanted to find out before I talked to anyone whether there was anything to the dreams.

"I looked for the name, Nathan Tompkins, in the phone book, and I found a name and address. I wrote the address down and asked Teddy to take me to the address. I wanted to drive by and see if I could remember anything of the place. We did drive by the house, and it was just like the one in my dream. Teddy turned around in the driveway so we could get a better look. Teddy was about to back out when a man came from around the house. He walked up to the car. He looked like the man in the dreams. He asked if he could help us, and Teddy told him we'd just missed our turn and were only turning around."

I stopped talking and looked at everyone sitting there. No one said a word; the house was absolutely quiet. I didn't know how Mr. and Mrs. Daniels were taking all of this; it felt like I was in the front of a class reading them a story.

Mrs. Daniels was about to speak but kept quiet when I started talking again. "I called the number many times but hung up before the phone rang. I finally got my nerve up to let it rang, and when the voice on the other end said hello, I asked to speak to Mr. Tompkins. I told him I needed to speak with him about something, and it would have to be in person. I added that it was important and asked when would be a good time to come over and discuss the matter. When he asked who I was, I told him it would have to be a surprise. I didn't know what else to say. He agreed and told me the date and time that would be good. It was today. That's where Teddy and I went today. I'm sorry I didn't tell you, but I had to do this on my own."

Mrs. Daniels started to speak, but this time I cut her off. "Please, Mrs. Daniels, let me finish." I told them about Teddy and me arriving and Mr. Tompkins inviting us in and saying he remembered us from the other day. I told them how Teddy had stayed outside and how I hadn't remembered anything when I walked inside the house. I explained how, when I'd asked if he was married or had children, Mr. Tompkins had told me about his little girl and how she and her mother had disappeared without a trace eleven years earlier. "As I sat there listening to him talk about his daughter, there was a lot of hurt in his eyes," I said. "In my dreams, my name was Nyah. I asked him his daughter's name, and he said Nyah. I couldn't hold back the tears or my feelings any longer. I told him I thought I was that missing daughter."

Then I described the combination of love and shock in Mr. Tompkins's eyes when he looked at me and how he'd said there had to be a mistake and how he'd never once taken his eyes off me. I told them about how Mr. Tompkins had shown me the scar I'd never known about until this day. "We knew then that I had to be his missing daughter," I said. "He hugged me, and we both cried together with joy. I told him you would want to talk to him," I added. "I have his number. He will be waiting to receive your call."

By the time I was finished, we were all in tears. Mrs. Daniels and everyone else hugged me and said how happy they were that I had found my dad.

Mrs. Daniels said she understood that I had wanted to do this on my own. She only said she would have been there for me if had needed her. She was glad Teddy was there for me. She said she would give Mr. Tompkins a call now. Mrs. Daniels hugged me tightly and said, "As much as I have grown to love you like my own, I surely hope that you have found your family."

Assuring me she was happy for me, she went to make the call. She and Mr. Tompkins talked for a while. When she got off the phone, she told me the two of them would go down to the social service office in the morning to tell them everything. She told me what to expect and explained that we would have a lot of paperwork to do and that I would have to take a test just to show proof that Mr. Tompkins was my father.

I was so happy. I knew that tomorrow was a school day, but asked Mrs. Daniels if I could miss school and go with her.

"Of course," she said. "I wouldn't have it any other way."

That night, Sara and Kaylin had many questions that I could answer but did not. I told them that all I'd had to go on was what was in my dream. I hated not telling them the whole truth, but I knew I couldn't tell them about my mother. I told them I still didn't remember him or the house. I didn't know if my memory would ever come back. I was just glad that I had found my dad.

The next morning, even though I was up early, Mrs. Daniels was up way before me. She had fixed breakfast for us, and Sara and Kaylin were getting ready for school. Mrs. Daniels said, "We have to be there at nine o'clock. Mr. Tompkins will meet us there."

We arrived fifteen minutes early. My dad was already there waiting. I remembered the truck from the driveway. I told Mrs. Daniels that was his truck. We pulled up beside it. When we'd parked and gotten out, I introduced everyone. We started talking about what was going on. Mrs. Daniels said she couldn't be happier for the both of us and that she hoped everything would turn out for the best. She knew that we'd both been through so much.

He told her he already knew I was his daughter. He had tears in his eyes, and so did I. We hugged each other tightly.

It was time to go inside. I had to stay in the waiting room while my dad and Mrs. Daniels went in to talk to the social worker. They stayed in so long I thought they were never going to come out.

Finally, Mrs. Daniels came out. "They want you to take the test here," she told me. "They will only swab your mouth. It will let them know for sure that he is your dad."

I was ready to get this part over. I already knew he was my dad. We went into another room, and soon, my dad walked in. We each took a seat while a woman wearing a lab coat filled out a bunch of paperwork. Then she took out a long thing that looked like a Q-tip and swabbed it all around in my mouth. After me, she did the same with my dad. She told me we were all done and explained that I needed to go back to the waiting room.

My dad and Mrs. Daniels went back into the room they'd been in earlier, and I waited another thirty minutes.

When they all finally came out, Mrs. Daniels said, "We are all done for today. We have to wait now."

Mrs. Daniels said we were going for lunch and added, "I invited your dad to come along."

I was glad. I wanted so much to be with him. I knew that he could tell me about my mother and me. He was the one who could tell me about everything that had happened to me up until the day my mother and I had left. Then I would have to tell him my part about me.

We went and had lunch and talked more. Dad asked Mrs. Daniels if she knew anything about my mother.

"No," she said. "Your daughter was alone without her mother when she was found." She told him how sorry she was that she didn't have any information on my mother.

Mrs. Daniels finally said, "We have to go." She needed to get dinner started, and she wanted to be there when the girls got home.

Dad smiled and said, "Thank you, not just for lunch but also for taking care of my little sunshine."

I smiled when he called me his sunshine. Looking into his eyes and, for once, seeing the happiness that was breaking through the pain and a heart that was shining and full of love for me was amazing. For once in my life, I was truly happy. And to be standing in front of my dad and seeing the same happiness wash over him after all he'd been through was overwhelming. I stepped up and threw my arms around him. "I love you so much," I told him.

He embraced me tightly, and tears fell from his eyes as he said, "I have loved you from the day you was born. You have always been the sunshine of my life, and you always will be sunshine in my life."

Mrs. Daniels was wiping tears away. "It's only tears of happiness for the both of you," she said, and she invited my dad for dinner.

"Sure," he said, beaming.

That night at dinner, we were like one big happy family. Everyone was happy for my dad and me. Even though the test results weren't back, my surrogate family could tell that Mr. Tompkins and I were father, daughter, and that we belonged together.

My dad thanked Mr. and Mrs. Daniels again. He said that, as much as he hated to go, he had to get up early for work and didn't want to keep us any longer. He thanked the Daniels for a good dinner, walked over to me, kissed my forehead, and said, "We have a whole lifetime."

I smiled as I walked him to the door. He gave me another hug and said he'd give me a call tomorrow.

After he left, a flood of questions I wanted to ask him filled me head. But I reminded myself that I would have plenty of time for that. I did not want him to go, even though I knew I would be with him soon after the test results came back.

The next day at school, I told Teddy about everything that had happened. I was glad to have Teddy. Having someone to talk to about my dad felt good. Teddy smiled and just listened.

That next week, the results came in. We all had to meet back at the same building. This time, I went in the office with Mrs. Daniels and my dad. The woman sitting behind the desk had a stack of paperwork in front of her, and my dad had to start signing on a bunch of lines.

"First," she said, "I'm going to read you the results."

All I heard was ninety-nine point something. My dad jumped up grabbed me and said he knew I was his daughter. "I have you now, and I will never lose you again," he said.

The woman went on and told us she would set up a court date for us.

"Court date?" I said.

"Let me explain," she replied. "We have found out that Mr. Tompkins is your dad. Now he has to get custody of you so you can be free to live with him. The only way for him to do that is by going to court. Then a judge can award him legal custody so that no one can ever take you from him."

I smiled and said, "I see."

"It won't be long," my dad said. "Then you can come home for good."

Hearing those words felt so good, but I was sad when I looked at Mrs. Daniels. I knew having to leave her and Mr. Daniels and Sara and Kaylin was going to hurt. I felt a familiar hurt start up again in my heart, knowing I would be leaving people I loved.

We left and went back home. I was the happiest girl on earth at this moment. Mrs. Daniels told me that she was very happy for me. "When you leave and go stay with your dad," she added, "you feel free to visit any time. And we could also come visit you."

"I would love that," I said.

In two days, the woman from social services called Mrs. Daniels and told her she would be sending the paperwork. She also gave her the date for us to be in court. She said she'd send all the necessary papers to both us and Mr. Tompkins tomorrow.

I was happy, but I still didn't have my memory back. I hated having no memories of my dad and family, and I wanted to know everything about my past. The next week dragged by.

When I got home from school that day, Mrs. Daniels called out to me. She said she wanted to talk to me and told me she had good news.

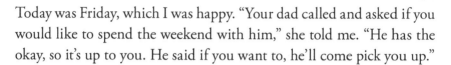

Today was Friday, which I was happy. "Your dad called and asked if you would like to spend the weekend with him," she told me. "He has the okay, so it's up to you. He said if you want to, he'll come pick you up."

I smiled. "Yes, I'd love to," I told her. I ran to the phone and called my dad right away. "I would love to spend the weekend with you," I told him.

He told me he too was excited to have me there. "Your grandmother and aunt also really want to see you," he added. He told me he'd be here at five to pick me up.

I hung up the phone and ran upstairs to pack. "Take enough clothes," Mrs. Daniels said. "You'll be staying until Sunday night."

Sarah and Kaylin helped me pick out outfits to take. Soon, Mrs. Daniels walked in. She had a huge smile on her face, and she told me my dad was downstairs waiting. Sarah and Kaylin gave me a hug and told me to have fun.

Mrs. Daniels walked me to the door, and Dad told her we'd be back Sunday night at seven.

I said good-bye and was off to spend the weekend with my family.

As we drove to my dad's house, I told him there was a lot I wanted to tell him.

"Yes," he agreed. "We have a lot to talk about and a lot of catching up to do." He looked at me with a smile said, "Sunshine, you are so beautiful."

I smiled back and said, "Thank you."

When we got to his house, there were many cars out front. When we walked in the house, a bunch of people shouted, "Welcome home!"

I smiled and kept a smile on my face. I didn't know what else to do. I didn't know any of the people in the room. My dad went around telling me who everyone was. Before long, I had met every one but my grandma. She came from around the corner in a wheelchair with the biggest smile on her face and tears running down her face. She was saying, "My baby, my baby." She held her arms out for me. I went to her, and she landed the biggest hug ever on me.

Grandma said she used to watch after me when I was a little baby. "You were my little angel," she said. "I am so glad you're home. I missed you so much.

"I heard you don't remember anything," she added gently, "but you will, angel. Just you wait and see."

The family had barbecued, and the food was good.

"I am glad you are here so someone can be here in this big house with your dad," my grandma said. It was a huge home for only one person.

As we ate, everyone had a story to tell about me when I was a baby. I loved them all. Listening to the stories was so much fun. But I realized that no one was saying anything about my mother.

"What was my mother like?" I asked.

Everyone got quiet and looked at my dad. I looked at him also. Was there something they didn't want me to know?

My dad started to talk. "We never said anything about your mom because we didn't know how you were going to take it with her still missing," he began. He went on to say how great a person my mother was. "You could not ask for a better person or mom than her." He met my gaze. "Your mom and I loved each other so much. I still love her. I don't know what happened to you two when you both disappeared. I am grateful that you are back here with us after all these years, and we pray for her safe return some day."

I felt the biggest lump in my throat. It was hard to swallow knowing what I knew about my mother and knowing I'd have to tell him all about her.

"Let's be happy for now and have a wonderful time," my grandma said.

My dad came over, sat beside me, and asked, "You okay?"

I smiled. "Yes," I assured him. "I am finally with a family that is all mines." I asked, "What happened to Grandma? Why is she in a wheelchair?"

"A car accident left her paralyzed," he explained, adding quietly, "Your grandpa didn't make it."

I was sad to hear that. "How long ago was this?" I wanted to know.

"Thirty years ago," he told me.

I thought of all the hurt my grandma had been through, and I felt sad for her. But knowing I might be able to help her felt good. I had to talk to my dad about me being different. For once, I was glad that I was different. I knew she might be able to walk again.

I could see the love the rest of the family had in their hearts for my mother and me as they talked about us. We laughed and talked for hours, until Grandma said it was getting late and it was time to go. She came to where I was sitting, held out her hands, and gave me a big, tight hug. "I love you, angel," she said. "I am so glad you are home safe."

Everyone else soon left, so Dad and I could spend some father-daughter time together.

I was happy being with my family. I only wished I could remember them as they remembered the times we'd shared together when I was younger. My dad looked at me and smiled, saying he was the luckiest man on earth. He went on telling more stories of my childhood that I could not remember. It made me feel good to hear him talk with much happiness about us together. I could see that he loved me very much then and even now.

Dad got teary-eyed again as he told me how happy he was that we were all were together and how he couldn't believe it when my mother and I had just up and disappeared one day without any trace. He told me that getting through day by day without us and not knowing if we were alive and safe had been difficult for him. He still didn't understand what had happened; no one had any answers.

I knew that I had the answers to some of his questions, and I knew that he needed to know.

"I talked to the police and updated them with the new information we have," he told me. "Hopefully your mother will be found alive and okay too."

Should I tell him everything now? I wondered. I knew I had to tell him, but not now. I couldn't bring myself to tell him about my mom. But I knew I would have to do so soon. I didn't want him to think I was keeping things from him. *Tomorrow*, I decided. *I will tell him tomorrow.*

How could my mother want to leave a person as good as my dad? I wish I didn't have to be the one to tell him so much bad news.

Dad said, "It has been a long good day. Let's go to bed and rest. We have the weekend to spend together and talk." He showed me around the house and then took me to my room. "Your room is the same as it was the day you left," he told me. "I couldn't change it or let anyone else come in here. I was afraid they would change something. I use to come in your room to feel close to you."

Tears rolled down my face as I walked into the room. It was beautiful, and I had many toys and stuffed animals. Three of them were on my bed. "Those were your favorites," Dad said. "They had to sleep with you every night."

"This is the perfect little girl's room," I told him.

I went to bed grateful to have a loving dad who cared so much for me. I only wished I could remember all the wonderful times together. His love for me shone through as he told me the stories of my childhood. He tucked me in, saying, "I know you are a little too big for tucking in, but you will always be my baby." He kissed my forehead said, "Good night. Sweet dreams."

I lay there thinking about how glad I'd be when I could come and stay here with my dad for good. I hoped it would be soon. I closed my eyes and went to sleep.

Chapter 12

The next morning when I woke, Dad was in the kitchen cooking breakfast for us. When I walked in, he grinned and said, "I hope you're hungry."

"I am," I assured him. "But could I help."

"Yes, you could, he replied. "But please, you sit and let me cook for you."

He was cutting up potatoes and onions, talking, and smiling. He looked up at me and started to say something. When he grabbed the kitchen towel, I knew something was wrong by the look on his face. I saw the blood and ran over to where he was standing over the sink. He said he knew he would need stitches.

"Let me take a look," I said.

He said he had to keep pressure on it to control the bleeding.

I knew I could help him but was afraid. I didn't know how things would go for us afterward if I did. I was scared to take the chance. Showing my dad the truth about me might even cause me to lose the only thing I had. Still, I knew he would need to know the truth eventually. I was willing to take the chance. I knew it was time to tell him everything.

"Sit down," I said. "I have something to tell you."

"We could talk on the way to the office," he offered.

"Dad, please just sit for a minute," I insisted.

He sat in the chair, keeping pressure on his hand.

"Dad, I can fix your hand," I told me.

He looked at me strangely. "I need stitches," he said. "Are you a nurse? I don't have anything to fix it around here. I'm a doctor," he added. "I know I need to have this cut stitched up."

"Please, Dad, let me show you. Then I will tell you what I need to tell you."

He looked up, and there was deep concern in his face. "How?" he asked.

"There is something about me that is different from any one else. When I help you, it will be different—something you have never seen happen. But you have to keep this between the two of us, please. When I am done, I know you will have many questions. I promise to answer them all. Please give me your hand."

He was hesitant but did as I asked. He held his injured hand out, still applying pressure with the other hand. I took hold of it and said, "What I am about to do ..." I gulped. "I don't know how you'll take it."

I could feel him trying to draw his hands back, but I held on tighter. I asked him to close his eyes.

He said, "Baby, what is all this about?"

"Please, Dad. Trust me," I said.

He closed his eyes, and I closed mine and began to focus on his hand getting better and healing. At first, nothing seemed to be happening.

Then I started to focus harder. That's when I felt the tingling in my hands. I knew it was healing his finger. I held on tightly until all the tingling had stopped. I took my hand off his and told him to look at his finger.

He opened his eyes, took the towel off his hand, and looked at his finger. The blood was still there, but his finger looked as if nothing had happened to it. With his mouth opened and his eyes wide, his stare fell on me; he didn't say a word. I didn't think he could say a word. His eyes stayed on me, and his mouth remained wide open. He fell to the floor.

I knelt down next to him. "Please be okay, please be okay," I heard myself muttering. I was afraid I had killed him or maybe given him a heart attack. I shook him, crying and calling his name. I didn't know what to do. I knew he was breathing but not responding. I shook him again. "Please, Dad. Don't leave me," I cried. "I am so sorry." I felt the tears rolling down my cheeks, and I threw my arms around him.

I could feel his body begin to move, and then his eyes slowly opened. He was still looking at me in shock. I didn't try to move him. I just asked if he was okay. I knew his finger was okay, but maybe something was going on in his body that I didn't know about. I was afraid to try to help him through focusing again. I asked, "Do you need me to call an ambulance to get you to the hospital?"

He spoke softly. "No."

I felt some relief and said, "Let's get you up."

I helped him up and to the couch. I tried to get him to lie down, but he shook his head no.

"Are you feeling okay?" I asked.

He nodded.

I said, "Stay here. Let me get you a drink."

He took a sip of the water I brought him, but he didn't speak and he never took his eyes off me. He was looking at me as if I was a ghost.

"Dad," I said, "This is what I wanted to tell you. It's time for you to hear the whole story. I will answer all the questions I know you have."

He still couldn't get his words to come out right.

"I don't know where to start, so I am taking your advice. You said just start talking. I was going to tell you everything today. I'm sorry you had to find out this way. I know I could have kept this to myself without telling or helping you. I could have just let you go to the office to have your finger stitched up. I wanted you to know I was different. I didn't want us to keep secrets from each other."

Before I continued, I asked, "Are you sure you're okay?"

Finally he spoke. "Yes … how did you?" By his words, I could tell he was still in a state of shock. His words weren't coming out plainly, but I could understand what he was asking.

"Dad, it's okay," I said. "I'm still trying to figure all this out myself. I am different because my mother was different."

He looked up. "What do you mean your mother was different?" he asked.

"Dad, she never told you who she really was or that she was different," I began. "I'm sure she might have wanted to tell you everything. I can't say why she didn't tell you. She was different. What you saw me do, she could do also."

Dad spoke quickly. "She never did anything like what I just saw you do." Then he added, "You got hurt as a child. We took you to the hospital."

"Dad," I said, "Mom was different. She wasn't from here. That's why she isn't here now." I took a deep breath. "Dad, I know you may not believe what I'm about to say to you. But everything I'm going to tell you is the truth. I recently learned all this information myself. I knew I was different when things started happening to me. I would get hurt and heal instantly. I was afraid; I even thought I was going crazy. Then I started having these dreams of a woman. The woman in my dreams said she was my mother. She started telling me why things were happening to me. She told me I was different and that I could do things that others couldn't do.

"As I told you, I don't remember anything about my life when I was smaller. I only know that I woke up in a field all alone without my mother, and I couldn't remember my mother or anyone else, not even myself.

"But I kept having dreams about this woman. She would tell me things about myself, explaining what I could and telling me how I should do things. Mother is different. And when I say different, I mean she was on this earth but not from this earth."

Dad spoke. "How do you know all of this if you have no memory of her?"

"I talk to her," I told him.

"Are you sure you're okay, Sunshine," he asked.

At least he still claims me as his daughter, I thought. That was a good sign.

"I don't know what to think of this and what you say about your mother. Where is she? Is she here?"

"No," I told him. "She's in the world she comes from—her world. I can talk to her through my mind. She's the one who told me about you.

I only found out recently—just before the first time Teddy and I were here, when we drove by that day. I was just finding out about you and came over to see you or to see if you had a wife or children. I couldn't tell you the truth then. I knew you would have thought I was crazy and wouldn't have wanted to see or have anything to do with me. I wanted to find out the truth for both of us. This is all new to me too. I know how you are feeling right now."

"You talk to your mother, and she told you all this?" he clarified.

"Yes," I said, "but not the way you think. It's not like talking on a phone. It's just." I struggled to find a way to explain. "Just like I focused to help your hand get better, I do that to talk to Mother. Believe me; I know I had the same feeling that you're having right now when Mother told me. I was scared and angry. Sometimes, I'm still angry.

"Mother said she wanted to tell you so many times when she was with you who she was. Only she didn't want you to think of her as different. She said she wanted you to love her for who she was—the woman you'd fallen in love with. I was angry and still am in many ways that she even wanted to leave and go away. The day she left, it wasn't as if she took a plane or a bus or something. She told me that we were in the park one day and the door to her world opened. She said she couldn't go and tell you. The door would only stay open for a few seconds, and then it would close. Mom said I was with her when she walked through the door, and just before it closed, I ran out. Then she disappeared from our world, and the door hasn't opened since. She had no way to get to me or to contact you or anyone else here.

"I stayed with this nice homeless woman in the park until she took ill and had to go to the hospital. When the people at the hospital found out I was alone, I was placed with foster parents, which is where I've been since.

"Mother isn't the same," I added. "I mean she's the same in terms of being herself. But when she went back to her world, her appearance changed. I see her how she look there. Here she would look like her normal self to you, but there, her looks are different. I have to be honest. She only looked like she did because she was here. And that's true for me too. I don't know being of you and from this world makes me different, but I am. In my dreams, I saw myself. And I looked like my mother. She told me I would look like I do now as long as I am here.

Mother said that, one day, the door would open for me. And it will be up to me whether I want to stay here or go there. She also said it would open again for her."

I could tell my dad hadn't taken all of this in.

"I haven't told anyone what I'm telling you or that I'm different. I have helped people, but they didn't know that I did it. I could help Grandma too."

He looked at me with hope in his eyes. He asked, "How can you do those things?"

"I don't know," I told him. "Mother told me it was a gift. I am learning to live with it. I'm glad I can help people when they need help, like I helped you."

He looked down at his finger and then back at me. "You are my daughter. I do know that. But what all can this gift as you call it do?"

"I don't know what all I can do," I said. "I only know how to help someone. That's all I need to know. Dad, I am the same person; I'm your daughter. Only I'm gifted to help people. You fell in love with a woman who was different. I came from her because I was part of her and part of you. I got the gifted part from her. I am part of both worlds. I don't know what all this means. I'm learning about it just as you are.

"I am glad I found out that you're my dad and that you're here with me. I haven't changed or anything. I'm still human. It's just that, when I get hurt, it heals instantly. Other than that, I am the same as you."

I told him how sorry Mom said she was for putting him through what she had.

He stopped me and said he did not want to talk about her but that he was glad I was back with him. I think that, after I told him everything, he felt like I did when I'd first heard all this from my mother—angry because she had decided to leave. She should have told him everything that I was telling him.

Dad spoke softly. "Thank you for helping my finger," he said and then added, "We can't change what has taken place. You are my daughter, and I love you no matter what you can or cannot do."

Even though I knew he had more questions, he wanted it to be a great weekend for the both of us. So he stopped with the questions for now. "I love you more than life itself. I will always be your dad, and you can always count on me, Sunshine, to be here for you. I will never leave you—never.

"Now let me finish breakfast for us," he said.

I smiled and told him to watch out for his fingers as he started chopping again. The way he looked at me made me hate that I'd said that. I told him how much I loved him and that I only wished I could remember our childhood together.

When he finished cooking breakfast, we sat down together to eat. I told him how good the food he'd cooked was. Silence hung between us as we ate breakfast.

I didn't ask any questions. I knew he had a lot on his mind and that he had to adjust to all that I'd revealed. I decided I wouldn't bring talk about our past this weekend anymore unless he brought it up. I wanted to spend the rest of our weekend living in the future and having fun with my dad.

We did just that. He said nothing about what had happened the next morning. He got a call from my grandma inviting us to dinner at her place after church on Sunday. I was glad I'd brought dress clothes, but I told my dad that I'd never been to church. The Daniels were always so busy they never took us to church.

"You loved going to church when you were younger," he told me.

"I know I will still enjoy it just as much now," I assured him.

"Today is Saturday," he said. "What do you feel like doing today? How about a movie? You name it."

"A movie would be great," I agreed, "only at home, and maybe some popcorn."

"That sounds great," he said.

I wanted to spend as much time with him as I could. Together time as father and daughter would do us both good. I felt good that everything was out in the open about me; he was my dad. That night, we watched movies, had popcorn, and had a wonderful time. He didn't look at me any differently even though he knew I was different. He seem like he loved me for who I was—his daughter.

The next morning, we both got dressed for church. He looked at me, smiled, and said, "You are beautiful. You look just like your mother."

I smiled at that. "Thank you," I said.

I could see the hurt in his eyes when he said anything about Mom, and I knew that, deep within his heart, he still loved her. Even through all the pain, the love in his heart was plain to see. I wished things were different for him and me. He had lost the woman he loved deeply, and had I lost the only real mother I ever had. The hurt was there for both of us. If two people had ever needed each other, it was us. All we had was each other. I knew he would be here for me, and I intended to be here for him.

Church was great. I felt very calm as I sat and listened to all the singing and the preacher. After church, the pastor came and hugged me. He said, "It is good to have you back, young woman." He went on to say that, when I was smaller, I would always clap my hands and that I had clearly enjoyed the service. "You have a great father," the pastor added.

I smiled, knowing he was right about that.

"It was nice having you at the service today," he told me. "I will keep you all in my prayers."

After church, we went to my grandma's for dinner. She had the table spread with tons of food. Grandma said. "Let's eat."

We all took our seats and held hands as my father said grace. His words touched my heart. I knew what he said came from his heart as he prayed and gave thanks. I could tell this family was close to each other and close to the one, they often prayed to. After the wonderful prayer, we ate and had a wonderful time, laughing and talking. I already loved the family, and I was glad they were mine. We stayed for a while longer, as everyone kept the stories of my childhood coming.

Then dad said we'd better get ready to go. We had to stop by the house and pick up my things before returning to the Daniels.

On our way to Dad's house, I told him how wonderful my weekend had been with him. I also told him I was sorry that I was different but that I loved him with everything in me.

He looked at me and said, "We have a lifetime together, Sunshine. Our days will be much brighter. You will see. Sometimes things don't go as we plan. But when we get down on our knees and pray, things always work out somehow in our favor." Dad said, "I prayed for you, Sunshine. I may have missed many years of being without you, not knowing what happened to you. But Jesus kept you safe and me in my right mind. He brought us back together, and we still have the rest of our lives to spend together." He said some families didn't get another chance to be together again. Things could have been so much worse; we could have lost each other forever. "Always pray," he told me. "Always be thankful, not only for the big things but also for the small things that we often overlook daily."

I was enjoying hearing him talk. It made me feel good inside. I asked him how to pray.

He looked at me for a moment and then said, "You talk to Jesus as if you were talking to me, but mean it from within your heart. Whenever you go through rough times, talk to Jesus. Even when you are doing well in your life, still talk to Jesus. Jesus loves to have you talk to him all the time and he loves to help us."

"Then I will start talking to him," I said.

We picked up my clothes and were on our way to the Daniels. Dad said, "I would love it if you would spend more weekends with me until you are able to stay for good."

I told him I would love that.

We arrived at the Danielses' place and Dad went in said hello and thanks to Mr. and Mrs. Daniels before he left.

Sara and Kaylin were all ears. They wanted to hear all about my weekend, and I was excited to tell them all about it. In bed that night, we talked and talked about all the fun I'd had. I told them about the rest of my family and about how we'd gone to church, how much fun it was, and how the pastor had remembered me from when I was smaller and had gone to church with my parents.

The next day, I had to tell Teddy the same thing over again. I didn't mind at all. I loved talking about my dad. The next time we have something at school that involved parents, I could bring my dad. Teddy asked if I wanted to go out that weekend. I told him I might be at my dad's and suggested that, if so, I could see if he could come over. I wanted my dad to get to know Teddy because I cared about Teddy a lot. I told Teddy I was sure it would be okay. He put his arm around me and walked me to my class.

All my friends were excited for me, and they all had so many questions. I tried to answer them the best I could. All I really wanted was to be back with my dad.

After school that day, I talked to Mrs. Daniels. She told me an attorney had called from the airline about the crash and would be sending information about it in the mail. She said she would turn all that over to my dad since he would be getting custody of me. I told her how much fun I'd had with my dad and the rest of my family. She was excited to hear all about my weekend. I told her I wanted to spend time getting to know my dad and the rest of my family, and she said it would be okay for me to spend more weekends with my dad.

Mrs. Daniels told me how blessed I was to have a family who loved me so much. She said she wished children were as lucky as me—to have parents who loved and wanted them in their lives. I didn't know for sure, but I think she was thinking of all the children without parents in their lives; she had a sad look on her face. She told me I should enjoy my family. "You are lucky you have a second chance with yours."

I told her thanks. I wanted to stay and talk longer with her, but I had to get started on my homework.

After all my homework, I lay on my bed thinking about all the things that had molded my life so far. I fell back on the old woman from the woods. I would love to go and visit her. I missed her so much. I called

Teddy to talk to him. He knew me well. As soon as I started to talk, he asked what was wrong. He knew something was on my mind. I told him that I wanted to visit the woman I used to live with, Miss Isabella. He said that was no problem; if I'd just let him know when, he would see about getting the car. I told him to let me talk to the Daniels and that I'd get back with him. Teddy and I spent hours on the phone before we hung up. I needed my own phone. Then I wouldn't have to keep this phone tired up. Maybe I could get one when I moved in with my dad.

I went out side with Sara and Kaylin talked with them. They were talking about boys they thought looked good at school. They were too scared to talk to boys, so they talked about boys to each other. I asked them why not just talk to the boys. They both looked at each other. Then in unison they said, "No," and laughed. I walked away and let them have their moment, talking and laughing about boys.

I went back in the house talk to Mrs. Daniels about wanting to visit Miss Isabella. She said that was a great idea but that she was going to be busy and wouldn't be able to get around to taking me right now. I told her Teddy would drive me there and back home, perhaps Saturday morning. I would call Miss Isabella's daughter first to see if it would be okay. Mrs. Daniels said if it was okay with Emma, it was okay with her. I said thanks and told her I'd let her know after I spoke with Emma. I decided I'd call tomorrow after school, as it was late now. We ate dinner and I went upstairs to read. I love reading and read a lot when I had nothing to do during the summer. Lately, since I'd been busy with all the things going on in my life, I had put reading on hold.

I picked up a book and started to read. As soon as I'd started getting into the story, my mind wandered over my own life. I considered that my life story would make a good read. *Maybe one day*, I thought. Sara and Kaylin came upstairs. They were talking so much that I decided to stop reading for now.

Chapter 13

I lay in bed letting my mind wander over my life. I had gone through many hard times, but I'd never been alone. I hadn't had my family with me, but I'd always had someone in my life that cared for and loved me. First was Isabella, who, although she didn't have anything, gave me so much love. Isabella didn't have a beautiful house, but she had a tent that kept us out of the rain. She didn't have the best of food or many choices, but we'd had something to eat every day. Even though our food came from a trashcan, it filled my empty stomach when I was hungry, and never once had I gotten sick. I loved and missed Isabella a lot.

Finding my dad felt like a turning point for the better, and I was very happy about that. I had a good life here with the Daniels. They were the perfect foster parents; any child would want to live with them. They were like family to me, but I longed to be with my dad and the rest of my family and to find more out about them and me.

When I heard my dad and my family talk about our past, I saw clearly that I'd been happy as a child and that my parents had been in love. Why had my mother wanted to go back to her home and leave this life behind if she was so happy? I hadn't tried to talk to my mother lately; I was busy getting to know my dad. If she had not chosen to go back, maybe none of the things that had happened in my life would have happened. Maybe I would have my memory and be living happily with the both my parents, rather than having to get to know my father and the rest of my family over again. If only she had chosen to stay.

I was distracted by Mrs. Daniels calling saying I had a phone call. It was my dad. When I got on the phone, he sounded tired or different. He said he needed to see me and to talk to me. He said it was about my grandma. She'd gone to the doctor, and the news was bad. He didn't' want to talk more about it on the phone but said he'd talked to Mrs. Daniels and arranged for me to go to his place tomorrow after school so we could go see Grandma together. He asked if that would be okay with me.

I felt a hard lump in my throat and tried to swallow, but it hurt. "Sure, Dad," I said. "I would love to see her."

He said he would be there after school to pick me up.

I swallowed and said, "I'll see you then."

Mrs. Daniels came and put her arms around me. "It will be okay," she said. "Your grandma will be fine. We will say a prayer for her."

"Thanks," I said.

I went to bed with a lot on my mind. I didn't know what was wrong with Grandma, but my dad had sound worried. Tears fell. I remembered what my dad and Mrs. Daniels had said about saying a prayer for her. I got out my bed and on my knees. I didn't know what to say, so I just started talking to Jesus. "Jesus, this is Nyah," I said. "I don't know how to pray. I have never come to you to pray before. I am sorry. Dad says I can just talk to you as I talk to him. He said you love us to talk to you. I hate to come to you on our first talk asking for something. I am sorry. My dad said you know everything. Jesus, this is what I want to ask of you. Something is wrong with my grandma. Please make her better. I will try to help her, but I need your help. My dad said you have all powers so please make her better and well enough to walk again.

"One more thing," I added. "Can you please help my mother come back home. I want this for me but mostly for my dad. He loves and misses her so much. I know many people want to talk to you, so I won't take up any more of your time.

"Oh, Jesus, thank you for loving me. I love you and will come talk to you more not just on bad times. Thank you and good night."

I got up feeling a lot better, lay down, and slept well. In fact, I was sleeping to well. Sara had to wake me. "Are you going to school?" she asked.

I jumped up and said, "Yes."

I dressed quickly and hurried to get breakfast and be on time for the bus. I could not concentrate on schoolwork very well that day; all I could think about was my grandma. Teddy tried to cheer me up. He told me not to worry, that everything would be okay. I told Teddy I was going to see my grandma after school and that my dad was coming to pick me up.

After my last class, I ran outside. My dad was already there, and no matter what, he always had a smile on his face. I got in the truck and said hello.

Before he had a chance to say anything else, I asked, "What's wrong with grandma?"

"Grandma went to the doctor, and her doctor told her she's going to need to have another surgery." I listened carefully as he explained what the doctor had said.

After he was finished, he looked at me and asked, "Do you think you could help your grandma like you helped me?"

"I will try," I said. "That's all I can do. But I did pray."

He smiled and told me that was good.

"I don't want Grandma to know that I'm different," I said. "Only you know. Dad, please, I want to keep it that way. I will try to help Grandma. I just don't want her to know."

"The doctor has her on some strong medicine that makes her sleep," he replied. "Maybe you can try to help her when she's sleeping."

"Would we be alone with her?" I asked.

"Yes," he assured me. "Your aunt has to leave when I get there. She has to go and get clothes so she can stay with her tonight."

"Okay," I said. "We can try." I looked at my dad, and he smiled back, but I saw the heavy pain and worry behind his eyes. I told him, "Dad, it will be okay. She will be okay."

He smiled and said, "I am sure she will, Sunshine."

When we got to my grandma's house, my aunt gave me a big hug and said it was good to see me. Then she left to get her clothes, saying as she went that she had given Grandma her medicine and that she was sleeping.

Dad and I walked in to my grandma's room. She was sleeping. We walked to the side of the bed. She turned her head toward us, looked at us, smiled, and closed her eyes again. I said, "Hello, grandma."

She didn't answer. The medication she was on meant she'd fallen back asleep. I told my dad that I was going to try now. I explained that I'd do the same thing I'd done when I helped him; I'd place my hands on her and focus on her getting better.

As I started, Dad asked, "Do you want me to leave?"

"No, Dad," I replied. "You stay with us."

He moved over as if he were afraid. I looked at him and smiled. "Dad, nothing is going to happen," I assured him. "You won't get shocked or anything. You don't have to be afraid."

He stepped closer to the bed.

I stretched my arms over my grandma's body, closed my eyes, and began to focus on her getting better. Dad was quiet as a mouse. I knew he was afraid. I blanked him and everything else out of my mind, focusing on Grandma only. I focused and focused harder; it took a while before I started to feel the tingling going through my hands. I knew she was getting better. I took my hands and placed them at the bottom of her feet, and then I moved them all the way up over her legs and body until I'd reached the top of her head. I kept my hands on her until the tingling stopped. Then I opened my eyes, removed my hands, and looked at my dad. His eyes were big.

I asked if he was okay.

"Yes," he said softly. "Is she better?"

I told him she'd be better. "I felt the tingling in my hand that I feel when a person is getting better," I explained. "I felt it when your finger was getting better."

He moved toward me and gave me a big hug. When I looked up at him, he said, "Thank you." Tears were streaming down his face. He said he knew Grandma wouldn't be able to thank me since she wouldn't know what had happened, so he said thank you for her.

"Your aunt cooked something," he added, wiping away tears. "She knew we were coming over. Let's sit down and eat."

We had spaghetti with garlic rolls, and it was delicious. After we ate, I cleaned the kitchen with my dad's help. Then we went to sit with my grandma while she slept.

My aunt returned and we talked a bit, but I had to leave soon. Dad said he wanted to get me back to do my homework. I went to see Grandma before we left. I kissed her even though she was asleep and told her how much I loved her and that she was going to be okay.

After I'd thanked my aunt for dinner, Dad and I left. On our way back to the Daniels, Dad and I talked. "Thank you, Sunshine," he said. "I don't know how you do the things you do, but you helped me. I had to ask if you could try to help your grandma. No matter how it turns out, I am grateful to you."

I looked at him and said, "Dad, she will be okay. And you are welcome. I was hoping that I could help her when I first saw her in the wheelchair."

We made it to Mr. and Mrs. Daniels' house, and I told Dad to call and let me know how Grandma was tomorrow after school. He said he would. He walked me to the door, hugged me and kissed my forehead, and said, "Tomorrow." He thanked Mrs. Daniels and left.

I told Mr. and Mr. Daniels how Grandma was doing and that she would be going back to see her doctor in the morning. "Dad will call me after school tomorrow to let me know how she's doing," I said. "I have to do homework."

Mrs. Daniels asked if I was hungry, and I told her I'd eaten already.

Upstairs, I joined Sara and Kaylin, who were finishing their homework. I did my homework and lay down. I was tired. I had drifted off to sleep when Mrs. Daniels woke me, saying the phone was for me. *I really need a cell phone*, I thought. It was Teddy calling to check on me. He went on telling me how he missed me. I told him about my grandma and said I'd tell him more at school tomorrow.

After we hung up, I went to bed and slept well. I was tired.

The next day was a long day; I really wasn't into school today. I was glad to see Teddy. I did miss him. I had started to care a lot for him over the years; we had been spending a lot of time together. During lunch, Teddy asked if I wanted to hang out this weekend. I told him that I would be at my dad's but suggested that he could come by. I was sure it would be okay. He said, "No. You go on. Have that time with your dad." That is why I liked Teddy so much; he always put my feelings first.

School was finally over, and it was time to go home for the day. Teddy did something that caught me off guard. Before I got on the bus, he pulled me close to him and kissed me, not on the forehead like before but on the lips. He held me for a while, and when he let me go, I looked at him and smiled. I felt a funny feeling in my stomach, only a good kind of feeling. He said he would talk to me later and then turned and walked away. I left with a smile on my face. I had never had that feeling before. I had never been kissed like that before. In fact, I had never been kissed on the lips before. That was my first real kiss, and I loved it.

After I got home, all I could do was think about that kiss. Every time I thought about it, that funny feeling came along with it. I smiled and thought about how I couldn't wait to see Teddy at school tomorrow. Maybe he would kiss me again like that.

We only had one more month of school, and then I would be out for the summer. I hoped I would be staying with my dad by then. But I really wanted to spend more time with Teddy.

That evening after school, my dad called. He said the doctor had said my grandma was doing better, so much so that he was going to postpone the surgery. He added that Grandma had said she hadn't felt so good in a long time. I told him I was glad and hoped she would keep getting better. We decided that I would stay with him that weekend, and we'd go visit her.

Before I hung up, I asked if it would be okay for Teddy to drop by.

"Sure," he replied. "That would be good."

I was happy because I wanted to see Teddy this weekend. I couldn't wait to see him the next day and give him the great news. So I called him as soon as I hung up with my dad and told him the good news. He was happy also. I didn't stay on the phone long, as I knew I couldn't keep the line occupied for long. I thought again, about how I really needed my own phone.

At school the next day, my heart started beating fast as I saw Teddy walking toward me. I had never felt like this before just by seeing him. He walked up to me, said hello, put his arm around me, and asked my friends if he could "borrow me. My friends all laughed, and one said, "Sure. Take her."

I wanted to be alone with Teddy; I felt good being so close to him. I didn't know what was going on with my feelings. I just knew it felt good to be with him. He took my hand, and we walked hand in hand toward the lockers. The bell hadn't rang yet, and as we stood in front of my locker, he told me how sorry he was for having kissed me like that, not knowing if it was okay to do that. I stopped him before he said another word and said, "I loved the kiss." I asked if I could have another one. He kissed me again the same way. I knew I had to stop, but I didn't want to. I enjoyed being kissed like that. But he cut it short. His next words were, "I love you."

I couldn't say a word. I just smiled. He walked me to my class, told me to have a good one, and then turned and walked away. I was a different person all the rest of the day. I couldn't wait until lunch just to be with Teddy.

When lunch came, we got our lunch and went outside to eat under the big tree where we always sit. We didn't get a chance to eat all our lunch for kissing each other. It was good we weren't in the front of the school. But we both knew we had to stop this while we were on

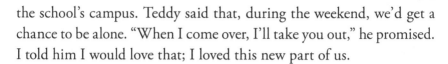

the school's campus. Teddy said that, during the weekend, we'd get a chance to be alone. "When I come over, I'll take you out," he promised. I told him I would love that; I loved this new part of us.

The rest of the school day, all I could do was think of Teddy. I couldn't wait until Saturday to be with him. At the end of the day, he walked me to my bus. We didn't kiss, but I wanted to. "We'd better just say good-bye," he said with a laugh. "Don't look so sad. You will get your kiss, young woman." He smiled and walked to his bus.

I was on cloud nine. I was in love and had learned what it feels like to kiss. I knew about the birds and bees as they say, but it was only kissing. Surely, nothing could happen just from kissing.

On the bus ride home, I thought about my mom. I wished things were different and that she was here with me. Yes, I had my dad. But I wanted a mother to talk to about boys and all the things a mother and daughter talk about. I needed my mother. I wished she were here with dad and me then things would be perfect. I would have my family.

However, that wasn't the case. I didn't have my mother to share my feelings with. I tried not to think of her, as it only made me angry and sad. She had chosen to go. I had two men in my life who loved me—my dad and my boyfriend. But I needed a mother to talk with.

Friday evening after school, I went home to pack so I could spend the weekend with my dad. I loved spending time with my dad, but I was more excited about Teddy coming. It was as if we were falling in love all over again, only it was better this time.

When my dad came to pick me up, he said we were going to stop and see my grandma before going home. I was glad; I had been waiting to see how she was doing. When we got to her house, we found her up in her wheelchair and happy. I walked in, and she was all smiles, her arms outstretched. She told me how she had missed me and was happy to see me again. She always had stories to tell, and I enjoyed listing to them.

In the middle of her story, which everyone there was listening to, she hit her leg, saying something was biting her.

My dad looked at her sharply. "Do you feel something biting you?" he asked.

"Yes," she replied.

Then she realized that she had feelings in her leg. She started to gingerly feel around her other leg. Tears begin to fall. "I have feelings in my legs," she said simply.

My dad took her shoes off and tickled her feet. She moved her feet away; she could feel that too. Her eyes filled with tears. "I have not had any feeling in my legs for more than thirty years," she said.

As she cried more, my dad cried along with her, tickling her feet and watching with glee as she jerked them back. Together, they laughed as she cried. I cried for the both of them seeing how happy they were. I was happy for Grandma. I ran and hugged her tight, telling her she would be walking soon.

She looked at me and smiled. "That would be a miracle," she said.

"Yes it would," I agreed and gave her another big hug.

We stayed for a while. Everyone there was crying and talking about how happy they were for her. Grandma told us she would go back to the doctor and give him the good news. She wanted to ask him what had changed. Dad looked at me and smiled. Tears rolled from his eyes, and he silently mouthed, "Thank you."

We slowly gave our good-bye hugs to Grandma, who always hated us to leave.

On our way home, Dad thanked me again. "I know her improvement has to be a result of you helping her," he told me. "The doctors have done so much for her for all these years, and we've never seen a change like this. I do not know how you do it, and I don't have to know. All I know is that I'm incredibly grateful."

I didn't quite understand all he was saying. I was just happy to be home and to help in whatever way I could. I was grateful for the help, wherever it came from. When we were home, we watched movies and ate popcorn until our eyes could no longer stay open.

I woke up early the next morning. I was excited to be spending time with my dad, but I was also excited that Teddy would be coming over today. Dad was up cooking breakfast. After we ate, I cleaned up the kitchen. He started asking me about Teddy. I smiled and answered his questions. He said he could tell I cared a lot for Teddy and that he was glad Teddy was coming over so he could get to know him. I told him that Teddy and I were planning to go to a movie and then out to eat and that, after that, we would come back to the house to spend time with him, if he wasn't busy." I told him a little about Teddy, saying I thought he'd find Teddy to be a sweet, caring person.

Dad said, "If he cares for my daughter, then he'll be fine with me."

Dad and I sat around the house and talked for a long time. He told me more about my childhood, and I reiterated that I hoped, one day, to remember that fun part of my life with him.

"You just give it time," he said reassuringly.

I asked about his job, and he told me he was a doctor and that he worked a lot. "The good thing about it is that I'm my own boss and set my own time off."

I smiled. "That's great," I agreed. "Why do you have this big home with no one but you here?" I asked.

His eyes saddened. "This big house was once filled with happiness, laughter, and little feet running up and down the stairs with me and your mother running behind you." He said he has been waiting for us to return and explained that he could never sell the house, as it held too many good memories. He looked at me and his smile returned. "You are here and will be moving in soon."

I returned his smile. "I'll be glad when that day comes," I said.

"Was Mother happy?" I asked him.

The look on his face became sad again, but he answered my question, telling me how happy we'd all been as a family. "I loved your mother like there was not another woman on earth," he said. "Your mother loved me too. I knew she did. She showed it every day. She was like no other woman I'd ever met. She had her own special way that she cared and loved. That's why I love her so to this day. When you came along, I never thought I could love anyone as I loved your mother. But you were my heart of sunshine. You were the seal of our love for one another. We were a family and a happy family. Your mother and I were happily in love, and we both loved you with all our hearts. When I lost both of you at the same time, not knowing what happened, I needed more than man's help to get me through it. I believed you both had been kidnapped. I never would have imagined that she left on her own accord."

As Dad talked, tears formed in his eyes. My heart swelled with love for him, but it was tinged with sadness too. I could see how deeply he missed my mother, and I could see that he was still in love with her. I threw my arms around him and told him how sorry I was about the pain he was feeling. I told him how much I loved him and assured him he would never have to worry about me leaving him.

He held me tightly and told me how much he'd loved me as a baby, adding that he loved me even more now as a young woman. He said his life was a lot better now that he have me back.

"I know it hurts you to talk about her," I said, sharing that it hurt me just as much and that I love her too. I said that I hadn't talked to her in a while.

"How can you talk to her?" he asked.

I looked at him for a moment, trying to decide how to explain our conversations. I did my best, and he seemed to understand.

"It's good that you could talk to her when you want, but it must hurt more to be able to talk to her and not be with her," he noted.

"Yes," I agreed. "I want her here with the both of us." Then everything I'd been thinking about came out. "I don't fault her that I'm here instead of with her; I'm glad I'm here," I told him. "After all, I was the one stepped out when she tried to take me to her world, and she couldn't get back to me. But I do fault her for going back period. She had a family here who loved her so much."

"I know that you're angry," Dad said. "So was I, but she is your mother, and I know for a fact that she loves you with all her heart. If there were any way she could have you with her, you would be there and not here. She is going through just as much hurt and pain as you and me. The love for your child always remains strong within your heart because that child is of you. To know your child is out there somewhere and you cannot be with your child feels like having something taken from your body that you need to live. Your mom has that part of darkness with her. Her love for you will always remain strong."

We had been talking for a long time, and I'd forgotten about the time.

Dad looked at the clock. "It's getting late," he said. "What time is Teddy supposed to be coming over?"

"Two o'clock," I replied.

When he said it was one fifteen, I jumped up and hugged him. "I have to get dressed," I said.

He smiled, saying, "It was nice talking to you."

I loved talking to my dad about our family. Even though it hurt both of us, I knew it also did us both good. The phone was ringing as I went upstairs. I heard my dad talking as I was getting dressed.

When I was ready, I went back downstairs. He told me how good I looked. "You look just like your mother." He said he had to go out for a little while but would be back before Teddy and I got home. He gave me a key to the house and said, "It's time you have your own key. This is your home now."

I took the key, but I didn't have a key chain.

He smiled. "I figured that might be the case, so I got that covered." He handed me a lovely key chain. "Thanks," I said. "I love it."

Just then, the doorbell rang and my heart skipped a beat. I knew it was Teddy. Dad went to the door, and Teddy came in. After greeting my dad, Teddy looked at me and told me how good I looked.

"Come on in and have a seat," Dad said.

The two talked for a bit while I went back upstairs to make sure I looked my best. I knew Dad was grilling Teddy, so I went back down to rescue him from the grill. I could tell Teddy was glad to see me come down the stairs.

My dad said, "You two have a nice time." As we walked out the door, Dad said, "Teddy you take care of the most important woman in my life."

Teddy smiled. "That's a promise," he said.

When we were in the car, Teddy said, "Your dad loves you."

"What did you two talk about?" I asked.

Teddy wouldn't tell me. He'd only say, "Man stuff," and then he smiled.

Chapter 14

Teddy drove away from the house. Then he stopped and gave me the kiss I had been waiting on.

"Let's just skip the movies and sit here like this," I suggested.

"No way," he replied. "You are too close to home, and your dad would kill me."

We drove around to the park. We had two hours before the movie started. We parked on the side next to the lake, but we didn't get out. Instead, we moved closer to each other, and soon we were kissing again. I was feeling feelings I'd never felt before, and I didn't want to stop.

We pulled ourselves away from each other, and Teddy said, "I think we should get out for a while."

"No," I said. Then we were kissing again, only this time, Teddy's hands started to rub my back.

Then he stopped and said, "I know it is time to get out and walk around the lake. I have bread for the ducks."

I thought it was nice that he'd planned to come to the park to feed the ducks. We got out of the car, and after feeding the ducks, we walked around the lake and talked.

I was the one to tell him that it was time we took our relationship to the next level.

"We need to slow things down a bit," he said, looking into my eyes.

"I don't think so," I countered.

He said we'd talk about it later.

"We can talk about it now," I insisted. "We're here alone together. Let's talk about it now." I pointed out that we'd been together for a long time and that we both loved each other. "I think it's time to go to the next step."

"As much as I would love to, I don't want to rush into something that both of us will end up regretting for the rest of our lives," Teddy said.

I stopped him and looked into his eyes. "I love you, Teddy," I told him. "I am ready to share a part of me with you."

He looked at me. "You do not believe in sugar coating, do you?" He told me how much he loved me and how hard it had been for him to stay on this level with me. "I did it because I loved you so much and never wanted to step out of boundary or disrespect you in any way," he said. "The same applies now. Taking it to the next level means opening up another chapter, and once you start it, you never stop."

I looked at him and said, "I am ready."

Teddy said, "We have to let it be the right way."

"Yes," I agreed. "I'll tell my dad we're planning to have sex for the first time."

His eyes got huge. "What?" he asked.

I smiled. "Calm down. I was only kidding."

He let out a sigh of relief. "Let's just go to our movie and dinner tonight," he suggested. "We'll talk later about moving to the next level."

I wondered if Teddy not being in a rush to move on had something to do with the talk he'd had with my dad. Whatever the case, I planned to win him over. We would talk about it, and sooner than he thought. I didn't mention it any more that night, though. I just enjoyed the rest of the night being with him and getting a kiss as often as I could. The movie was good, but I think I was more into Teddy than I was into the movie. Dinner was great too. Teddy had picked out a good Italian place.

After dinner, we were back in the car kissing again and getting carried away. I said, "Let's stop by the park again."

Teddy said no, but I begged until he gave in.

"Only for fifteen minutes," he said. "Then I have to get you home."

We stopped and things got a little out of hand. We both had our hands on each other where they had never been before.

Then suddenly, Teddy stopped. He started the car and said, "It's time to go now."

I smiled and agreed with him. He was right; if we didn't go then, things would have gotten entirely out of our hands.

When we pulled up in front of the house, we held each other's gaze. Teddy said, "Nyah, I love you so much, but I think we need to slow down."

I looked in his eyes and said, "I love you too, Teddy. But as for slowing down, the answer is no." I smiled and then asked, "Could I have a kiss?"

He smiled back. "The answer is no. Now let me get your door for you."

As we walked to the door, I turned to him. "I had a nice time," I told him. "It was the best date ever."

He looked at me and smiled coyly. "I bet it was," he said.

I knew we both loved each other. Teddy did kiss me on the forehead before we went inside the house. He said, "I had a wonderful evening with you, but it is always wonderful whenever I am with you."

I took my key out and opened the door. My dad wasn't in the living room. He was upstairs. He called down, saying he was finishing some paperwork and would be down in a minute. We turned on the TV and watched it for a little while. I tried to get Teddy to kiss me while my dad was upstairs, but he wouldn't go for it. All he said was, "Are you crazy?"

When Dad came down, he asked, "How was your evening?"

"Great," Teddy replied.

I told Dad about the Italian restaurant and how great the food was. "I'll have to take you there one day," I promised.

He asked what our plans were after high school. We told him that we planned on going to college.

"That's great," He said.

"Teddy and I are planning on going to the same college," I added.

My dad looked at us and said, "You two remind me of your mom and me so much. Always aim high. You can be whatever you put an effort into being. It may take a little more time when you aim high. But in the long run, it's worth it."

We talked a little more before Teddy said he had to be getting back home. Dad told Teddy he enjoyed him and that he was welcome any time.

Teddy stood up to leave and said, "Thanks."

I walked him to his car and said I hated him to leave. "Could I have a kiss?" I asked.

He looked at me and shook his head. "Don't push it," he replied. "We are standing in your dad's driveway. Your dad could be watching us."

"Good," I teased. "He would see how good a kisser you are."

Teddy kissed me on the forehead and got in the car, saying, "You are crazy." He told me to go into the house; he didn't want to pull away until I was inside. I did put my head into the car and kissed him on his lips. He smiled and said, "You are going to get me killed."

I turned and said, "Until next time," and walked back to the house.

I went back into the house. Dad was sitting and watching something on TV. "Tomorrow we are going to see about getting you a cell phone after church," he said.

I was happy to hear that. I had wanted my own cell phone.

On Sunday morning, we got up late and hurried to get ready for church. We didn't even have time for breakfast. Dad said, "We'll go over to Grandma's after church. She cooks for everyone every Sunday. Before you go home, we'll stop and get you a phone," he added.

"Okay," I agreed.

I hurried and fixed my hair, and we were out the door to church. Church was good. I was sleepy and struggled to stay woke, but I managed to make it through the service. Dinner at Grandma's was excellent. I was hungry by then. Grandma was doing well getting around, but she was still in her wheelchair.

After dinner, I asked, "Grandma, since you have feeling in your legs, have you tried to see if you can stand or walk?"

"No," she replied. "I've been in this wheelchair so long; I never thought of not being without it."

I suggested she talk to her doctor about the possibility, and she agreed that, when she went in for her next appointment, she would ask.

She hugged me. "There is something special about you, baby," she said. "That's why I love you so much. You are my angel."

We had to end the day short. We told everyone I was going cell phone shopping. Dad said he would pass my number along to everyone.

At the mall, I looked at a few different phones before I finally found the one I liked. Dad got it for me. He told the salesperson he wanted everything unlimited on the plan. I picked out the case while he finished the paperwork, and then we were done.

I added my dad's number, and he added mine. "Thank you," I told him.

He said he always wanted me to have a way to get hold of him, day or night. I hugged him and told him how much I loved him.

As we pulled up to the Danielses', he told me how much fun he'd had and said he hated to bring me back. He hoped this dropping me off situation would end soon. He walked me to the door, thanked Mr. and Mrs. Daniels, and said good-bye until next time.

I was happy to be back. I missed them, and everyone was glad to see me back home too. I told Mrs. Daniels that my dad had bought me a cell phone, and I gave her my number. She said that it would be nice for me to have a phone of my own.

I went upstairs to talk to Sara and Kaylin. They were happy to have me back. Sara said, "It won't be the same when you are with your dad for good and stop coming back here to stay."

"Maybe we could work out something where you two can come and spend some weekends with me," I suggested.

I showed the girls my phone and gave them my number.

Just then, it started to ring. It was my dad. "I just wanted to say thanks for a lovely weekend," he said, adding that he was looking forward to many more soon and that he loved me.

"Thanks again for the phone," I replied. "I love you."

He reminded me to use my phone wisely and with respect for the others there and then said good-bye.

I called Teddy. He didn't know my new number, and when I said hi, he was surprised to hear my voice on the other end. When I told him about my new phone, he was excited to be able to text me and that we could chat more often. I told him I really enjoyed his company and had had a great time with him. Then I said I had to go and that I'd see him tomorrow at school.

I lay in my bed and thought about my weekend. I couldn't wait until tomorrow to talk with my friends about my weekend. They always talked about all the hot, juicy gossip with their boyfriends. Now I could add to the discussion for a change; my news wouldn't be as juicy as theirs would, but it was a step farther. I was excited at that moment. I wished I had my mother to gossip with. I just knew it would have been fun living together as a family with both her and dad.

The next day was a good day at school. I talked and gossiped with my friends and talked with Teddy, which was always great. We talked about the summer how we plan to spend it. The months had flown by. We only had three more weeks to go, and school would be out. Teddy said he would be working full time during the summer. I told him I planned to find a job as soon as I moved in with my dad. We talked about the different colleges we wanted to apply.

Teddy said something to me that shocked me. I mean I wasn't thinking about it yet. He said he wanted to marry me. He wanted me to become his wife one day. He said, "I know this is early yet, and we haven't finished high school or gone to college, but I want you to add that to your future goals—that you will be my wife, that is, if you want that also."

I smiled and planted a kiss on him.

When we were done, he said, "I take that as a yes."

"I would love to add that to our future," I said.

"Then get ready," he told me. "I will be asking you again one day."

He walked me back to my class. The rest of the day went by quickly. It was time to go home before I knew it. After my last class, Teddy met me and walked me to the bus. He said he'd call me later. "I have to work on getting a car so I can drive you home," he added, looking into my eyes.

I smiled. "That would be great," I said.

When I got home that day, I heard the news we'd all been waiting. The court date had finally been set. It would be the following Tuesday morning. "If everything goes okay," Mrs. Daniels told me, "You'll be able to move in with your dad." She told me how happy she was for me but added that she'd miss me too.

I was ecstatic.

My dad called later, and I confirmed that Mrs. Daniels had given me the news. I could tell how happy dad was. I was happy and ready to move in with him. We didn't stay on the phone long; he was working and said we'd talk later.

Grandma called and told me she was going to the doctor tomorrow. She planned to talk with him about her chances of walking again. She said she was happy I was finally going to be able to move back in with my dad. I told her I was glad to hear that she was doing so well.

My phone stayed busy with calls from my family, and I had no complaints. I loved it.

Teddy finally called, and we talked about many things. He wanted to get a car during the summer before school started again, and he was excited to work full time and save more money. I was happy he would be able to work so much, but I knew I would miss him. I sure hoped I'd be able to get a job this summer somewhere.

I pulled out my books and did my homework. Sara and Kaylin were still working on theirs by the time I'd finished, so I walked downstairs and went outside.

My mind had been on Isabella lately. I decided to give Emma a call and give them my number. I wanted to keep in touch with her family.

When Emma answered, she said she was glad to hear from me. I told her the news about finding my dad and getting ready to move in with him. "How's Sadie doing?"

"Great," she said.

Then I asked about Isabella.

"She's doing great also," Emma said. "She's up and walking around again. We're keeping a close watch on her."

"I would love to visit Isabella soon if that's okay," I told her.

"That would be great," Emma replied. "I know she would love to see you."

I told her about the court date Tuesday and said I'd give her a call after next week. Then I gave her my cell number and told her to call any time. "Tell Isabella hello for me and that I'll be there soon to visit," I said before we hung up.

The rest of the week went slowly for me. I was excited for the court day to come. The weekend came and went, and Monday was especially slow.

Then finally it was Tuesday—court day. I missed school to go, and Mrs. Daniels and I were there early. My dad was already there and waiting. We all walked in together. We had all the necessary paperwork, so we expected the proceedings to move quickly.

We had to wait for a while for some other cases that had been scheduled before ours to conclude. Then our time came.

The judge asked each of us some questions. He had all the paperwork in front of him. He asked about my mother, and Dad told him she was still missing. After the judge had gone over all the paperwork and asked all the questions he wanted to ask, my father was given custody of me. I was able to move in with him that very day.

I was only asked one question. Did I want to live with my dad? And my answer was yes.

I was nervous and glad that was the only question for me. My dad picked me up and hugged me right there in the courtroom he was so happy.

Mrs. Daniels told us both how happy she was for the both of us. She was in tears; only she said they were happy tears. She said, "You can get your things whenever you come by. We will leave you two to celebrate."

We both hugged Mrs. Daniels, and Dad told her we'd come by later in the day. We all left happy. I was finally able to move in with my dad and be part of my family.

I called Teddy to give him the good news. He was at school on break. I told him we would celebrate later.

Dad and I went back to his house—a house to call my home with my family. We walked into the house and Dad said, "Welcome home, Sunshine."

Dad tried to talk me in to taking one of the bigger rooms, but I'd already fallen in love with the one I was in my room.

"Okay," he said. "You can make any changes you want with the color or furniture."

"Nope," I told him. "I love it just the way it is. It'll be a perfect room for me."

He told me he needed to run to the office for a while but said he could take me to get my things first and bring me back so I could start putting them away. I said that would be fine and called Mrs. Daniels

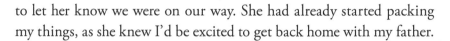

to let her know we were on our way. She had already started packing my things, as she knew I'd be excited to get back home with my father.

When we arrived, Mrs. Daniels said she'd packed what was in the drawers but hadn't gotten to the things in the closet. I was glad she'd started. I had a lot of stuff. We finally got it all together and loaded it into the truck.

By the time we finished, Sara and Kaylin were walking in the house. They were already looking sad. I knew I couldn't stay long, as my dad had to get to the office. I hugged them all, and by the time we were through, we were all in tears. I told them we would see each other again soon and reminded the girls that we could have some nights over at each other's house. Saying good-bye was hard. I felt a lump in my throat that I couldn't swallow.

We were finally out the door and into the truck. As we left, Dad said, "It'll be okay, Sunshine. You can visit whenever you want."

I was on top of the world. When my phone rang, I looked at the caller ID it was Emma. "Hello," I said.

Emma apologized for bothering us but said she wanted to let me know she had taken her mother back to the hospital. She didn't know what was going on, but Isabella had just passed out again. I told Emma I would come as soon as I could.

I hung up and told my dad what was going on. He said he'd drop me off at the hospital and promised I could call when I was ready to leave. We went straight there.

I rushed into the emergency room. Emma was in the waiting room. I ran over, gave her a hug, and asked how Isabella was doing.

Emma said she hadn't heard anything yet. I sat and waited with her. Emma asked how I was doing, and I told her about Dad getting custody and that I'd be moving in with him today. She told me how happy she was for me. She kept talking, but I didn't really hear her. I was thinking about Isabella. I had to know what was going on.

The doctor finally came in. He told Emma it was her mother's heart and they were waiting on more test results to come in. Tears were rolling from Emma's eyes. I put my arms around her and told her everything would be okay. It was good Sadie wasn't here. I was having a hard time trying to keep Emma together. Emma asked the doctor if she could see her mom.

He said yes but added that only one of us could go in. I knew Emma had to be with her mother, so I stayed in the waiting room. I also knew I had to get in to see her somehow.

It wasn't long before Emma returned. "I didn't stay long," she told me. "I knew you wanted to see her. The doctor said it was okay, but you can only stay for a minute or so."

I rushed into Isabella's room. She lay there helpless. Tubes were running from her body in every direction. She wasn't awake. I walked over to her and held her hand. "Hello, Isabella," I said. "This is Nyah." I knew that, deep within, she could somehow hear me. I told her I was sorry she wasn't feeling well and that I hated to come see her on these terms, rather than better ones. I told her everything was going to be okay.

I knew I didn't have much time, so I placed my arms around her and began to focus on her getting better. Tears fell from my eyes. I cared for this woman as if she was my very own mom. She was all I'd had; when I'd had no one else, she had taken care of me as if I was her own. I couldn't stand to see her going through this. My hands began to tingle, and I knew then that she would be okay. Even after it was all over, I sill lay on her, telling her how much I loved her. I told her I would always be there for her—always.

The doctor came in and told me that Isabella needed her rest I left feeling relieved.

Emma was there waiting on me. I told Emma not worry; her mother would be fine. Emma asked if I needed a ride, I told her my dad was picking me up. We hugged, and I told her to keep me posted on how Isabella was doing.

I called my dad and told him I was ready. I sat down, and I thought of Isabella while I waited. Dad called and said he out front. I walked out feeling good. My dad asked me how Isabella was, and I told him she would be just fine. He asked if I'd help her, and I told him I had. He smiled, saying he did not know how I did it, but it was good that I could help.

Back at home, I started to put my clothes away and settle in. Dad said he was going to start dinner, but I told him I wasn't hungry and said I'd make a sandwich later.

"Okay," he said. "Sandwiches sound good."

I loved my dad and knew I was going to enjoy staying with him. When I went downstairs for a drink, Dad was sitting in front of the TV. "It is good to have you back home," he said. "I have prayed for this day to come for so long."

I walked over, sat beside him, and hugged him. I could see the tears in his eyes. "I never thought this day would come," I told him. "I never really believed that I would be with my family again or even find you." I told him how happy I was to be home. I only wished I could remember my dad and our home. But I was happy to be here with him, knowing he was my real dad.

I smiled and asked if he'd like a sandwich.

"Sure," he said. "Everything you'll need is in the kitchen."

I went into the kitchen, which was big. *Anyone would love to cook in this kitchen*, I thought. I had to ask where the refrigerator was; I couldn't see it. Dad came in and showed me where everything was. The refrigerator and dishwasher looked just like the cabinets, which I thought was cool.

After I made the sandwiches, we ate, talked, and then watched TV for a while before we both went to bed. I slept like a baby that night.

When I woke the next morning, Dad was in the kitchen drinking coffee. He said he would go in a little late so he could drive me to school. I told him I'd get the bus schedule that day.

School was great that day. I felt good. I was living with my dad. I was in love with a wonderful person. I was happy for a change. I only wished my mother were here, not just for me but also for my dad. I knew he still loved her very much.

Chapter 15

I talked to Teddy during lunch at our favorite spot under the tree. It was nice to get away from around the crowd. I asked him when we could go out again.

"After what you pulled the last time," he said grinning at me, "maybe in two years."

I hit him on the arm. "You know you loved every moment of the fun we were having," I protested.

Teddy hugged me. "Yes, we did have a nice time," he agreed.

I asked when it was going to be our special day.

He looked into my eyes and said in a serious tone, "We have to talk about that."

"We're talking about it now," I responded.

Just then, my friend Sandy came over to invite both of us to her birthday party on Saturday. By the look on Teddy's face, I could tell he was glad she'd come over. I looked at him and smiled. "This isn't over with," I said. Then I turned my attention to Sandy. "We would love to come," I said.

She gave us an invitation and said she hoped we could make it before walking off.

I looked at Teddy with a smile. "Where did we leave off?" I teased. "What day is good for you?"

He smiled back at me. "Okay, if you are sure, we will talk about it and make plans," he said, "but not so fast."

I hugged him. "I know it will be a wonderful day," I said.

Too soon, it was time to go back to class. I spent the rest of the day daydreaming of the time we would be spending together.

My final class was gym, which I enjoyed. Today, we were playing volleyball. We were all dressed and out on the field playing. Everything was going well until one of my teammates, Sandy, tried to spike the ball. When she came down, she collapsed on the ground not moving. Coach ran over to her. He hollered for one someone to run and call for help while he stayed with her.

Cathy, one of our teammates, ran off to make the call. We all stood there. Everyone had Sandy surrounded. There was no way I could get close to her. I knew I could do something if I could only get close, but too many people were standing and watching every move that was being made with her.

The ambulance arrived quickly, and the EMTs were soon working on her. I stood there helpless; I couldn't do anything but watch.

I had to leave to catch my bus, but I knew I had to go to the hospital.

My cell phone was ringing. It was Teddy, saying he hadn't seen me before his bus left. I told him what had happened and said I'd call when I get home. It was too noisy on the bus.

As soon as I got off the bus, I called Teddy. I asked if he could get his dad's car, pick me up, and take me to the hospital. He said he'd call me back. It didn't take long before he called to say he was on his way.

I called my dad. He was with a patient, so I left him a message telling him what had happened at school and that Teddy was taking me to the hospital and would bring me home. Teddy pulled up in the driveway. I told him to come in while I changed.

When we arrived to the hospital, Sandy's family was there. I told them we were classmates and asked how Sandy was doing. Her mother said the family hadn't heard anything from the doctor yet. *It's always a wait*, I thought. So Teddy and I sat and waited with them.

Finally, the doctor came out with news of Sandy. He told her family she was stable and doing well but that there was a problem with the blood flow to her heart. He said they were waiting on more test results to come back. Her parents could go in with her for a little while, but she really needed rest. Teddy and I waited while Sandy's parents went in to visit. Sandy's mom came back crying.

She looked over at me and said, "You can go see her for a few minutes."

I jumped up. "Thanks," I said and headed for the room.

Teddy was behind me. I needed to be alone. I could not think about Teddy there with me. I was worried about Sandy. When I got to the room, I saw that Sandy was asleep. I stood beside her bed. I knew what I had to do, and I didn't have much time. The nurse had warned us we'd only have a few minutes.

I looked at Teddy. "Can you get me something to drink?" I asked.

When Teddy walked out, I put my arm across Sandy and began to focus on helping her get better. Just when I started feeling the tingling in my hand, Teddy walked in. I had my eyes closed and I tried to keep focused on what I was doing and block out all the questions Teddy was asking. I didn't say a word to Teddy, and he finally walked out.

After it was all over, I walked out of the room. I was thinking of Teddy and how I was going to explain what he'd just seen. I walked back to the waiting room. He was sitting there in a daze, which was broken when he saw me. His first words to me were, "What was going on in there? What were you doing to her?"

"Let's go," I said. "I'll explain later."

My mind was all messed up. I knew I loved Teddy and was scared that, if I told him the truth, I would lose him. All the way home, the questions kept coming. I wanted to tell Teddy everything, only I couldn't. There wasn't enough time to explain everything I wanted to explain. I told him I couldn't tell him now and said we'd talk later when we had more time—even though I still wasn't planning to tell him the truth.

Teddy pulled into my driveway without saying a word. I opened the door and turned to the window, thinking he would get out and walk me to the door. Instead, he put the car in reverse and backed out without saying a word, not even a good-bye.

Teddy had never left with me standing in the driveway. Tears rolled down my eyes. I opened the door and wiped them away. My dad was watching TV. He turned to me and asked if everything was okay. I faked a smile and said yes; the doctor had said Sandy would be okay. I didn't tell him what happened.

He asked if I was hungry. I didn't know if I was hungry or not after what had happened between Teddy and me. I told him I'd fix a sandwich later and that I had to do homework. I ran upstairs. I tried to call Teddy, but there was no answer. I started my homework but stopped soon after to call Teddy again. Still no answer came. I knew he was upset. He never didn't answer his phone when I called. I gave up calling and finished my homework. Then I took a shower and got into bed. All I could think about was Teddy. He hadn't returned my calls.

As I lay there in my bed crying, all I could think about was how I was going to explain the other part of my life to Teddy. I knew I loved Teddy. I also knew I could drive him away if I told him the truth. But telling the truth hadn't driven my dad away. He was my dad, though. He would love me no matter what, because I was his child. Teddy and I didn't have any ties. He could walk away, find someone else, and move on.

I didn't know what to do at that moment; I needed my mother to talk to—not through my mind but here with me. I wanted her to be here with me. I wanted to talk to her. I closed my eyes and concentrated on her, but my mind drifted. I tried again, and soon I felt myself connecting with her. I opened my eyes, and there she was, as if she was standing right in front of me.

Mom was smiling and happy to see and talk with me again. She told me how she missed and loved me, and I could see tears in her eyes. I told her I'd found my dad and was staying with him. After I told her how great a dad he was, I asked the question that had been filling my mind. "Why would you want to leave him?"

Her face fell, and she cried as she answered. She explained that she hadn't thought she was leaving for good. When she saw the open door to her world, she'd thought she would be able to step through and step back into our world whenever she wanted. By the time she learned how wrong she was, it was too late. "I know now," she told me, "you cannot come and go when you want. If the door ever opens for you, make sure, before you step through it that you plan on staying. Don't make the same mistake I made, which I am still regretting."

"Will it open again for you to come back?" I asked tentatively, half afraid of the answer.

"Yes," she assured me, "someday. I am so sorry for all the hurt I have caused you and your father. I still love your father and always will."

I told her I knew he still loved her—that it showed in the way he talked about her and in his eyes. She smiled, and the tears flowed as she told me to tell him how sorry she was.

"This house is huge and beautiful," I said. "I wish you could come back, so we could all be a family." I told her that we both needed her.

She asked about her beautiful garden. "It's wonderful," I told her. "It has every kind of flower you could want."

"I loved that garden," she said wistfully. "Your father used to tell me that I'd stay there all day working in it. And then we would sit for hours just looking at the beauty of it."

In a way, I felt sorry for her. I could tell she really wanted to be here with us.

"Is everything okay?" she asked me.

I assure her that being here with Dad and the rest of the family was great. "I love them all. They are all kind and love me dearly. And they talk about you with much love."

"Yes," she agreed. "They are all good people."

"I do have a boyfriend, Teddy," I told her. "We're close. We've been together for years. Only he doesn't know the real me. I mean he knows about my memory loss. That's all I told him."

Then it just spilled out of me. "I was at the hospital with a classmate helping her get better when he walked in. He had so many questions. I couldn't take the time to answer. I was afraid if I told him the truth about me, he would not want to be with me. I do care for him."

She looked at me sadly. "I do wish I was there with you," she said. "The only thing I would do if I was you," she added, "is sit him down and tell him the truth. I wish I had told your dad everything about me. I wanted to so many times. But like you, I was afraid I would lose him. I loved him too much to lose him. I still love him."

Mother took a deep breath and said, "You have to be honest with your boyfriend. If he really loves you and is the one for you, he will be with you until the end. Even if he leaves, he will come back to you somehow.

"Tell him the truth," she urged, "because if you don't, you will always have to lie and then lie again to cover another lie. That's no way to live your life with the one you truly love."

She said that maybe one day she would have a chance to come back and make things right with me and my dad and that she'd give anything for another chance. "Tell your dad I am sorry and that I'm looking forward to asking him to forgive me in person," Mom said. "You have choices in life. Making the right decisions means always being honest, no matter what. If you give your all and are honest, you're doing what is right in life. Then you'll know you've done your best, and no matter how things turn out, you will always come out on top."

She told me she loved me with everything inside her and told me to take care of my dad.

I told her I loved her and would keep in touch. Then I closed my eyes, and she was gone.

With my eyes closed, I soon drifted off into a calm sleep.

I woke up early for school the next morning. I could hear Dad downstairs saying he was about to leave. "Have a great day," he called.

I told him I would and said I loved him. He was out the door. I dressed and was off for the bus stop, but my mind was still on Teddy.

Normally, when my bus pulled up at the school, Teddy would be waiting. But he wasn't today. I didn't see him anywhere.

I walked to the cafeteria. No sign of him there. I went to our spot. He wasn't there. I went to my first class and then the second, and still I'd seen no sign of Teddy. I knew then that either he hadn't come to school or he really wanted to be alone. My day was all upside down. I wanted so much to call him. Instead, I gave him his time to be alone. I went all day without talking to him. It was like having a cell phone but leaving it home; trying to function all day without it was hard.

When school was out, I got home and still I hadn't heard a thing from Teddy. I dialed his number more times than I could count, but I never could hit the call button.

When Dad got home, I was making dinner for the two of us. Mrs. Daniels had taught me how to cook. Dad said, "It smells great."

We sat down to eat dinner, and he knew something was wrong. I told him what had happened with Teddy and me. He said he was sorry. "Just give Teddy a little time," he suggested.

"I hope so," I said as I gathered the dishes from the table.

Dad offered to wash dishes since I'd cooked.

"No," I said, "it's okay. I'll clean the kitchen." I wanted something to do to keep my mind off Teddy. It didn't work; he was all I thought of. This wasn't our first fight, but none of the previous ones had been like this. He'd always called before, and we'd never gone this long without talking.

I watched TV with my dad, and he tried to cheer me up. I laughed with him, but through all the smiles and laughter, Teddy was there on my mind. Dad said he was tired and was turning in early. He'd had a long day. He told me not to worry about Teddy too much; he just needed time. Dad was sure that, after he'd had time to think, he would be back.

I went upstairs and watched TV for a while before I fell asleep.

The next day was Friday, and Teddy showed up at school. He walked up to my locker. When I saw him, I felt a thrill of joy going through me, only to have it taken away right away. "We need to talk," I said when Teddy was standing beside me.

"Yes," he agreed, "but not here. I'll call you."

He then walked off, leaving me at my locker alone. I was hurt and angry at the same time. It wasn't as if I had done him wrong in anyway. He didn't understand what was going on, and because I didn't want to tell him, he was acting as if I'd done something to him. I walked off angry. I didn't try to talk to Teddy anymore that day. Between breaks, I tried to get to my locker early, so that we wouldn't be at our lockers at the same time; his locker was close to mine. It worked out, and we didn't see each other the rest of that day. I left my last class early, rushed to my locker, and boarded the bus well before it would take off. That worked too, and I was off and headed home without seeing him. I was still angry, and I was also hurt.

I had the weekend ahead of me, and I planned to stay busy, not think of Teddy, and avoid calling him. That was going to be hard no matter how mad I was with him. I loved him no matter what. I would spend time with my dad. That would keep me busy. Sandy's party had been canceled. I hadn't talked to her, as she hadn't been back to school. But I'd heard she was out of the hospital. I just wanted to stay home this weekend, doing nothing but kicking back and watching TV.

I got home, changed my clothes, and got into the doing-nothing mood. My dad came through the door full of joy as always; he was like that, even if he'd had a bad day. Dad asked, "How's it going with Teddy?"

"We're not talking," I told him.

"Just give it time," he counseled. "Don't try to rush it. Teddy has a lot on his mind, just like you do."

He asked if I wanted to go out for dinner, but I didn't want to eat; I wasn't hungry.

"Well," he suggested, "how about a good movie tonight here—just the two of us—and a bowl of popcorn."

"Now that's a date," I said.

In truth, all I wanted to do was be alone, to think or just cry. I wanted this difficulty between Teddy and me to be over and things to get back to the way they'd been before the hospital with Sandy.

Dad's phone was ringing. When he hung up, he told me he'd have to take a rain check on the movie night. He would be going to the hospital later to check on a patient.

I was glad in a way. It would give me an opportunity to be alone tonight. I had a lot of thinking to do. I had to decide what I was going to tell Teddy. I knew that, at some point, we would have to talk, and I needed to be ready to tell him something. I thought about what both Mom and Dad had said about honesty. I wanted nothing more than to tell Teddy the truth. Only I didn't know what would happen between us if I did. I didn't want to lose Teddy. He wasn't just my boyfriend; he was also my best friend. He was someone I could laugh with and tell all my problems to. He knew most of my secrets, and I'd use his shoulder to cry on through so many of the problems I'd faced. Teddy was the one who people say is hard to find. I'd been through so much, and Teddy had been there for me through most of it. I knew we were both young.

But when you've been with a person for so long and the two of you had gone through so much together, something grows between you. Some say its love; some say it's just that you have been together for so long. Whatever the case, I couldn't take the chance of losing everything Teddy and I had.

How would Teddy look at me when I told him about the other part of me? I still had problems understanding it myself. How could I possibly put this on him? No, I decided, I just can't. I had to think of something else; there had to be some other way. But what?

Dad came back downstairs. "Are you still sitting there watching TV?" he asked. "And you're not hungry yet?"

I didn't notice that time had gone by so fast. I had been deep in thought. When Dad asked me what was I watching, I didn't even know what was on. My eyes were on the TV, but my mind was far away. I didn't answer his question. Instead, I changed the subject, saying I hoped everything went well with his patient.

"It's going to be a long night," he said. He kissed my forehead and said, "Good night."

I was surprised that Teddy hadn't called at all that night. I turned the TV off downstairs and went upstairs to watch some more. I called and talked to some of my friends from school. They all asked what was going on with Teddy and me. I told them we were having our differences and left it at that.

I didn't call anyone else. I didn't want to talk about Teddy and me. I knew Teddy was missing me. It had to be hard for him not call, because it was driving me crazy. I really didn't have anything to do, and I didn't want to talk to anyone. So I got out a book and tried to read to get my mind off Teddy. It didn't work. The only thing left to do was cry, and that is what I did until I went to sleep.

My phone woke me up. I grabbed it thinking it might be Teddy. It was my dad calling to check on me. Since I was awake again, I turned on the TV and fell asleep with it on. I slept through the rest of the night and didn't even hear my dad when he came in.

I woke up to the sun shining through the windows that Saturday morning. Somehow, that put me in a good mood. I got up. Everything was quiet. I knew my dad was still sleeping since he'd had such a long night, so I kept it quiet. It was early still. I walked out to the front and got the paper. I looked across the street and noticed a man coming out his house. He was using a white cane to help him walk. I sat on the porch and watched the man as he made his way down the steps. He was blind, but he was coming out to get his paper out of the paper box. As he picked up the paper, it fell to the ground. He kneeled down and patted the ground looking for it.

I stood and started over to help him, but I waited and watched as he gathered most of his paper, stood, and turned and walked back into his house. I wanted a reason to visit him. I walked over to his yard and gathered up the rest of his paper.

When I knocked on his door, I heard him come to the other side of the door. "Who is it?" he asked.

"Your neighbor," I answered. I told him I had the rest of his paper. He opened the door and told me to come in. When I walked in, he thanked me. I noticed a girl in a wheelchair with the paper in her lap.

"Please tell me you have the comics with your stack," she said.

I smiled. "Sure do," I said, pulling the comics from the pile. "Here it is." I walked over and handed it to her.

She asked if I liked to read them.

"Yes," I said. "They're my favorite."

"Sit," she said, "I'll read them to you."

I sat, and we laughed as she read the comics aloud. Before she was finished, we were all three laughing.

When she was done, I looked over at her. I wanted to ask what was wrong but wasn't sure how.

She answered as if she'd read my mind. "I've never been able to walk," she told me. "I'm used to it now."

I told her I was sorry to hear that.

"Me too," she said. "But I'm okay. I don't get out much, so my uncle goes out and gets the paper for me. He usually gets the entire paper; only sometimes he leaves some behind." She smiled playfully in her uncle's direction. "My aunt brings the rest in when she gets home from work.

"This is my uncle Joe," she added. "He got hurt at his job. The accident left him blind. He's been blind almost as long as I've been in this wheelchair. He helps me out by bringing me things. He knows this place like the back of his hand and never knocks down a chair or bumps into a table. The only problem he has is getting the entire paper. But he's getting better."

"Do you both stay here?" I asked.

She laughed. "I know it looks weird—a blind man taking care of a girl in a wheelchair.

"No," I assured her. "It looks good." I stood and told her I had to go.

She asked, "Could you please help me before you go by rubbing this cream on my leg for me? I always make a big mess."

I stood and said, "Sure."

She handed me the cream. My mind was already there helping her. As I rubbed the cream on her leg, I kept my head down, closed my eyes, and started to focus. I kept rubbing the cream in and focusing. Finally I felt the tingling. I rubbed until it stopped.

"Thank you," she said.

"You are welcome," I replied, adding, "Oh, I'm Nyah. I stay across the street."

"With Mr. Tompkins?" she asked.

"Yes," I told her, "and I'm his daughter, Nyah."

"Sorry, I'm Kim," she replied.

I told her I had to go and she thanked me for the company as well as the favor. I walked out of the house knowing Kim was going to be walking out and getting her own paper soon. I knew that I would return to help Joe as well soon.

I walked into the garden in our backyard and sat on a bench. Sitting there thinking—and I had some long, hard thinking to do—somehow made me feel close to my mother, and looking at the beautiful garden always made me feel better.

I knew what my heart was telling me to do what my parents had advised—be honest. I knew when the time came for Teddy and I to talk, I had to be honest with him, even if it caused him to break up with me. I realized too that he might not believe me. I knew if I was in his shoes, I wouldn't.

I looked around at all the beautiful flowers. I could see why my mother loved flowers; they were beautiful. I stayed in the garden for a while, picking off all the brown leaves and pulling out the weeds and doing all the other work that needed done. Before I knew it, I'd been there for hours.

When my dad walked over, he smiled. "You look like your mother here. She loved her flowers."

I told him she still did, and he gave me a funny look. He didn't respond though, but just smiled. He said he tried to keep the garden up, but work kept him from it too often. I stood up and got out the hose to water the flowers. I had dirt all over me.

It occurred to me that not once had I thought of Teddy or what was going on while I'd been out here in the garden. Maybe that was why my mother had loved gardening so much. It keeps your mind from thinking of your problems. I knew she'd had a lot on her mind, keeping so much from my dad.

At that moment, I knew I had to be honest. I had to tell Teddy the truth about me if I was planning to be in his life a long time. I just hoped my honesty wouldn't change things for us.

Dad looked at the garden after all the work was done and told me it looked good. "In fact," he said, "I've never seen it looking this good before."

"It was already beautiful," I told him. "It only needed a little caring for. That always brings the best out in everything or person."

"You have spent most of your Saturday in the garden," he said. "What's next, young woman?"

Dad and I both stood looking at the garden. Dad said he'd tried to plant all the flowers that he thought my mother loved. Whenever he worked in the garden, somehow he felt close to Mom. I told him I felt the same way.

Then I told him that I'd talked to Mom recently. He looked at me in surprise. But I continued. I wanted him to get her message. I told him that Mom had said she was sorry for all the hurt and pain she'd caused us both and that she'd left thinking she could come back. "She told me to tell you she will always love you," I said. "Mom wanted me to ask you to forgive her and said that one day maybe she could ask you yourself."

When I looked over at him, I saw tears on his face. "Your mother is a woman that any man would be blessed to come home to and never want to leave. She had a heart that cared and was full of love. She loved in a special way." He cleared his throat. "I will always love your mother. That's why I am alone today. Another woman could never replace your mother. I could never love another like I loved her."

He put his arms around me, and I wiped his tears as he wiped mine. He said, "We will get through this together. We have each other. Now let's get something to eat. You've worked hard."

After lunch, dad said he wanted to stop by Grandma's for a little while. He wanted to show me something.

When we got to Grandma's house, she opened the door. And she wasn't in her wheelchair! Instead, she was walking with a walker.

I threw my arms around her as she stood there in tears. She told me she'd never thought she would live to see this day—to be able to walk again. "I walk too much," she added. "The doctor told me I might be overdoing it." She chuckled and said how grateful she was to be walking and that she was sure that, soon, she wouldn't even need a walker.

I was so happy for her. She wanted us to stay and have lunch. Dad told her we'd just had lunch and were only stopping by. He told her we were having a father-daughter day.

When we were back in the truck, Dad looked at me for a long time. "Thank you," he said, "for helping your grandma. Thank you for giving her that part of happiness in her life again." He wiped his tears, saying, "These are what you call happy tears."

I smiled and wiped my own happy tears away.

Chapter 16

*D*ad was treating me to the mall to do some shopping. We shopped the rest of the evening from store to store, and I got clothes, shoes, and purses—the works. We had so much fun together. Dad took me to a Mexican restaurant that he said my mother had loved. I'd never had Mexican food, so he helped me by telling me what was good and what my mother had loved.

"Order me what Mom always got," I told him.

The food came, and I started eating it. I immediately saw why my mother had loved this restaurant; the food was great. And we had so much food we had leftovers to take home.

On the way home, my dad said, "I knew you would love the food."

Dad and I got home, and I snuggled on the couch, ready to watch movies the rest of the night. Dad couldn't keep his eyes open. So he said, "Good night," and left me to finish the movie alone.

My mind returned to Teddy. I hoped we would work things out soon. I really missed him. I finished watching the movie and decided to go upstairs and lie down to watch more TV, even though the TV always ended up watching me.

I woke up that Sunday morning feeling great and went out early to water the flowers. I was falling in love with the garden. I sat among the flowers, watched the sunrise, and listened to the birds singing. I heard this funny, low chirping sound over by the trees on the fence side of the yard. I walked toward it and found a little baby bird lying on the ground chirping. I looked up. In the big tree over me, I could see the nest and hear the rest of the baby birds chirping. I picked up the bird, and when I looked close, I saw that one of its wings had been broken, maybe from the fall. I rubbed its little head as it chirped and thought of it being alone without the others; it made me think of the time I'd been alone. I felt badly for the poor baby bird. I closed my hands around it and focused on helping the little creature. The tingling feeling went through my hands, and I knew the bird was going to be just fine. When the feeling had stopped, I opened my hands and looked at its wing; it was back to normal.

I couldn't reach its nest, so I went to get a ladder from the shed. I placed it under the tree and climbed up. When I looked into the nest, I saw the mother wasn't there, but three little birds were there chirping. I placed the baby back in the nest with the others. They were all chirping together as I left them.

Back inside, Dad was up. He said he was making us a breakfast sandwich before we went to church. "You know your grandma will have a ton of food for dinner," he added. We ate breakfast, dressed, and left for church.

Everyone was so happy to see grandma walking with her walker and out of the wheelchair; church started late because everyone wanted to hug her and tell her how happy they were for her. I was happy to see her smiling and walking.

After church, we went to Grandma's for dinner. As usual, she had more than enough food, and this time she'd made a chocolate cake that melted in your mouth. I felt full just looking at it all. Our family, as well as a number of close friends, met here every Sunday for dinner. Grandma said she wouldn't have it any other way. She loved to cook. I knew she had to get up early to cook all the food that was there.

I always hated to leave when it was time to go. When I was gathering my things, I looked at my phone, and my heart seemed to stand still. I had a missed call from Teddy. He'd left a message. I didn't call back or listen to the message right away. I wanted to wait and get home so I could be alone.

As soon as we got to the house, I ran up to my room and listened to the message. Teddy started by apologizing about how he'd been acting. Then he said that he didn't know what was going on at the hospital. Then when I'd acted weird and hadn't even tried to tell him what was going on, everything had seemed even stranger. He said he'd been angry and confused and had needed time to himself, but now he thought it was time to talk. He left it up to me to pick a time and place.

I wanted so much to talk to him, but I didn't think this was the right moment. I chose not to respond to him that night, knowing I would see him tomorrow. I went to bed feeling somewhat better. I was glad that he'd called. Still, I was worried. I knew we had to talk, and I didn't know whether, he would just call it off and walk away. I went to sleep pondering deep thoughts.

The next morning when I got off the bus, Teddy was standing there waiting. I was happy to see him but also afraid.

"Good morning," he said and added again that he was sorry.

I told him I was sorry too and that I knew it wasn't fair to have left him not knowing what was going on to not have talked to him. He said we needed to talk—that things couldn't go on like this. I asked if he could come over after school today. He agreed and walked me to my class. Things were different; he was quiet as we walked. When we were at my class, he said he would see me later and turned and walked away. I felt somewhat hurt, but I think he felt the same. We didn't sit together at lunch since he didn't show up for lunch, and I didn't see him anymore that day. I was somewhat glad because the tension, or maybe hurt, between us was too much.

When the end of the school day arrived, I called my dad to let him know Teddy was coming over to talk.

"Okay," he said. He told me he'd be home late and wished me luck.

"Thanks," I said. Hanging up the phone, I knew I was going to need not only luck but also a miracle to help me through this all.

Soon, everything would be out in the opening with Teddy. I was glad I'd decided to be honest with him. I felt good in a way.

I arrived at home and waited. I used to be excited whenever I was waiting on Teddy. Today wasn't like that at all. I thought of my dad and what he'd been through and was still going through. No matter how much he loved my mother, he didn't really know her at all. I didn't want to put Teddy through anything like that. We were both young. We did love each other and were best friends. Teddy had gone through a lot with me. I loved him so much I had no choice but to tell him the truth. I hoped he'd still feel the same toward me after our talk.

Through the window, I saw his father's car pull up. He sat there for a while before getting out. It seemed this was as hard for him as it was for me. No, it would be harder for me, I decided. I was the one who had to tell him about me. All he had to do was listen. I knew what he'd seen at the hospital had confused him. I hoped he wouldn't run out of here after I told him everything about me. As I stood watching him, I thought of us being together and happy, of him always coming to my rescue, of the times he'd lent his shoulder for me to cry on or his ear for me to talk and cry out my problems. No matter what it was, Teddy had always been there helping me through situations I'd thought I would never get out of. I was the type of person who never wanted to wait on anything. Whenever I thought of doing something, I wanted to make it happen right away. Even when I had time, I wanted to jump ahead of things. Only Teddy had always been there to slow me down or keep me from doing something that most likely would have gotten out of control.

I watched Teddy as he walked slowly up the driveway toward the house. He looked sad and was looking down toward the ground. He rang the doorbell, and I opened the door and invited him in. He followed me into the living room, and I told him my dad wasn't home so we could talk here.

I sat across from him, and looking into his eyes, I could see the concern and hurt in them. I sure hoped he was ready to hear what he was asking me to tell him.

Teddy started to talk, but I interrupted. "Please, let me talk first," I said. I knew if he talked first, I wouldn't be able to tell him the truth about me. I'd felt the same hurt and fear not too long ago in this same house when I'd had to tell my dad the same story I was about to tell Teddy.

I started by saying, "Teddy, I am sorry for all the hurt and pain I have put you through. You are the last person other than my dad I would want to hurt. I never meant to hurt you or leave you in suspense about what was going on at the hospital. You have been here for me since the first day we meet. You know almost everything there is to know about me. As I said, *almost* there is this other part of me I am trying to know more about.

"As I got older, I started to see and feel things about myself that were different—what I mean is that I started to learn that I was different somehow from anyone else. I still don't have any memory of my early childhood before I woke up in the woods. Certain things have happened to me over the years that have taught me about this difference between me and everyone else. I don't know how to explain who I really am because, to this day, I don't really know myself. All I do know is that

I am not like you or any other person you know. I mean I am like everyone else; I'm just different in some ways. I don't know how or why. I've just learned to accept that I'm different and go on with life.

"At first, I started having dreams of this woman that seemed so real it was almost scary. I kept dreaming of the same woman. She told me she was my mother, and I've since found out that she is my mother. She told me I was different—special, as she called it. I could do things that other people couldn't do. I was in the woods one day and I fell and cut myself. I was bleeding, and I help my hand over the cut to stop the bleeding. When I stopped on the way back to the house to check on it, the cut had healed by itself. There was no sign of the cut at all."

I looked at Teddy. His eyes were big, and the expression on his face made him look like he was watching a horror movie.

Still, I knew I had to keep going. I shared with him the other times that I'd concentrated and had been able to help people with the tingling feeling in my hands.

The entire time I'd been talking, Teddy hadn't tried to say a word. I asked him if he was okay.

"You're kidding me, right," he said.

I looked at him and held his gaze. "I wish I were, but I'm telling you the truth. You saw me with Sandy and you wanted to know what was going on. I was helping her get better. I can help people get better. I didn't want to tell you the truth. But I finally decided that if I was going to tell you anything, it was going to have to be the truth. I know that, other than this, we haven't kept anything from each other. But this was different. I didn't want to drive you away, and not knowing how you would take it, I chose not to tell you. I was wrong, and I'm sorry. I'm being honest with you about myself. Please, no matter how things go after this, please let this stay between us."

Teddy cleared his throat. He seemed to be trying to say something, but the words just wouldn't come out.

"I know this is hard to believe," I said. "And you have many questions that I am willing to answer."

He tried again, clearing his throat. This time he managed, "Is what you just told me true?"

"Yes," I answered.

"How?"

"I got this from my mother," I explained. "She was different like me. I don't know how though. I've told you all that I know; this is all new to me. I hated it when I found out that I was different, but now I'm glad because I can help people who are in need of help. I am still the same person. I'm just a little different, but in a good way."

He smiled for the first time. Seeing that smile brought tears to my eyes. "I thought you were going to tell me next you were from another world or an alien," he said, his lightheartedness only half-real.

My heart skipped a beat again. I knew what he was joking about was also true, but I said nothing in response.

He then asked me something that made my blood boil with anger. "Is this that witchcraft stuff?"

I couldn't believe he would think of me that way. The hurt went deep, cutting me like a dull knife going through flesh. Tears began to fall as I looked into his eyes. "Do you really think I'm that kind of person—that I would deal with such things? If I were, you'd be a frog by now. But if you really think that of me, then you've never known me at all. You have been with me for this long, we've been through so much, and yet you think so little of me?"

Teddy asked, "Is there anything else you need to tell me?"

"Yes," I said. "My mother is different too. She's alive, and I talk to her sometimes. She isn't from here. I don't know from where she's from, but I can talk to her through my mind."

He had a look that said he was ready to run.

"I close my eyes, focus on my mother, and she's there," I continued. "She's the one who led me to my father. I'm sorry I couldn't tell you then."

"Are you not from here?" he asked slowly.

"Yes. I was born here," I told him. "But I am like my mother" I didn't get into any more details. I figured I'd already given him enough information. Besides, he had started looking at me as if I was a ghost. "You're standing here with me, looking at me, and talking to me just the same as always," I said. "Do I look different in any way to you?"

"No," Teddy answered. "But you are standing here telling me things that we would only ever see in movies or on TV. This is no movie; it's you.

"Nyah," he added softly, "you're this person I've grown to care so much about. Yet I know so little about you. I'm sorry that you've gone through so much in your life. But I don't know what to say. I don't know how to take all of this."

I looked into his eyes. I could see that this was hurting him, but most of all I saw fear as he looked at me.

"We've been together a long time," Teddy said, looking away. "I care deeply for you. I've never had any reason to be afraid of you or think twice about you in any way. I am sorry to say this, but I'm afraid you're a completely different person standing here telling me all these things about yourself. I do know you, yet I don't know you." He looked at me, and sadness seemed to come over him. "I don't know how I feel about you, me, or anything anymore," he said. "I don't know what to think."

I spoke softly to him, telling him, "You have no reason to be afraid of me. I could never do anything to harm you. The only thing I could do is love you and help you if you ever needed it. I will always be there for you no matter how things turn out. I am sorry that I am different. I'm sorry I make you afraid or that you feel differently toward me after hearing this. However, I will never be sorry for being the person who loves and cares for you or for helping someone have a better life, free of pain, and seeing a smile afterward. For that, I am thankful. I know this is a lot for you to hear, and maybe it's hard for you to see me as you once did. But I am the same person you've always know. So how you feel now or what decision you need to make about us is yours; I can't make that choice for you."

Tears were rolling down Teddy's cheeks now. I knew that he was serious when he finally talked. "Yes," he said. "We have been through a lot together. And I know you've been through so much. Dealing with family issues and still working them out. I love you deeply, but this is too much for me to deal with. Thank you for being honest with me.

I don't know how to take it when I look at you now; I see this other person. I have to be honest with you as well. I am sorry. I can see that what I'm saying is hurting you. I've never wanted to hurt you, ever. It's hurting me just as much."

He talked on, tears falling the entire time. And finally, he choked the words I'd feared so deeply. "We should go our separate ways and see other people. We need to give each other space."

I felt my heart stop; or at least it seemed that way. I couldn't believe what I was hearing. Tears streamed down my face as I listened to the one guy who I cared for more than almost anyone else break up with me. I looked at him, and I knew I was in shock. I felt the entire range of painful emotions swell up inside of me. I could hardly speak as I opened my mouth to tell him I was sorry I had hurt him and made him look at and feel differently toward me. "I'm sorry it has to lead to this, but I will always love you, Teddy," I told him. "You have your feelings, and the choice you're making is yours. I'll respect that, and I'll give you the space and time you need." I told him again that I was sorry.

He said he was sorry too. Then he stood and walked toward the door. I followed him. At the door, he turned and looked into my eyes. He was still crying, but all he said was, "Good-bye." Then he opened the door and walked out. No hug or kiss, which I wasn't expecting.

If I had heard what I'd just told him, I would be bolting for the door too. From the window, I watched the one man I loved dearly, my best friend, walk to his car. I watched him wipe his tears from his eyes, get into his car, and drive out of my life. I didn't know how to take what had just happened. All I wanted to do was cry, and that is what I did.

What was I going to do without Teddy in my life? School would soon be out, and I'd have the whole summer to be myself without Teddy.

The next week was hard for me at school. Teddy and I didn't talk to each other. I never saw him at school, even though I knew he was there. My friends knew we weren't together, and they kept me updated with all the gossip.

I told my dad what had happened, and he kept telling me to give it time. Things had a way of working themselves out. But I knew this time was different.

I knew Dad, who was without my mother, was feeling the same pain I was going through. I knew his heart had been full of pain for a long time, as he'd been hurting during all the time he'd gone without Mother and me.

One day, Dad and I were sitting around the house talking and he went into his bedroom and returned with picture albums. "Your mother took a lot of pictures of us," he told me. "I could never look at them. It was always too painful. It still is, but I thought you should see them."

I figured this was his way of trying to cheer me up. And I was very happy to see the pictures. I hadn't known how my mother looked here; I only knew how she looked there. I opened the book, and there was my dad, a woman, and a baby. I didn't have to ask him who they were. Mother was beautiful. Everyone told me I looked like her. My dad and she looked so happy.

He spoke softly, saying he was sorry that I couldn't remember my mother or him or my childhood time we'd spent together.

Dad was right. Mom had taken many pictures. It was as if she'd known how important these pictures would become. *Did she know this day would come?* I wondered. There were pictures of her in the hospital and of them coming home with me. I came to a series of photos capturing a family vacation. I felt lost looking at my family together; it was weird to see myself there and not remember any of it. We seemed like a happy family. I knew how empty my dad must feel. I felt empty just looking at all the pictures.

He left me to look through the rest of the pictures alone. As I looked through the pages, I cried for my dad, my mother, and me. Even though our life was better, it still wasn't complete.

It was our last week of school, and Teddy and I still weren't talking to each other. I dreaded going to school and was glad that the end of the year was coming. It had been almost three weeks, and Teddy hadn't called once. I didn't call him either, though I wanted too many times. But what more could I say? I had been honest with Teddy. He knew how much I cared for him. The only thing I could do was respect his wishes and go on. I had decided my life must go on; only it was hard to make that happen without Teddy.

At this point, it was hard trying to get through the day without talking to or seeing him.

The last day of school finally arrived. It was a fun day, with no work. I was happy being with all my friends. I did see Teddy from a distance that day but only for a second. He was walking to his class with his friends. I didn't see him waiting for the buses anymore; he must have started riding home with his friends.

I went home that day happy that school was out and that I had the summer ahead of me with no homework. I hoped that I'd find a job soon. I had started seeing less of my dad. He was working long hours at the office, and when he get home it was always late and he was tired. So I didn't bother him about going out.

I started to hang out with my friend Sissy. She had just brought a car, and she'd always pick me up and we'd hang out. Most of the time, Sissy's boyfriend was with her, and I was tired of being with them all the time. Plus, I could tell her boyfriend wanted to be with her without me tagging along. I started telling Sissy I was busy.

I really missed Teddy. I figured he was working full time at his summer job; at least that had been his plan back when we were talking. I knew that my life had to go on, so I decided I'd try to forget about Teddy being part of my life and get over him.

Summer was soon on its way, and I was dealing okay without Teddy. It was easier now that I wasn't seeing him at school. I spent most of my days with my grandma and aunt. They were cool, and spending time with them kept me busy, since I didn't get the job I'd been hoping for at my dad's office. The woman I was going to fill in for had decided to stay, so I had to say good-bye to my promising summer job.

I'd looked for a job at other places, but either no one called back or the place wanted night help. I wanted to work days. My dad told me to just relax for the summer and have fun. He said something would come along for me.

I was the kind of person who wanted something to come along now. I wasn't a waiting-on-something-to-come-along person. I was more of a right-this-minute person. Waiting was hard and stressful for me. It gave me too much time to think and feel alone. Inevitably, I would start thinking of Teddy.

I had gotten used to taking the bus where I wanted to go. So one day, I decided to go spend the day with Isabella. I had called and gotten the okay from Emma. I told my dad I'd be spending the day there.

I caught the bus and arrived at Isabella's early. I was happy to see everyone. Sadie and Emma had to go out. I was glad, as it gave me time to visit Isabella alone. I told Emma I would stay with Isabella until they returned.

When I walked into Isabella's room, she turned and looked at me. She smiled, and I knew she was as happy to see me, as I was to see her. I hugged her tightly and told her how much I missed her. Then I started talking. I told her about my dad, and I ended up telling her about Teddy and myself. She let me know she was listening by smiling and giving me an occasional nod. I knew she could talk, and I wondered why she'd chosen not to talk for so long.

"Why don't you talk?" I asked her. "I heard you talk in the woods."

She looked at me. Her eyes saddened, and she dropped her head.

I didn't want to push her. "I'm sorry," I said. But I kept talking. "Thank you for letting me stay with you and taking care of me," I told her. I always thanked her for that.

As usual she looked at me, smiling again, and gave me a nod.

"I miss living with you," I told her. "I mean, I love being with my father. But you are as close to me as a mother could be. How have you been feeling?"

She smiled and nodded.

"One day, I hope you will be able to talk to me," I said. I told her how much I loved her.

She stood, walked out of the room, and came back with cookies and milk.

I smiled. "Thank you," I said and ate a cookie.

We sat there watching TV and eating cookies. I talked, and she smiled and nodded. I was happy being there with her. I didn't know what it was about Isabella, but she made me feel differently than I did with anyone else. Even though she never said a word, I was happy, and I knew we were communicating with each other.

I told her I wouldn't hate it if she had been my mother and that she'd showed me just as much love as any mother could show her child. I hugged her and told her I loved her so much. And I wasn't just saying it. I felt tears forming as I hugged her. "The love I have for you comes deep from within my heart," I told her. "It's a special kind of love."

Isabella wiped my tears, patted my head, and looked in my eyes. I smiled. I could see all the love she had coming through her eyes.

Just then, Emma walked in. Sadie wasn't with her. Emma saw how her mother looked and told me, "Mother is a different person when you are with her. She blossoms when you're around."

"Isabella is special to me and I enjoy being with her," I told Emma. I looked at Isabella and smiled. "We enjoy each other."

Isabella smiled back. Emma said, "Mother smiles often around you."

I said, "She smiles all the time."

I finally said I had to get back home. I stood and gave Isabella a big hug. "I will come back soon," I told her.

She nodded okay.

Emma walked me to the door. "Mom cares a lot for you," she told me. "She rarely smiles or nods to anyone."

"She likes for you to talk to her," I told Emma.

"Mother doesn't talk back," she replied.

"But she does in so many ways," I said, "through her caring eyes, her sweet smiles, and her precious nods. That's enough for me."

I said I had to go and promised I'd come back soon. Like always, I felt bad leaving Isabella. It was like leaving something you care deeply for behind. Inside, I felt all alone. It wasn't the same alone feeling I got from losing Teddy. It was the alone feeling that told me I was still not whole—that part of me was missing.

Was there more to me? I had the feeling there was. I wished I knew myself.

Chapter 17

*H*ow could I be so happy yet sad? How could someone go through so much in life and be so strong for others but unable to figure herself out? How could I not know who or what I was?

I had gained so much. Yet still, a part of my life was lost. I wasn't referring to Teddy but to my life, my family. I knew my dad and my mom. But it was hard not knowing a part of what you know for yourself. Accepting who you are or who your family based on what someone else has told rather than what's in your mind is strange. I had to learn to believe the pictures that had been painted rather than the ones my memory would have created, and I had to learn to live with that and accept it. It was like sitting in a classroom and listening to someone tell you a story about a person and her family—what she was like and what she'd gone through—only that person was you.

One day, as I sat wondering about my life and trying to fill in some of my blank life, I started to cry. I asked myself, Why me? Why did my life have to be so different? Why did it have to be my family and me going through this? Why was I not like any other normal girl with a happy family?

Summer was here, I had friends from school to hang out with. Only I wanted something different in life. This was going to be a long summer if I didn't find a job. I decided to look in the newspaper and see types of jobs, if any, were out there. My dad called to say he'd be late. He asked if I wanted him to pick up something to eat. I said no.

I watched TV the rest of the evening while I looked through the paper for jobs before falling asleep.

Dad kissed me on the forehead and woke me as he came in. He asked me if I had eaten.

I said, "Yes," and headed off to bed.

He followed me upstairs. He said he was tired and going to bed too. He had a long day tomorrow. I turned the TV on in my room and tried to watch. But sleep took over again.

The next morning, Dad was up and out early for work. I dragged around the house and fixed a bowl of cereal, which was mostly what I ate for breakfast and dinner since my dad had started working late. I kept the house cleaned and worked in the garden most of the day. That kept me from thinking a lot. I did not need to think a lot.

My phone rang, and I saw that it was my friend Terry from school. We'd been good friends at school, and now she was calling because she knew I was looking for a job. The hospital she was working at needed some help. Terry, who was older than I was, said the hospital always hired help during the summer.

I asked if she would pick up an application for me and swing by after work so I could fill it out. When she agreed, I thanked her and told her I'd see her later.

I hung up the phone happy. I called my dad to give him the good news. He was happy for me.

That evening, Terry stopped by with the application. I filled it out and asked her, "Does it matter if I've never had a job?"

"Everyone has to have a first job, and they get it without ever having had a job," she pointed out." Don't worry. I hadn't had a job when I started here."

Terry asked if I wanted to ride with her to get something to eat, and I said sure.

While we were out, she told me all about the job and asked if it sounded like something, I might like to do.

"I would just like to have a job," I told her.

We ate and talked more about the job, and then she dropped me off at home. She promised to take the application in and put in a good word for me.

The next week was hard. I was impatiently waiting to hear something from the hospital.

Then, it was going on the second week of hearing nothing. I talked to Terry a lot during that time and she told me to be patient. "It takes time," she would say.

I knew she was right. But I was not a patience person. I hated waiting, but I had no choice.

One early morning, my phone rang. It was someone calling about the job. The woman said her name was Alice Bradshaw and that she was from the hospital. She asked, "Are you still looking for work?"

"Yes," I answered.

"Can you come in tomorrow at one thirty for an interview?"

I said I'd be there and hung up feeling very happy. I realized I'd told her yes so loudly that I must have woken up some of the neighbors.

I started to call my dad but decided to wait to see if I was going to get the job first. It took all I could not to say anything about the interview, but I didn't say a word.

The next day, I was ready early for the bus. I didn't want to be late. It turned out that I arrived early. I saw Terry, and she told me that Alice was a nice person and easy to get along with and assured me I'd be okay.

It was time for the interview. Terry walked me to Alice's office. When I went inside, she smiled and introduced herself.

"Have a seat," she said. She was looking at my application in front of her. She asked me questions that were easy to answer, and then she asked me to tell her about myself and why I wanted to work at the hospital.

I told her about me and said that I loved helping people.

She had a smile on her face as I finished. She went over my references and asked about my dad, saying she knew him well as a doctor.

Alice explained the job in detail and asked if it was something I thought I'd like to do.

"Yes," I assured her quickly.

She smiled and asked if I had any questions.

When I said I didn't, she said, "Okay. Welcome aboard. She gave me the paperwork I'd need to get my drug test and said she'd call me when she got the results.

I stood and thanked her and then went to find Terry and tell her the news.

"Welcome to the working world," Terry said. "See you next week when you start."

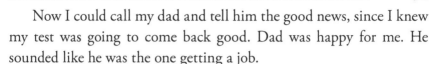

Now I could call my dad and tell him the good news, since I knew my test was going to come back good. Dad was happy for me. He sounded like he was the one getting a job.

The rest of the week went by slowly, even though I had a great weekend hanging out with my dad, going to church on Sunday, and visiting my grandma after church.

I wished Teddy and I were talking and still together. He would be happy for me. I hadn't talked to him since our breakup, and I knew he was working. I missed him so much. I hoped he was missing me as much as I was missing him. It hurt so badly whenever I started thinking of him.

I finally got the call I'd been waiting on—no, not from Teddy. It was Alice, telling me that my test results had come back and I was good to go and asking if I could start working tomorrow.

"Yes." I assured her.

We arranged that I'd be in her office at eight o'clock to do paperwork, and she told me to bring two forms of identification and to wear white comfortable shoes (it could even be sneakers) and some blue scrubs.

I thanked her, hung up, and called my dad to share the news. I told him I had to go buy some white shoes and scrubs for work tomorrow.

I called Terry and told her I would start tomorrow. She was off for the day and had planned to do some shopping, so she agreed to pick me up. That way, I could go with her to get what I needed. It was good she had a car.

I got everything I needed for work, and then we went out to lunch to celebrate.

Terry told me she'd seen Teddy, and my heart skipped a few beats when she said his name. She'd seen him with some of his friends at the burger joint where we hang out. "I spoke to him, and he was alone. I mean, he wasn't with a girl, but his friends had their girlfriends with them.

"Teddy asked how you were doing," she added. "I told him I didn't know. I thought if he wanted to know, he should give you a call himself. It was no place of mine to tell him anything about you."

I smiled as she said that, I told her I was okay. Then being honest, I said, "Yes I miss him, but I'm making it day by day."

We hung out the rest of the day. Then Terry said, "Let me get you back home to rest. You have to work tomorrow."

That night, my dad talked to me. He was happy for me and asked if I knew what time, I would have to be to be to work. He went by the hospital every morning and could drop me off on his way to work. I told him I had to be there at eight the next day, and I'd know more later. He said he could drop me off tomorrow.

We popped popcorn and watched a movie before going to bed.

The next morning, Dad was up and had fixed us both lunches for work by the time I came downstairs. I was wearing my scrubs and white shoes, and when he looked at me, he told me how proud he was of me.

"Thank you," I said.

We got our lunches and were off to work. He dropped me off fifteen minutes early. When I got to Alice's office, she was already. "Good morning," she said. "Come in and have a seat. Let me get you your paper work." She asked for my two forms of identifications. I was glad my dad had gotten them earlier for me.

I filled out all the paperwork. Then Alice went over my hours. She said I'd be on day shift, which was from seven o'clock to four, and explained that I'd get an hour lunch each day. She told me what my pay was and then took me to meet the person who was going to be training me—Terry.

I smiled when Alice took me to Terry and felt relieved.

Alice said, "Terry will teach you everything you need to know for this job." She smiled and walked off.

I looked at Terry and asked, "Did you know?"

"Yes," she said, "and it was hard to keep it inside."

I hugged her and thanked her.

"You are welcome," she said. "Now let's get to work."

I would be transporting patients to and from different places within the hospital. I knew that I was going to enjoy working here for the summer, and I already planned to stay on part time once school started back up.

Terry and I worked up to lunch, signed out, and went to lunch. I was happy to be working with Terry. That made me more comfortable with the job I'd be doing. Everything was going great.

Terry and I finished the rest of the day, and I was given a badge before I left.

That evening at home, I told my dad all about the job. He smiled. "You show pride in what you're doing," he said. "That is a good thing. You will be good at your job because you love what you do, and I can see how proud of it you are when you talk."

The rest of the week, I had my job down pat. Terry said she would be working with me for another week, and then she'd let me do it all on my own; she would step in only if I needed her. I was sure I would be fine; there was nothing to it. I had to make sure to look at the patient chart and the armband to make sure I had the right patient. Then I just had to get them where they had to be.

The next week went by quickly, and it was a payday Friday. I got my first check ever. I was happy that day when I received my check and even happier when I opened it and saw how much it was for. I couldn't believe it.

The next day was my Saturday off. We all took turns working Saturdays. I slept in that morning and woke up to the smell of food. My dad was up and cooking breakfast. I got up, took a shower, and got dressed. Then I went downstairs and had breakfast with my dad. He asked what my friends and I had planned for the day. I told him I had planned to spend the day with my dad if that was okay.

He grinned at me. "That would be great," he said.

"I know we don't get to spend a lot of time together since we're both working."

We smiled at each other. Dad and I had fun that day together. We went to the bank to deposit my check, and he told me again, how proud he was of me.

I worked the next week by myself. I wasn't the only one there doing what I was doing, and now I was doing it alone like everyone else. The job was easy, and I knew what to do.

One day, I had a patient who was a little boy. I looked at his chart to see where he was to go and saw that he was going to get a scan. He had cancer. My heart went out to him. He was so small. I had to try to help him. I did everything I was supposed to do and got him to the room to get the scan.

No one was in the room but us. His mother was still at the front desk finishing paperwork. I was to stay with him until the doctor called for him. I asked him if he wanted to play a game. He said yes, but I could feel the sadness in him. I could tell he was weak and feeling badly. I told him to close his eyes. When he did, I put my hands on him and began to focus hard. I knew I didn't have much time. The feelings came into my hands, and I knew he was going to be better. I held onto him until the feelings stopped. When I removed my hands, he sat up in the bed. His whole look had changed. He looked like he had energy.

He asked, "Are we going to play a game?"

"Yes," I told him. I showed him some tricks I had learned with my fingers and taught him how to do them. He was happy and talking a lot. He looked like a different little boy.

Soon it was his time to go in. The nurse looked surprised when she saw how much energy he had. I told him good luck and said I'd see him later. I felt happy knowing that he would be okay. That day I helped three more children as they came through. I felt good knowing that I was helping people and doing a good job.

The next week, I heard a nurse talking about the children's condition. She was amazed at how things had changed for the better for all four of them and said it was like a miracle. She had no idea what had happened. The kids' parents were happy. I saw some of them shedding tears of joy for their children. Tears rolled down my cheeks when I saw how grateful they were that their children had gotten better. I knew this was going to be a good job. Here, I could help many people.

Terry and I went to lunch every day together. One day, she asked how I liked my job so far. I told her I loved. "You seem like you enjoy doing what you do," she said.

"What's going to happen when school starts back up?" I asked. "Is the hospital going to let me go?"

"If you're a good worker, they'll let you come in part time after school and on weekends," she told me. "That's how I get to keep my job."

I was happy to hear that, and I hoped that would work out for me as well. I had started to love this job.

Time went on, and I settled into a routine at the hospital. One day, just as my shift was about to end, a strange thing happened. I went to pick up my last patient of the day—a little girl who was about six or seven years. She gave me the oddest look and just kept staring at me. I grabbed her chart and started rolling her off to where she needed to be. She told me to stop, and when I did, she looked straight at me and said, "You're the one."

I was puzzled. What was she talking about?

"My mother cries a lot for me because I am sick," she said. "I know that I am dying and that I don't have long to live. I heard the doctor tell my mother when they thought I was asleep."

I looked at the girl. For as small as she was, she sure had a lot of information about her health.

"I see things," she said.

I asked what kind of things.

"Things only I can see," she replied.

She went on to tell me that her mother said it was the medicine talking, but she knew that what she saw had nothing to do with the medicine. "You could see things," she said matter-of-factly.

What is she talking about? I wondered. I too thought that perhaps her medication was behind what she was saying. "We have to go," I told her.

"Roll me slow please," she requested. I did, and she asked, "Let me hold your hand."

I gave her my hand, trying to comfort her. Only she started telling me things about me. I pulled my hand from her quickly.

"You could help me," she said.

"How do you know that?" I asked.

"I can feel it inside me," she replied.

"Does your mother know you can see and feel things like this?" I wanted to know.

She said she'd tried to tell her mom about her abilities, but her mother had told her never to talk like that again—that the doctors would think she was crazy and put her in a crazy hospital. She explained that now she keeps things to herself.

I couldn't believe what she was saying. I handed her my hand again, and she told me that I'd had my heart broken by a boy I cared for. How did this girl see or feel this? I didn't know, but she was right. I was heartbroken. She said, "You have helped a lot of people, but there are many more people that will need your help." Then she asked me, "Could you heal me please? I knew this was my day—that you would be here for me today."

I rolled her to the waiting room. The nurse came out and said it would be a minute or so. The little girl took my hands and placed them on her. I began to focus. Soon, I started to feel the warmth come into my hands. The tingling took longer than usual to stop, but eventually, it did.

When I removed my hands, the girl looked at me. "Thank you," she said. "My cancer is gone. I feel fine.

Then she cocked her head and added, "And that boy who broke your heart, he will be back in your life. He loves you." She lay back down, closed her eyes, and didn't say another word.

The nurse came out a moment later. She looked at the girl with pity in her eyes. "Poor thing," she said. "She's been in a coma for four months. We still scan her often."

"So you're telling me this patent hasn't spoken to anyone in four months?" I verified.

The nurse answered, "Yes."

Now this was scary. She had undoubtedly just talked to me. I didn't say a word to anyone. I would make sure to check on the little girl later.

Before I went home, I heard the talk all over the hospital—a little girl had came out of a coma and was doing great. The doctors had been talking to her family about pulling the plug.

I was so grateful that I had been there to help. But I couldn't get over the things the little girl had told me. I wanted to stop by her room and look in, even if I didn't get a chance to go in. I headed that way as soon as I was off the clock. Her mom and family were in her room. I stood in the doorway looking at all the tear-filled faces. One of the family members knew who I was—she'd seen me working upstairs— and invited me to come in.

I said I didn't want to disturb them; I'd just wanted to check in on the little girl. I walked over to the bed, and she was all smiles. "Thank you," she said.

"I was only doing my job," I replied.

No one else in the room had any idea what we were talking about. I told her to take care, told the family I was happy for them all, and walked out. This was a strange but happy end to a workday. I was able to meet someone else who was special, which is what I would call myself.

I had been working at the hospital for over a month now, and things were going well. I hated that I would have to stop working full time when school started. But I'd learned that I would be able to work part time after school, so that was great. I got home feeling good inside.

My mind fell on Teddy. Oh how I missed him. I even missed just being able to talk to him. I wondered if he missed me as much or sat and thought of me as often as I did him.

I pushed thoughts of him out my mind. He was going on with his life, I was happy for him. I was tired. I wanted to take a shower and just rest in front of the TV for the rest of the day. I had tomorrow off. I was happy to do nothing, except maybe work in the garden.

A couple of my friends from school called and asked if I wanted to hang out at the mall tomorrow. That didn't sound appealing, so I told them I had plans to work in the garden and had a lot of work around the house to do. I was not up for hanging out or shopping. I did love working with the beautiful flowers in the garden. I worked there all day and still hadn't gotten to everything I wanted to get done. I would finish on my next day off.

After getting cleaned and freshened up, I got a glass of cold lemonade and went back into the garden to sit. I heard someone crying; it sounded like a little child's cry. It was coming from the next yard. I followed the cry to the little boy from next door. He was sitting in the yard with his puppy, only his puppy was lying on the ground all bandaged up. I sat next to the fence. After saying hello, I asked the little boy what his name was and why he was crying.

He told me his name was Bobby and about how a bigger dog had fought with his very small pup. He told me his dad had taken his puppy to the doctor and that his puppy couldn't walk after he'd had surgery. Even though the puppy was in pain, he still wagged his tail while he was with the little boy.

"Would you like to pet him?" the little boy asked.

"I would love to," I said.

He move the puppy closer to the fence, and I was able to get my hands close enough to rub him. I asked, "What's your puppy's name?"

"Brownie," he replied.

"Brownie's a good name," I told him. "Brownie will be running and playing again soon. You'll see."

I already knew what I was going to do. I had to help this puppy. Bobby made that possible by asking if I could stay with Brownie while he went to use the bathroom.

"Sure," I said. "I'll keep petting him until you return."

As soon as Bobby walked off, I began to focus on getting the dog better. I started to feel the tingling in my hand, and I knew the dog was going to be all right. I was still petting Brownie when Bobby returned.

"Thanks," he said. "I didn't want him to be alone."

I told him I was sure Brownie would be up and playing again in no time. I told him I had to go. When I stood up and began to walk away, I heard the dog bark. I turned, looked back at the boy and dog, smiled, and kept walking.

I sat in the garden with all the beautiful flowers. I began to think. I had been through a lot in my life and had been too many different places. I always ended up finding someone who needed help. Was this how my life was supposed to be? I still had many questions. Maybe there were no answers. I had come to accept the strange life I had and even be happy with it. I still had a mind, though, and a mind never stopped wondering and thinking what if. I lay back in my chair, closed my eyes, smiled, and said aloud, "I love this strange life of mine, and I am happy."

The next day I slept in. I could hear my dad getting ready for work. He knew I was off today, and he was trying not to wake me. "Good morning," I hollered.

"Good morning," Dad said. "Did I wake you?"

I said no, even though he had. He asked what was I going to do today, and I told him I planned to stay home and do nothing.

"Sounds great," he said. "I have to go. I'll see you this afternoon."

I just lay there resting for a while before I got up. It did feel good to lie in bed. I thought, *I should go to school to become some type of nurse. I could help people both ways.*

Yes, I decided, that was a great idea. I would study nursing in college. I knew my dad would be glad to hear about my decision and that he'd be there to help me in any way possible.

I got up. I wasn't hungry, so I skipped breakfast and headed toward the garden. I wanted to finish the work out there. I started by pulling all the weeds and dead leaves. It was a job that took a lot of work. Only it was work I felt good doing. Being among the beauty of the flowers made me feel so refreshed and peaceful.

Time went by quickly. I had been working nonstop for a while. My phone wasn't on me. I did not think of anyone while I was here working in the garden. The work helped my mind be at peace. When I looked up and saw that it was late in the day, I stood up to take a break. I needed a drink. Lunchtime had passed; it was already one thirty.

I still had a lot I wanted to do out here. I poured a large glass of cold lemonade, turned it up, and it was wonderful. I drank it down more slowly that I normally would. It was ice cold.

As soon as I was finished, I was right back in the garden where I'd left off. I worked two more hours before calling it quits. After I was done putting away all the tools and buckets I'd been working with, I stood back and took it all in. This garden was beautiful.

I had just sat down for another glass of lemonade when my dad walked out. He smiled and told me how great the garden looked. I could tell he loved the garden as much as I did. It showed in his face. "You work just as hard as your mother did in this garden," he said.

I didn't say anything, but his comment made me wonder if, one day, Mom would be back here with us. I sure hoped so, for both our sakes. I only hoped Dad would still feel the same when that day came as he did for her now. I looked at him, and I could see that he was thinking of her too. "If Mom ever came back, would you still love her and want her back?" I asked.

He turned and looked at me. His smile faded away slowly as he thought. After a moment, he said, "It has been a long time since your mother went away. Her love is still with me in my heart. There is never a day that goes by when I don't think of her in some way. I don't think there ever will be. Now that you are back and you are like her in so many ways, I think of her more. So often, something you do or say reminds me of her. When you truly love from the heart, it is pure love. Life may take you in different directions, but that pure love is always there. Even if you try to let go, that love will never depart—no matter how long you are apart. The love alone in all the memories you made will keep itself close in your heart."

"I could have another woman," Dad said. "But what I still feel for your mother is so strong in my heart, I could never be with another. It wouldn't be fair to the other woman. No matter how hard I tried to love her, I could never love her as she deserved to be loved because your mother still has my heart. I only have love for your mother; she is the only woman besides you, young woman, who has my heart."

I looked at him and saw tears in his eyes. "I will always be here for your mom," he said. "I love her."

I reached over and hugged him tightly. "Dad, I love you so much," I told him.

He held me tight for a while, saying he was so glad to have me back in his life. Then he said, "Let's go out and get something to eat." He said he knew how it is when I was working out here and figured I hadn't stopped to eat.

I smiled at him and admitted, "You are so right."

We both got dressed. Then we went out to eat and shared some wonderful father-daughter time for the rest of the night.

Chapter 18

A person screaming for help woke me up. I jumped out of bed and looked out my window. I saw a woman across the street kneeling beside a man. It was the blind man from across the street. He was lying on the sidewalk in front of his house. I ran out and across the street.

The woman said she was about to leave for work when she'd seen him lying on the ground. She was their neighbor from next door and needed to call an ambulance. She asked if I could stay with him while she went to call for help and let his family know what was going on. I said I would. As soon as she was gone, I kneeled beside him, put my hands on him, and started to focus. I didn't know what was going on, but I wanted to help him. I focused harder, and soon I started to feel the tingling in my hands. I felt relief wash over me; he was going to be okay.

He started to move.

"What's wrong?" I asked him gently.

He kept trying to get up. I helped him into a sitting position and told him to stay sitting until help came.

He started screaming. I thought he must have been hurting badly. I tried to calm him down, but he kept screaming at the top of his voice. I asked him what was hurting him, and he turned his face toward mine. He calmed down, and he put his hand on my face. He kept rubbing my face, which I figured was normal, given that he was blind.

Looking into his face, I saw that he was crying. "I have been blind for twenty-eight years," he said. "I have lived in darkness, feeling my way through this world, accepting the limits as to where I could go— that I was afraid to go farther than the mailbox. I've sat on the porch for many years, listening to the voices as different people went by and wondering how they looked. I have held my grandchildren many times and not been able to see how they look. Children would often stop and talk on their way home from school, and all I could do was sit there and wonder whose neighbor child it was. I couldn't tell by looking if the sun was out or whether it was night or day. I saw nothing but a world of darkness."

He was trying to get up as hard as I was trying to keep him still. I couldn't hold him. He put his hand on my face again and said, "You have the most beautiful brown eyes. I can see as plainly, as if I was never blind. I don't know how it happened. I was lying on the ground after I fell, and I started to feel a warm feeling come over my body. Then I felt a burning in my eyes. I opened my eyes, and I could see a light that began to get clearer and clearer. And then I saw your face with those big brown eyes."

Kim came out of the house. She was not in a wheelchair but walking with a walker. She was asking if her uncle was okay.

"He's fine," I told her. I helped him up.

The woman who'd gone to call for help came back, and then an ambulance arrived. Joe was hugging Kim and telling her he could see. He told her she looked good in pink. They hugged each other, and both were crying.

I looked down at myself and noticed I was out with my pajamas on. I told the woman from across the street that I was going since the ambulance was taking over. "Thanks for your help," she said.

As I went back home, I felt good.

I enjoyed being with my dad. He took me out to dinner that night, and I told him about my plan to go into the medical field when it was time to go to college. He was happy for me. He told me all about the good schools out me and said it wouldn't be a choice I'd regret.

After dinner, we went home and watched a show together before we both went to bed.

The next day at work, we had a full schedule. I was tired from yesterday, but I kept up with my work. I had a patient who was just a baby. My heart went out to the little girl. I didn't know what her problem was yet, but since she was in here, something had to be wrong. I took her chart and saw that something was going on with her leg that was keeping her from being able to walk. She was only two years old, and her name was Jenny.

"Hello, Jenny," I said.

She was all smiles, as if she didn't have a care in the world. She seemed to be the happiest girl on earth, yet she couldn't walk. In the hospital, I had seen that the sickest children always seemed to be the happiest ones—often more full of life than children who were well and had no problems.

Jenny's mom was with her. Only she wasn't as happy. I saw sadness in her face, and the redness of her eyes made it clear that she'd been crying. She said that, if she could trade places with her daughter, she would. The doctor had told her that a complicated surgery was Jenny's only chance of being able to walk.

"Hang in there," I told her. "Everything will be okay."

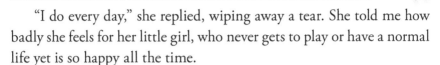
"I do every day," she replied, wiping away a tear. She told me how badly she feels for her little girl, who never gets to play or have a normal life yet is so happy all the time.

When Jenny's mother went back to her room to get something, I told Jenny I would be here with her until the nurse was ready for her. The little girl was lying still. I put my hand on her and began to focus. The tingling came and left and I smiled. I looked up at her, and she was smiling at me. I told her she was a big girl and that she'd be fine.

Her mother returned just as the nurse was getting ready for her. I looked at her mom and told her everything would be fine.

My next patient was a teenage girl. She lay there quietly. I watched her, not saying anything at first. Then I noticed the tears rolling down her face. I said, "Hello."

She wiped her tears and said, "Hello. Is this going to take a long time? I just cannot go through this." I watched her as the tears rolled more.

I looked at her chart and said, "It shouldn't take too long."

"That's what they always say," she said, "and then I'm here most of my day."

I saw her name on the chart and told her Candice was a beautiful name.

"Thank you," she said

"It won't be that long," I told her.

"It doesn't matter," she replied. "I don't have a life anyway. All I get to do is sit and sit more. I can't go out anymore. My boyfriend doesn't even call anymore because of my illness. How am I supposed to have a life like this? Even if I get the tumor removed, there's still a chance I won't be normal. I am fifteen years old. I'm supposed to be happy and enjoying my life. Only I'm always at a doctor's office or feeling bad. I have these terrible headaches, and it's too painful to even move my head at times."

I stood behind her bed and put my hand on her shoulders, trying to comfort her. At the same time, I closed my eyes and began to focus. I tried to block out her talking and told her, "Everything will be okay."

"That's easy for you to say," she replied. "You're not the one lying here."

I blocked her talking out, closed my eyes, and focused, rubbing her shoulders all the while. Finally, I felt the tingling go through my hands. It lasted longer than usually, but it eventually stopped. I opened my eyes.

She was still going on and on talking. But then she got quiet. "My headache is gone," she said. "My head doesn't hurt."

I told her that was good. The nurse came to take her in for her scan. "Just believe that everything will turn out well," I told her.

"Thanks for listening," she said.

That day, I had many more patients who'd come in for only minor things.

My last patient was an elderly man who had been paralyzed for many years. We had one patient ahead of us, so there was a wait, and I had to stay with him. We started talking. He told me how he'd been in a bad accident on his way home from visiting his daughter and grandchildren.

"The accident left me paralyzed from waist down," he said. "I've never been the same since. I lost everything, even my wife. It was too hard on her with me as I am. I lost all my friends. Baby, you find out who really cares when you get down. My wife left. My friends stopped coming around. I was alone. I lived in another state at the time, and my daughter lived here. She couldn't come as often as she wanted. She was a single parent with two small children staying in a two-bedroom apartment. She told me she was getting a bigger place with more room for me, so I went into a nursing home for a while. She moved me here when she was able, and she takes care of me, making sure nurses are there to help while she works. I enjoy being there with her and my grandchildren. I just hate that I'm not able to do anything. I can't even play with my grandson. He loves throwing the football. I wish things would be different—that I wouldn't have to be a burden to my daughter."

Then he looked at me as if remembering I was there. "I am sorry, baby. I know I have talked your ears off."

I told him no, that I enjoyed listening. "I hope things get better for you," I said.

"Yes," he agreed. "I am hoping the same. I've been hoping for many years now."

I rubbed his legs. "One day, they will be back in use," I assured him. I left my hand on his leg, and while I listened to him talk, I began to focus, trying to make him better. The tingling started in my hand, and it didn't last long. When it was over, I patted his leg and told him to hold on and keep believing.

"Always," he said, adding, "I've been so busy talking, I didn't get your name. By the way, mine is George."

I smiled. "Nyah," I said.

The nurse came for him. "Nice talking to you, Nyah," he said.

I was grateful to have this job. It gave me so many opportunities to help people without anyone knowing.

When my shift was over, I was glad to see the day end. I was tired and needed a long nap. I clocked out and checked my phone for any messages. I had several. I decided I'd call them all back later when I get home. I was still catching the bus home. I knew the phone calls were from friends wanting to go school shopping. It was almost time to go back to school.

I did have to take some time out to go school shopping. But today wasn't the day. I was too tired. All I wanted to do was get home from this bus ride, take a shower, and crash in front of the TV and sleep.

I got home, returned all my missed calls, and sure enough, everyone was talking about shopping. I told my friends I was too tired to join them today but would catch them on the next round. I knew everyone would be taking a number of shopping trips before school started. I was too tired to eat, so I took a shower and headed for the couch with a pillow and blanket. I turned on the TV, and that was all I remembered. I was asleep before I got a chance to watch any movies.

My dad woke me when he came in the door. I must have slept a long time, as it was dark outside. I smelled the food he'd brought as soon as he walked in. I was glad because I was hungry. "I brought dinner," he said. "I figured you were sleep since you didn't answer your phone. Hope you're in the mood for Chinese food."

I told him that sounded good to me. I hadn't had anything since lunch. I got up, but I still felt tired. So after Dad and I ate and talked we both decided to go to bed. It really felt good to relax in bed, and I soon fell asleep.

Work the next day was the same. I'd had enough rest, so I wasn't tired.

Friday finally came, I was glad to see Friday afternoon. I was ready to clock out and go home. I had only ten minutes left to clock out when a man came in who looked familiar. I knew I had seen him somewhere before. Only I couldn't remember where. I watched him as he went to check in. Then I walked over to the desk and went around on the other side. I saw his name, but I still couldn't place him.

"Hello there," he said when he saw me. "Good to see you again. This is a small world."

I didn't know what he was refereeing to. I was still trying to figure out where I'd seen him before.

"You don't remember me, do you," he said.

"I'm sorry," I admitted, "but I don't."

"The plane," he reminded me. "I was on the plane with you—the one that crashed."

Then I remembered him. He was the older man whose back had been hurt.

"You stayed with me when I was in so much pain, remember," he coaxed.

I smiled. "Of course," I said. "How you are?"

"Great," he replied, "only my daughter wants me to get this test done—to stay on top of things. It's the strangest thing though. I haven't had any pain since that day on the plane when I met you, and I'd doing just fine today."

I smiled and told him how happy I was for him.

"Do you work here?" he asked.

I told him I did and was just about to finish my shift. "Take care of yourself," I told him. "I'm sure everything will be just fine with you."

I went and clocked out. It was Friday, and I was looking forward to a weekend off.

I decided to call my friends and see if anyone wanted to go school shopping. After all, school was only two weeks away. In a way, I was glad to start back to school. But I wasn't so thrilled about the prospect of seeing Teddy. The hurt was still there, even when I saw him from a distance. I still cared so much for him, and I really missed all the little, simple things we'd done together.

How could a person turn and go in another direction, as if he'd never known you and said he loved you? I didn't see that as love. I knew Teddy might have been confused. But true love didn't turn off that easily. I wondered sometimes if he'd ever really loved me as he'd said he did.

I caught up with my friends and we went shopping that evening—and the next day. My friends had all the gossip on everyone. When I asked how they had possibly found out everything on everyone so quickly, they laughed, saying I was too busy to get the scoop on things, so they had to keep up with everything for me.

"Do you still communicate with Teddy?" Sissy asked.

"No," I replied. "Why do you ask?"

"Well," she said slowly, "we heard he's talking to someone—or might we say hanging out with this someone."

Before I knew it, I'd asked, "Who?"

They were glad to fill me in on whom Teddy was supposedly spending time with and where they'd hang out. They also informed me that Teddy had a car now.

All I said was that I was glad for him, which got me some strange looks.

"You should get your man back," Sissy said.

"Teddy is not my man to get back," I replied. "I don't need him if I have to get him back. I feel if he were my man, he would be with me and not this new girl." I asked, "Can we talk about something else?"

Hearing them, talk about Teddy with someone else was hurting me so bad inside, and I was trying hard not letting it show. All I wanted was to go off by myself and cry out the pain building up inside. If felt as if I could hardly breathe. But I got myself together and finished out the day of shopping. We decided to hang out for the rest of the evening as well.

After a day of shopping, we figured we should go get something to eat. We wound up going to the same place we always went to eat and hang out. As soon as we pulled up, the first person I saw was Teddy— with his new friend. My heart seemed to stop beating. Everyone looked at me, and someone asked if I wanted to go somewhere else.

"No," I said stubbornly. "There's no reason we should leave. So Teddy's here with someone else; we are no longer together."

We parked and got out. I was glad I'd taken the time to make sure I was dressed nicely and looking good.

As we walked by Teddy and the girl, I said hi.

Only he spoke back. "Hello. How are you?"

"Fine, thank you," I answered, never slowing down.

I joined my friends at the seats they'd chosen, and of course, they'd picked a table that gave them a view of Teddy and his friend. I sat with my back to them. Only you know I knew their every move, thanks to my friends.

Teddy's friend's back was to us, so only Teddy could see our table. My friends keep telling me that his eyes stayed on our table. That didn't make me feel any better. I knew Teddy, and he knew my friends. He knew they were the news channel bunch, and he knew perfectly well, what was going on—that he and his friend were being watched like a movie. I didn't understand why he'd stayed. I'd thought for sure he would have left by now. Maybe she wanted to stay.

I knew I was ready to leave when we first pulled up and I saw him. But I didn't want my friends to know, so I'd played it off. I was staying to try to prove a point to them—that I was over Teddy. In truth, my heart was taking all the hurt and pain for me and keeping it inside my chest.

When Teddy and his friend got up to leave, my friends continued to narrate their every move. Teddy waved in our direction, and one of my friends said, "No, he did not just wave good-bye."

"That's Teddy," I said. He knew what was up. I could only laugh.

We stayed and talked for a bit after we'd finished eating. I discovered that the girl Teddy was talking to was someone my friends did not get along with. I, on the other hand, had nothing against the girl. She had never done or said anything to me. I just hated that it wasn't me sitting there with Teddy. Neither the pain in my heart nor the lump in my throat would go away.

I told my friends I was tired and wanted to stop for the day. They were going to the movies and asked me to tag along, but I told them I wanted to spend some time with my dad. They dropped me off home and said they'd call me later.

I was glad to be home. My dad was out, and I was glad to be alone. I went straight upstairs, put all my new clothes away, and fell on the bed. I turned on the TV and had a long cry. I thought I had gotten over Teddy more than I had. I'd thought I'd be able to handle the situation by now. It's just that this was the first time I'd seen him with someone else, and it still hurt. I cried and cried. I still had a long way to go to get over him. I'd seen and felt that clearly this evening.

In truth, I still wanted to be the one with him. But things were different now. I tried to accept that, no matter how hard it was for me, I had to go on. I got on my knees and prayed to Jesus give me strength to do what was right and to help me with this issue. No matter what happened between Teddy and me, I could never hate him. I prayed for Teddy. I prayed that Jesus would keep love in my heart, no matter how bad thing got in my life.

I always felt better after I talked with Jesus, and it worked this time to. I got up feeling a whole lot better.

My dad prays for my mother even though she isn't with him. Dad always says that, one day, we will be a family, if it was God's will. Well I decided I'd say the same about Teddy. We would be together again if it is God's will.

I looked at all the clothes I had gotten for school. I had bought a lot, even shoes. My dad had given me plenty of money to buy clothes. He always told me to save my money, so I did have a nice amount in my bank account.

I knew that, one day, I would be on my own. I wanted to save now so I wouldn't have to depend on anyone taking care of me. I wanted to be able to stand on my own and take care of myself.

I found myself wishing again that my mother were here. Even though I had no memory of her here, I longed for those talks that only a mother and daughter can have. With a mother, you could have girl talk and get womanly advice. Yes, I have a dad, but that was different. About some things, a girl needs a mother to talk with, and only a mother will do.

My dad came home. I went downstairs and spent the late evening with him. We talked about our days, and he went into the backyard. I followed. We always ended up sitting in the garden. It was a nice evening to sit and feel the breeze and laugh with each other.

The next couple of weeks went by fast. I spent them working and getting the last of my school shopping done. Then the first day of school arrived. It felt funny going to school instead of work. I would be working after school some days and some on the weekends, though. I didn't want to work too much, as I wanted to keep my grades up to get into a good college.

I didn't see Teddy on the first day. But I got the gossip on him from my friends. I knew most of it was only gossip. I knew Teddy, and I knew he kept his life private. My friends weren't happy that he was with someone else and not me. I hoped they'd soon see that I was okay with and let it be.

After school, one of my friends pointed out Teddy's car—a nice mustang he'd always wanted. I was glad that he had one. I sure hoped that I would be able to get a car soon. I hated riding the bus.

Dad and I talked about many things. He asked me how school had been and about Teddy. I told him Teddy was talking to someone else. Like always, he told to me to hang in there, that sometimes things in front of you aren't always what they seem. I didn't quite know what he meant by that, but I guessed that it was good. He saw my confused look and went on to explain. "Sometimes when you love someone, things go wrong and you go separate ways. You may seek someone else's company, even trying to start another relationship simply because you're trying to get over the pain of missing the one you broke up with. The new relationship goes nowhere because that new person is only there to cover the pain, not fill your former partner's shoes. If its true love, the love will bring the original couple back and keep them together."

I loved talking to my dad. He always said the right things to make me feel better whenever I was feeling down. I didn't know if it was all true, about the love and feelings, but contemplating the possibility sure made me feel a lot better.

Teddy hadn't called me since the incident at the hospital, except for the one time—to break up with me—but somehow I'd managed to go on day by day. Everything was going well at school and work.

After school had been going for months, I even had someone trying to talk to me. Only my mind was still on Teddy. Steven Myers was a nice person, and he was on the football team. He told me he'd always had a crush on me and wanted to talk to me, but he'd known I was going out with Teddy. Steven said he'd heard that Teddy and I had broken up, and after seeing Teddy talking to someone else, he asked for my number and whether it was okay to call me some time.

"I know you may not be ready for another relationship," Steven said. "But if you need a friend or someone to hang out and have fun with, I would love to be that friend."

I smiled and said, "There is nothing wrong with that."

After I gave him my number, I looked up and saw that my friends were there, waiting for him to walk away so they could give me their input. They all said they could not believe it when they'd seen Steven Myers standing there with me smiling and laughing. They wanted to know what was going on and what he'd said. I told them he wanted to take me out and had asked for my number.

"Did you give it to him?" one of them asked.

I smiled said no—that I was waiting on Teddy.

Everyone jumped in at once, saying I was crazy and that I should just go out with Steven until Teddy and I got back together.

I laughed. "Yes, I gave Steven my number," I told them. "But he will only be a friend."

They all teased me, saying it was about time I started dating again.

"Yes," I agreed. "You guys are right. Every girl would love to get a chance to go out with Steven and he asked me."

I told myself I sure hoped Steven didn't think I was like the other girls he'd dated. I was different and not easy, if you know what I mean. It hadn't happen yet, and I was not eager to let it happen. So I hope Steven had the right intentions.

Steven didn't waste any time. He called the next day. We talked. He did most of the talking. I mainly listened. Someone had once told me that you could find more out about a person just by listening and not being so quick to talk. I did just that. And he seemed kind and very polite. He asked, "Please bear with me. I haven't been on a date in a while, not because I don't want to but because I'm not into what many of the girls at our school are about. I'm concentrating on my future and keeping it real."

He also told me that I'd always been different. "You stood out in a good way," he explained. "You were with your boyfriend. I have been noticing you for a while. I just never would have thought about coming between you and him. I'm not that type of person. And if you tell me at any time that you and he are getting back together, I will respect that, step back, and that'll be it.

"If you do not mind going out with me," he added, "I would love you to come to our game Friday night and maybe get a bite to eat afterward. I could pick you up, if that's okay with you."

I didn't give him an answer right away, and we kept talking. Before he hung up, he asked me again.

"Sure," I said this time. "That sounds like fun."

He said he'd pick me up at six o'clock and told me the game started at seven thirty but that he had to be there by six thirty.

I knew I wouldn't have to work and that my friends would be there. When I hung up, I considered what the gossip was going to say about Steven and me after Friday night. I didn't care. I was on my own, and I was not dating anyone. It was time to spend time with someone else, even though it was only going to be on a friendship basis.

My friends were very excited that I was going out with Steven. A few of them even said that, if I changed my mind, I could give him their numbers. I was kind of excited and sad at the same time. All I could think about was how Teddy was going to feel after he heard the gossip. Then I thought that he should be happy for me—happy that I was going on with my life. That's what he was doing, regardless of how I felt. I shook off the bad feeling that came with that thought and started to feel happy to be going out with Steven. I would see how it went.

That night when my dad came home, I talked to him about Steven. I wished my mom were here. But she wasn't, so my dad filled in. He talked me through things or just had an open ear; he was willing to listen to anything I needed to talk about. I told him about my date Friday night and the football game. Dad knew Steven Myers, which I hadn't known. He said Steven's parents were good people and that he'd meet Steven through them. Dad said he was glad I was starting to go out and have fun again. He told me that he knew I cared for Teddy still, but reminded me that what will be will be. "Always remember that," he said seriously.

I finished my homework and decided to watch a movie before going to sleep. It couldn't be a long movie though. I had to go to school and had to work after school. I knew I needed to get some sleep.

Between school and working afterward, the week went by quickly. Friday morning came, and I was excited. I had been seeing and talking to Steven at school. He always ended up at my locker talking to me. I knew people had started to talk about him and I my friends kept me updated on the gossip. I was glad he was taking the time out to stop and talk with me, which made many of the girls stare as they walked by, maybe wishing they had the same chance.

Teddy's locker was close to mine, but not once did I meet up with him now. I used to see him every day at his locker. I did see him and his friend sitting during lunch and talking as we used to do. I always sat in the same place Teddy and I had sat during lunch, under our tree.

One day, Steven stopped and asked if he could join me for lunch.

"Sure," I said, "the company would be nice."

I sat with my friends most of the time. But some days, I just wanted to sit alone in my spot. It was good having Steven join me for lunch. It made me think of Teddy how we used to laugh with each other.

Steven said, "I know this used to be your and Teddy's spot, and if you want to be alone, I'll understand."

"No, its fine," I told him.

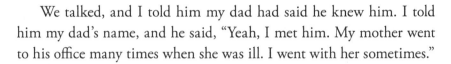

We talked, and I told him my dad had said he knew him. I told him my dad's name, and he said, "Yeah, I met him. My mother went to his office many times when she was ill. I went with her sometimes."

We talked and laughed throughout the lunch hour. He even asked if he could walk me to my class, and I said sure. We were laughing as we turned the corner toward the classroom, and there was Teddy. When he saw us together, his facial expression completely changed. I kept walking. Steven asked, "Are you okay?"

"Yes," I said. "We've both gone on with our lives, and life goes on."

Outside my class, Steven told me that if he didn't see me again today, he'd pick me up at six. He said he had practice.

"Okay," I agreed. "Thanks for the company."

He smiled. "I enjoyed it more," he said. "Thank you."

When I walked into the classroom, I could see a few girls whispering. I knew they were talking about Steven and me. I held my head high. I knew every one of those girls wished they were in my shoes having a chance to talk to Steven.

After school, I went home and rummaged through my clothes for something to wear to the game. I'd never bothered to attend one before. I picked out some nice jeans and a nice shirt. I did my hair and even put on a little makeup. I stood back, looked at myself, and smiled. "We're only friends," I said to the image in the mirror.

Even though Steven and I had only been talking for a little while, I was beginning to enjoy his company. Then my mind fell on Teddy. I wondered how he was feeling and figured he likely felt about the same as I had when I'd seen him with his friend for the first time. This is what he wanted. Even though I didn't totally understand, I hoped that, one day, even if we didn't get back together, we could be friends.

Chapter 19

Steven picked me up for the game. He was on time, and he asked if I wanted to stop anywhere, saying that we had time. I told him no.

His phone rang, and he said, "Excuse me." He answered, telling someone he would swing by before he got to the game.

When he got off the phone, he asked if I minded him making one stop. He had to run by his house to drop off some tickets.

"No," I said. *His place*, I said to myself.

He lived close by, and it didn't take long to get there. His family had a beautiful home.

Steven jumped out. He asked me to get out, and said I could meet his family.

I did, but I truly hadn't expected to meet his family. I walked behind him. He opened the door and announced us coming in. His mother, father, brother, and sister were all in the living room in front of the TV. Steven introduced me to the family. They were all very polite and happy to meet me. His dad even told me how beautiful I was. Steven smiled a big smile. He told them I was Dr. Nathan Tompkins's daughter. His mother smiled and said to tell my dad hello. She went on to tell me how good a doctor he is.

"Thanks," I said. "I'll be sure to tell him."

Steven gave them the tickets to get in the game, and we said good-bye and left for the game. He also gave me a ticket. He told me his parents never missed a game. I felt good about them. My dad had already told me about them.

When we got to the game, Steven walked in with me and sat with me until it was time for him to leave. He showed me were his parents always sat and said they'd be arriving any minute. I told Steven I was sure my friends from school would be here dragging me off with them. Steven smiled and said he was sure they would but asked if I could get away from them after the game to hang out with him. He said he usually went out with his family but had told them he was going to hang out with me after the game. I smiled, feeling special again.

Just then, my crazy friends joined us. They talked with Steven and me until he had to leave. Sissy told me that as long as they had been coming to the games, they'd never seen Steven with a girl. He was usually with his family before practice. I smiled and said that we were only friends. They all laughed. "Sure," Sissy said, "just friends."

I sat with them in a spot not far from his parents. I waved at them as they walked in. Of course, my nosy friends had to ask, "You already know the family?"

I told them Steven had stopped by his home to drop off some tickets and that, yes, I'd met his family.

Sissy pointed out Teddy and his friend had arrived. I looked at them and felt a bit envious of her being there with Teddy.

I jumped up, cheering for Steven's team as they ran on the field. The team played well, and Steven was good at the game. Everyone kept calling out his name all throughout the game. Going out with the most popular football player on the team felt good and eased the pain of knowing that I wanted to be over there with Teddy.

We fans all stood cheering after our team won. We made our way down from the benches and swarmed onto the field. Steven was with his parents, and I didn't want to interrupt them. Then Steven left his family and ran over to where my friends and I were. He asked them if he could borrow me for the rest of the night and pulled me into the middle of the field with him. People were taking a bunch of pictures, and I was in all of them with him. He seemed happy to have me by his side, and his parents seemed happy I was there with him.

I did glance over at Teddy and his friend. I didn't know who was staring the most—Teddy or his friend. If no one knew about Steven and me before, they knew now. Steven had his arm around me as if I was his girlfriend. I knew we'd said we were friends, but I also knew that in the eyes of others, we certainly looked like more than friends.

I was happy we'd won the game, and I was happy to be there by Steven's side. But I was even happier that Teddy had seen us together. I wanted him to see how it felt. In a way, it made me feel sad inside. I knew Teddy was experiencing the same feeling I'd had when I'd seen him and his friend together for the first time.

Then I had to ask myself, *Am I doing this to make Teddy jealous?* Was I hoping this would make him want to come back to me? That would be good, but no. I was having fun talking and hanging out with Steven.

He told his parents we were leaving to get something to eat, and they told us to be careful and have fun. Steven held my hand and led me off the field. On our way, he said good-bye to the team and coach, introducing me to most of them.

At his truck, he put his arms around me and said, "Thank you."

"For what?" I asked.

"For just being there," he replied. "A man could easily fall in love with you because you are different—only in a good way. You are beautiful. I can't imagine how anyone in his right mind would let you go, but I am truly thankful." He kissed my forehead, which reminded me of Teddy.

I couldn't hold back the tears. I was glad it was dark so he couldn't see them falling. I got it together when we got in the truck. I felt good about what Steven had said and hoped he was speaking from his heart. I could see that he'd started to care for me. Was this what I wanted? Should I stop him or slow him down? Should I tell him we were only going to be friends?

I liked his company, and knowing that he cared made me feel good. It was nice to have someone show me he cared. No, I decided, I wasn't going to stop him. I enjoyed his company as much as he enjoyed mine.

Steven took me to this pizza joint. All his friends ended up there. It was the after-game hangout, and the pizza was good. Steven enjoyed showed me off, as if I was his girl. I knew everyone knew about Teddy and me and knew we were both with someone different now. All of Steven's friends were nice and welcomed me into the group with open arms. All the guys had their girlfriends, and we were all having fun. I enjoyed myself.

Steven spoke up and said we had to leave. He told everyone it was fun, and we said good night and left. Steven asked me what was my plans were for tomorrow. I said nothing as of yet. I hadn't talked with my dad to see if he had plans. We always hung out on Saturdays when we both had time. Steven said he'd call me tomorrow. I told him I'd had a great time and that the team had played a good game.

At my house, Steven pulled into my driveway and walked me to the door. He kissed me on my forehead and said, "Thanks for a wonderful evening. Can I call you later tonight?"

I smiled and said, "Okay, I'll talk to you later."

I opened the door and walked in. Dad was watching TV. He smiled and, looking over at me, said, "I can tell your evening went great."

I smiled and sat down beside him. I told him all about the game and where we'd gone to eat afterward. I also told him about seeing Teddy and his friend at the game and how they'd both been staring hard at me. I figured that maybe they were surprised to see me there with Steven. "But I really had a wonderful time," I added. "Oh and he asked me out tomorrow, but I wanted to see if you wanted to do anything tomorrow."

Dad put his arm round me, smiled, and hugged me. "Thank you, Sunshine, for letting him know your dad is number one."

"Always," I said.

"No, you go out and have a good time," Dad said. "I just want to stay here and cut the grass and catch up on some work around the house."

I said I was going to take a shower and turn in. I knew Steven was going to call me later, and I wanted to be in bed watching TV. I was excited for once as I waited on him to call.

I was lying in bed thinking of the fun I'd had tonight when my phone rang. I looked at the phone. It was not Steven. It was Teddy. I could not push the button to answer. I just froze as I looked at his picture while the phone rang. Of all the times to call, he would have to call now when things were going well with Steven. I wondered what he wanted.

The chime let me know he'd left a message.

The phone rang again. This time it was Steven. I hit the answer button and said, "Hello." I was glad Steven called. He could tell in my voice that something was bothering me. I went on to tell him about the phone call from Teddy, saying that I hadn't answered his call.

Steven tried to lift my spirits and make me feel better. He asked me how I felt about Teddy calling.

"I didn't feel anything," I replied. "I was mostly shocked that he would call now of all times." I told Steven that Teddy hadn't called once since we went our separate ways. "Then he sees me with you tonight and he decides to call. In a way, it makes me angry. He has his friend and have gone on with his life. Why call now?" I told Steven Teddy had left a message but that I hadn't checked it.

"Keep an open mind and listen to what he has to say," Steven suggested. "Go from there."

I asked him how he felt.

He said he was okay with it all and thanked me for asking. He went on to tell me he'd started to care for me a lot. "But whatever way you choose to go," he concluded, "I'll respect your decision." He asked me to keep him informed and then said he knew it was late and would call me tomorrow if that was okay.

"Sure," I said, adding that I was free for tomorrow.

"Great," he said. "We will talk tomorrow."

I listened to Teddy's voice message. "Hi, Nyah," he said. "I know I'm the last person you were thinking would call you. I wanted to talk to you and not by leaving a message. You know me. I'd rather talk to you. Would you please call? You know I hate talking to a machine. I will wait for your call even if it's late. Call me please."

I looked at my phone. I didn't want to call. I knew I still had strong feelings for Teddy. I was trying hard to go on with my life. Then on the other hand, I wanted to call to hear what he had to say.

I called, and he answered on the first ring. He said, "Hello. Thank you for calling me back."

"Hi," I said. "No problem." I was trying not to sound too thrilled to be talking to him.

"I want to say I am sorry for how I ended things between us," he said. "Can you find it in your heart to forgive me?"

"You know I forgive you," I replied. "Only the hurt is still there."

He said he knew he'd said we should see other people and give each other space. He'd been trying to do that and had even been trying to talk to someone else, but it wasn't working.

After all the time we've been apart, he sees me looking happy with someone else, I thought. *Now he wants to call and talk.* I could not believe this. I started to tell him I had to go, but I didn't. Instead I said, "Teddy this is how you wanted things to go. I didn't want you to walk out of our relationship. You knew how much I loved you. I wouldn't have done anything that would come between the two of us. Teddy, you were a part of my life I cherished like nothing else. You had a part of my heart that no one could touch or even come close to touching. I was planning to spend the rest of my life with you. Of all people, you knew me better than anyone did. I loved you from my heart, and you knew that. I was honest with you about my life, only you chose to turn and walk away, hurting me more than anything that has happened in my life.

"Of all people, I thought you would never be the one to fill my life with so much pain. Only you were the one. I cried many nights, Teddy, not because I had done something wrong or hurt you by being dishonest but only because I'd been honest and shared a part of me that I do not share with many.

"I loved you, Teddy. You walked away, never calling once no matter what I was going through. You chose to go on with your life."

Teddy spoke up. "I was confused and scared," he said. "I never stopped loving you."

"You never tried to see if we could work things out," I countered. "You chose someone else. Teddy, are you happy?"

"She's not you," he answered, "and I know she will never be you. I am sorry for all I put you through and for not communicating with you or giving you the heads up when I started talking to someone else."

"Was I that bad that you had to turn to someone else?"

"No," Teddy answered, "and I am sorry. It tore my heart apart to see you with someone else having so much fun."

"Yes it hurt a lot, Teddy," I told him "That is something I have been dealing with."

"I am so sorry, Nyah," he said. "I do still love you so much."

I stopped him, saying, "Teddy, if you loved me like you said you did, love would never have let you turn to someone else. Love would have let us work it out. Love would not have us talking about our past but our future. And love would have us together now. However, love took you in another direction. You are with someone else. I am talking to someone else. I don't want anyone else to get hurt."

He asked me if Steven knew I was talking to him now.

"Yes," I told him. "Does your friend know you were going to call and talk to me?"

"No," he answered.

"Be honest with her," I said. "Don't hurt her. I for one know how hurt feels." I was trying all I could to hold back the tears that were trying to come. "Teddy," I said, "you have a good life and take care of yourself. I do hope somehow some day we can both get over the hurt and be friends. We are both with someone else. I don't think it's a good idea for us to be calling each other like this."

Tears were rolling down my cheeks. I knew this was good-bye for us. I wanted so much to tell him I wanted to be with him. I knew I still loved Teddy. Saying good-bye for good was tearing my heart open. But I was talking to Steven. I didn't want him to go through what I was going through. I told Teddy I had to go, and he said he thought we should talk in person to say our good-bye for good. I knew that could never happen. I could never say good-bye face-to-face without breaking down. I knew I would end up in his arms. I said, "It has ended. We are with other people. So this is our good-bye for good."

"One day, I'll win you back," he said. "Our love we have for each other will bring us back together. I will love you always. Take care."

I told him to do the same, said good-bye, and hung up the phone. It did hurt. Yes, I loved Teddy. I always would. Only it was different talking to him. Maybe that was because of the timing of the call or knowing it had taken him seeing me with someone else to pick up the phone and call me.

I shook my head, thinking about how he'd waited all this time to call. He had said he was sorry. I was sorry too. I knew then that our lives or that part of our life was over. I didn't cry long. Maybe I'd cried too many tears over Teddy. I did know that he would always have a special place in my heart because he had been there for me through many rough times, but I knew I was letting go. I closed my eyes, smiled, and drifted off to sleep.

Chapter 20

I heard the lawnmower going. My dad was in the yard working. I looked at the clock. It was ten fifteen. I had slept late. I got up and opened my window. The breeze felt good coming in. I waved down to my dad. He smiled and kept mowing the grass. He had a big yard, both in back and out front, and he loved doing the yard work himself. I knew he would be out there all day.

I jumped in the shower and got dressed. I knew Steven was going to be calling with plans for today. I was glad my dad would be home to meet Steven when he came over. I was dressed and downstairs when my phone rang. It was Steven.

"How are you this morning?" he asked.

I asked if he was up and ready for the day.

He said he'd been up since five and had already taken a morning run.

"Five," I said.

He laughed. "Yes," he told me. "I run every morning."

"Do you want to get together today to do something?"

"That sounds great," I said.

He asked when would be a good time to come over.

"Any time will be great," I said. "My dad is here doing yard work. He'll be here all day."

"I'll be there around one," he said.

It was twelve when I looked at the clock. I had an hour before Steven would be here. I wasn't hungry, so I skipped lunch even though I hadn't had breakfast. I told myself I'd eat later.

I did my hair and even put on a little makeup. Then I walked back downstairs. When Dad walked in, he smiled and said how beautiful I was and that I reminded him of my mother. I told him Steven was coming over at one. He said that was fine and that he would love to see him and to remind him to take extra care of his Sunshine. He was grinning when he said that last part. I knew he wanted to grill Steven. You know how dads are about their daughters; no matter how old they get, daughters will always be their father's baby girl.

I told dad I'd fixed him a sandwich and a cold glass of lemonade. "I'm just looking out for you," I said. "I know you. When you start yard work, you don't take the time to stop and eat." I also said I'd be cooking dinner tonight.

He smiled and said he couldn't wait. He knew I could cook some; he had given me plenty of cooking lessons.

"Don't worry," I told him. "It will be something simple but good."

Dad ate his lunch and walked back out the door, saying, "Thank you for lunch. I know dinner will be good. Why don't you invite Steven?"

"We'll see," I said.

I heard the mower start back up, and a moment later, the doorbell rang. It was Steven. I opened the door, and he came in smiling. He told me how nice I looked.

"Thanks," I said. I walked back into the kitchen, clearing up Dad's lunch. I offered Steven a glass of lemonade.

"Sure," he said. "I haven't had lemonade in a long time"

I smiled and poured him a glass. He turned it up and drank the whole glass.

I laughed. "You were thirsty," I said. "Want another?"

"Yes, please," he answered. "This is good. I am thirsty from the run this morning."

I walked into the living room and turned on the TV. We sat next to each other. He asked, "So what do you want to do today?" Then he added, "First, I would like to go outside and speak to your dad."

"Sure," I agreed. "I'm sorry. I'll take Dad something to drink."

We walked into the backyard, and Dad stopped the mower. "Dad," I said, "you remember Steven."

"Sure," he said.

They shook hands and started talking. My dad asked how Steven's family was doing, and Steven told him they were great. I gave Dad a drink told him I had something to take care of in the house—to give them their man time alone. I walked back into the house. But I kept looking out the window. I wouldn't let Steven stay alone with my dad too long. I knew my dad was into his grilling role, so I went to rescue Steven.

"Dad," I said. "I think I'll take this guy off your hands. I know you want to get back to your yard work."

Dad smiled and told us to have fun. "Oh, Steven," he added, "Nyah is cooking dinner today. It would be good if you would join us."

I could not believe Dad had done that. I looked back at him, gave him a frown, and walked away.

Steven said, "So what time is dinner, so I can have you back in time to cook. I know how you women get when you are cooking."

"Excuse me," I said, raising my eyebrows at him.

"I'm referring to my mother," he replied. "She stays in the kitchen all day, but it's is worth it when the food is done."

I smiled. "Cooking takes time," I said. Now I was wondering what I was going to cook. I still couldn't believe Dad had put me on the spot like that.

"What's for dinner?" Steven asked with a smile.

"I haven't thought that far yet," I told him. "I had just told my dad I'd cook because I know he'll be in the yard all day and won't take time to eating. I told him I'd cook something good and simple."

Steven smiled. "Simple is good," he said.

We both got into his truck and left. I waved at Dad, and he threw his hand up with a smile. I was going to get him back. I didn't know how or when, but I knew the time would come one day.

Steven ended up driving to a big park that I'd never been to before. He took a blanket from the truck and spread it out under a tree. We sat and watched all the different things going on in the park. People were fishing at a pond. Others were skating on one side of the park. Children were playing at the playground. There were even people barbecuing.

We lay back on the blanket, looking up at the beautiful blue sky. We talked about lots of things. He never once brought up Teddy's name or asked if I'd called him, so I brought it up. "You haven't asked about the talk I had with Teddy," I said.

"I didn't want to pressure you," he told me.

"I will always love Teddy in a special way because he was there for me when I needed him," I said. "But the fact that not once did he think about calling or reaching out to me until he saw me with someone else tells me a lot and hurts even more. We're both seeing someone else and going on with our lives.

"Now to you, Steven," I added. "Yes, I am moving on with my life. Yes, I am free of all connection with Teddy. So you don't have to think you're coming between anything. There is nothing to come between. He has his girl. I am talking with you."

Steven looked at me. "I am sad to hear that," he said. "I'm sorry it didn't work out. But I have to admit that I'm more than glad it didn't at the same time. I know we're starting out as just friends, but I would love to call it more than that. I would love it if you'd be my girlfriend."

He admitted he didn't want anyone else trying to move in and said now that everyone knew I was free, they would be trying.

I smiled. "Yes," I told him, "we can say officially say that we are dating, but we'll take it slow." I felt good saying that, and I could tell by the smile on Steven's face he enjoyed hearing it.

Then Steven asked if he could kiss me. I smiled and said, "Yes." It was a wonderful kiss. I must admit it did feel good to be in those big arms of his.

"Now you have my brand on you," he said. "All other hands off. You are my woman. I am not planning on letting you slip away from me. You'll see. I will always do my best to make you happy and feel special."

I hoped he was talking from his heart. "From this day, I can say that I am yours and proud to be yours and will do everything within me to make us both happy," I told him.

He kissed me again, this time without asking. We lay back, and I knew I'd have to get used to doing this all this over again. Being with someone else was something I'd never thought would happen. But here I was doing it over again with someone new.

Steven was a sweet person. Now that I was starting over, I was glad it was with Steven. Then my thoughts turned to how I was going to tell him about me—the other part of me. Should I tell him now and give him a chance to turn away? Or should I just wait to see how things would turn out with us?

I decided to wait. It was early. We hadn't had time to get to know each other. I told him again that I wasn't going to rush into anything but take it slow.

Steven asked, "Have you thought about dinner? What you are going to cook?"

"No," I said. I asked him what he thought and reminded him that I wanted something simple.

"I love tacos," he said.

I thought about it and asked if he'd cooked them before.

"Yes," he said. "Everyone loves my tacos."

"Tacos it is," I replied, "with you helping in the kitchen. I'll need to stop by the store to pick up some items for them."

"No problem," he replied. "I would be glad to help you out in the kitchen. We are a team now."

I smiled, and we lay there for a while longer talking. He told me about his plans for the future, and I told him I was planning on something in the medical field.

"I thought you would," he said, "being that your dad is in the medical field."

I smiled, saying I would have good help when I needed help studying.

He wanted to play football and had his goals set high. I was glad to hear that and told him I hoped everything would turn out just as he planned.

We decided we'd better get going so we'd have time to stop by the store and get the things we needed for the tacos before going home to cook. *This is going to be fun*, I thought.

One we'd gotten what we needed, we headed back to my house. Dad was still in the yard trimming hedges. He waved at us as we pulled into the driveway. We walked into the house, put the things away until we were ready to cook, and headed out to the backyard Steven told me how beautiful it was, and we sat in the garden together for a little while. He said this would be his favorite spot if he lived here. It was beautiful nice and quiet.

"This is my special place here in the garden," I told him. "I keep this part up and enjoy doing it."

We sat and talked for a while, and he asked about my mother. I told him that she and my father weren't together—that she wasn't here—and left it at that. He told me he was sorry.

"So am I," I said, "but Dad and I are happy. And maybe one day, I'll tell you all about my life's adventures. Come now, show me your skills in the kitchen."

He smiled and followed me. I went to the front of the house where Dad was finishing up and told him I'd have help cooking dinner.

Dad smiled. "Good," he said. "I've worked up an appetite."

I asked Dad if he like tacos and he said that sounded great. He hadn't had tacos in a while. "Can't wait."

Steven and I walked into the kitchen. I showed him around and then climbed up on the stool and told him, "You take over. It's all yours."

He smiled. "Really," he said, "because I can do this."

I jumped down. "I am sure you can," I said, "but I would love to help."

"Okay then, let's do this," he said.

He started washing and cutting the meat up into small chunks and seasoning it with different spices. I had the easy part—cutting up the lettuce and tomatoes. I watched him worked, and he seemed to know what he was doing. As we worked, we talked and laughed, and were having fun.

Dad came in and said how good it smelled. He was going to get a shower and change and would be down to join us.

I finished cutting up everything and went to stand next to Steven, asking if he needed any help.

"No," he said, "but you could stay here close to me."

I smiled and stayed, watching as he added all the seasoning. Dad was right; it smelled good.

Steven finished the meat and started doing the taco shells. Dad came downstairs and turned on the TV, and I poured him a glass of lemonade and told him to relax. Dinner would be ready soon. I set the table while Steven finished up in the kitchen.

When Dad sat at the table, he had a big smile on his face. "It feels good to come to the table and a good cooked meal," he said.

I smiled and agreed. "Dad, you've been working hard all day. You need to just eat and rest in front of the TV after dinner."

Dad said grace, and we started to eat. I had to say, the tacos were great. Dad even went for seconds. He told us we'd done a great job and the food was great. I had to admit that Steven had cooked the food; I'd just done the cutting part.

I started clearing the table and told Dad to go and rest. I would take care of the kitchen. Of course, Steven said he would help. Dad got up with a smile and headed for the living room. There was plenty left over, and I told Steven to take some home for later if he got hungry; we'd still have plenty for Dad if he wanted some for later.

The evening went well. After we cleaned the dishes and finished up in the kitchen, Steven and I went into the back to sit in the garden for a while before he left. When I went back into the house to get us drinks, I noticed my dad was asleep in the chair. I joined Steven and told him my dad was tired; his meal had put him to sleep.

Steven put his arm around me and told me how happy he was for this chance to be in my life. I did feel good with Steven. But it was nothing like being with Teddy. I had to get to know Steven more. I wasn't as comfortable with him as I had been with Teddy. We talked and laughed more before he said he had to get home. He didn't want to overstay his welcome the first time visiting.

I said I'd had a wonderful time and thanked him for cooking. I went into the kitchen, got his doggy bag, and walked him to his truck. He put his arms around me and told me he wanted so much to kiss me, but not here. I pulled him close and gave him that kiss anyway, and he kissed me back. Afterward, he said, "Please do not get me banned from your home on the first visit."

"My father is asleep, and it was only a little kiss," I told him.

"You call that a little kiss? I cannot wait to get a big kiss." He told me he'd had a wonderful time and said to tell my father good-bye and thank him. He started his truck, and I waved good-bye as he backed out of the yard.

I sit in the garden looking at all the beautiful flowers. I came here when I needed to think, which I'd been doing a lot lately. I really enjoyed spending time with Steven. My dad liked and approved of him. Then there was Teddy—I couldn't push him completely out of the picture. I would see what life had in store for me.

I had a good feeling as I walked into the house. My dad was still sleeping. I walked over, bent down and gave him a kiss on the forehead, and told him I loved him.

He smiled and said he loved me too and thanked me again for dinner. "It is good to see you happy and smiling, Sunshine," he added.

I crawled up next to him on the chair and told him Steven had said good-bye and thanks. I started watching the movie while he slept.

When Dad got up and went to bed, I was still watching the movie. My phone rang, and it Sissy checking up on me.

"A lot has happened," I told her. "Steven and I are officially dating."

She was excited to hear the news and told me she was happy for me. I knew she couldn't wait to tell the others.

"Steven is a good choice," she said. "He hasn't been dating anyone. At least I haven't seen him with any girl at this school."

"Good," I said. "Then there won't be any drama with any of the girls over him." I told her that he'd cooked tacos for Dad and me and that we'd a wonderful time.

"He's already up in your house cooking," she replied. "Yes, he's going to be the special guy in your life."

"I am starting to like Steven a lot, but I still think of Teddy when I'm out with Steven," I admitted. "I am trying so hard to block Teddy out. Only he keeps coming back inside my mind."

"You have to give it time," Sissy counseled. "You and Teddy were together for a long time. I'm sure you still care for him a lot. It takes time to get over someone like that."

"I am trying so hard to close that chapter in my life," I told her. "Only the more I try pushing him out, the more I find myself thinking about and missing him. I even sit wishing he were with me instead of Steven. It's so hard. Steven is with me saying he cares. I want to take it slow to make sure both of our feelings for each other are real. I don't want to be hurt again. It's such a bad feeling, and it's hard to get over. Plus, I don't want to hurt him in any way. So we're going to take it slow together."

"You make sure of your feelings," Sissy said. "I know you still love Teddy. I know he still loves you even though he is with someone else. Make sure there is nothing there to go back to." She told me she had to go and that we'd talk later.

I finished watching my show, cut the light off, and went up to my room. As soon as I'd turned the TV on, my phone rang again. It was Steven. I smiled and snuggled under my covers. I was glad he'd called. We talked for hours and by the time we got off the phone, it was late. I turned off my TV, closed my eyes, and went to sleep.

I was up early the next morning getting ready for church. I always enjoyed church. Plus, I knew we'd visit Grandma later and enjoy some of her excellent cooking. I loved spending time with Grandma. She was walking now with her walker, and her legs were getting stronger. She wouldn't need the walker soon. Grandma looked more alive and happy now that she was no longer in the wheelchair. She wanted it out of her house, and she'd been walking every day since she got out of it. I was so happy for her.

When we got home Sunday evening, Dad and I did nothing but rest. I called Steven and talked to him for a while. He said he missed me, and I missed him too. I told him I would see him at school tomorrow.

When I got off the phone, Dad came into the living room and asked me when I wanted to go get my license. He said we could start looking for a car. I told him I would pick up a drivers' handbook to study and then let him know. I was happy about the prospect of car shopping.

I asked my dad if he wanted ice cream. I knew he loved ice cream.

"Yes that would be good," he said.

I fixed us each a bowl with all the toppings and nuts, and we ate and watched TV together. *What a good weekend this has been*, I thought. I'd had the weekend off from work, and I'd had a wonderful time with

Steven and my dad. I sure hoped Teddy's life was going as well as mine. I was looking forward to seeing Steven tomorrow.

The next day at school, I walked to my locker. The first person I saw was Teddy. He was standing at his locker. All this time, I had rarely seen him at his locker when I got to school. Teddy looked at me, smiled, and said, "Hello."

I smiled and said hi. Just then, Steven showed up. He had noticed Teddy at his locker. He said hi and walked over to where I was, smiling and not paying Teddy any attention. Steven took my hand, and we walked away hand in hand. I hated to see Teddy look so sad, but he'd chosen this, not me.

I saw him again later, this time with his friend. He was smiling with her, and I had a bad feeling when I saw them together. Still, I was happy to see Teddy smiling.

During lunch, I would go out to my little spot under the tree. Steven would join me, and we'd eat lunch there. Today, Steven and I were sitting there talking. I looked up and saw Teddy coming out the door. I hadn't seen him come out here since we'd broken up. He noticed us sitting in the spot that used to be ours, turned, and went back inside.

Steven asked, "Are you okay?"

"I'm fine," I said. "Maybe he just wanted to come outside, saw us, and decided to give us our time." I told Steven, "We are together now. You don't have to worry. Enough about Teddy. When is your next game?"

"Friday," he said. "It's away."

I told him I'd be there. I knew my friends would be going and would love me to ride with them.

It was time to go back to class. Steven walked me to class. I told him I had to work today after school and said I'd call him on my break. I knew he had practice and I wouldn't get to see him the rest of the day. He asked if he could give me a ride home; it wouldn't be out of his way. I said sure; I was happy not to have to ride the bus. "Great," he said, and we agreed to meet back up after school.

Before the end of the day, my friends had spilled all the hot gossip about Teddy's friend, which they were clearly dying to get out. I listened, but I didn't want to hear about Teddy and his friend. I was trying to be happy with Steven. When I was with Teddy, I'd never noticed how good Steven looked. I'd been too in love to notice any other person. My eyes had been on Teddy. Steven was really a handsome person. When I'd watched him cooking at our house, I'd noticed how tall and muscular and in shape he was. Now he was all mines. I smiled as I thought of him.

I finished the rest of the day in a daze, but somehow, I got through it. When school was out, I hurried to my locker. I didn't want to keep Steven waiting. I knew he had practice and I had to work.

Just as I was closing my locker, Steven walked up. "Hi," he said. "You ready?"

I smiled and told him I was.

We talked all the way to my house. He didn't get out; he had to get to practice. He did kiss me good-bye and said he would call me later.

Chapter 21

I walked into the house and fell on the couch to rest. I had time to relax since I hadn't ridden the bus. It was nice to get home a little early and not have to rush. I sure would enjoy this extra time when I got my car. I fixed a sandwich and watched TV for a while before it was time for me to leave for work.

When I walked outside, the blind man, Joe from across the street was outside. He saw me, waved and said hello, and commented on what a beautiful day it was.

I agreed and said it was good to see him doing well.

He smiled and went back to planting flowers in the yard. It was good to see him seeing again. I got to work feeling great. I didn't have too many patients, which was good. I didn't have to work hard.

When I finished my shift and clocked out, I decided to take a walk around the hospital and look around. I even went to different floors I didn't normally work on. As I was walking, a voice called out to me. I stopped and saw an older woman who asked if I could give her a drink of water. She knew I worked in the hospital because of my uniform. I poured her a cup of water, and she started talking. I wasn't on the clock, so I sat down to listen to her talk. She told me about her condition, a bone disease, which she'd been living with for a long time. I asked her if she was in any pain, and she said she wasn't at the moment, as she'd taken her pain medication not long before.

She was so sweet and glad to have someone to talk with. I asked her if she had any family here, and she told me, her son lived in another state. "Baby, I don't want to hold you up," she said. "I only needed a drink of water. Thank you for sitting awhile."

I smiled and told her I was off the clock for the day. She apologized for bothering me on my time off, and I assured her she was never a bother. I already knew I was going to help her, but I wasn't sure how. I told her I had a little time to sit and talk, and she smiled. Her eyes lit up with joy.

She was sixty-nine years old and had grandkids she never spent time with because she was always ill and couldn't travel to see them often. When the grandkids did get a chance to visit, she was always in too much pain to walk.

When she asked me about my life, I told her I was still in school and living with my dad. She asked about college, and I told her about my plans to get into the medical field.

She smiled and said that was great. I could tell that whatever medicine her doctor had given her was started working; she was getting drowsy. I asked her if she was getting tired. She smiled, closed her eyes, and said, "No, baby."

I stood up, put my hands on her legs, and told her I would come back to visit her. I asked if she needed another drink before I left, but she didn't answer. That's when I started to focus on helping her. It took a while. I began to feel the tingling in my hands, and I stayed there until it had completely stopped.

As soon as I took my hands off her, she spoke. "Thank you," she said.

I told her she would be a lot better and promised to come back to visit on my next workday. I walked out glad that she would be better so she could visit her grandchildren and spend time with them free from pain.

I'd walked a little farther down the hospital hall when I heard a woman moaning. Her door was halfway open, and the nurse was coming out. "Hi," she said. "Are you stopping to visit her?"

"Yes," I replied.

The nurse told me to go on in; she was done.

I walked in and saw a young woman. Her eyes were closed, and she was shaking her leg. I figured her leg was hurt. "Hello," I said.

She responded without opening her eyes.

I asked if the nurse had given her something for pain.

"Yes," she said, sounding exasperated, "but it doesn't stop all the pain. I have had back pain for way too long."

I asked if her leg hurt, and she explained that shaking her leg made her feel better. "I cannot keep it still," she said. "It hurts too much." She took a deep breath and sighed. "I didn't want them to put me on that strong medication, but I don't know how much more I can take of this pain."

I walked closer. One of her legs was stretched out. I laid my hand on her leg and rubbed it, telling her it would get better. She kept talking about her pain, she didn't seem to even noticed that my hand remained on her leg; she was completely preoccupied with the pain she was in. I began to focus on her getting better. I felt the tingling started in my hands and held on until it stopped. When I removed my hands and backed off, she stopped shaking her leg.

"How did it stop?" she asked. She opened her eyes and looked at me. Then she sat up in the bed and asked, "What happened?"

I asked what she meant.

"All the pain just stopped completely," she said, sounding perplexed.

"No pain anywhere?" I asked.

She smiled. "No pain in my back," she said, "not anywhere."

She looked at me. A tear fell. "I have never had no pain. I've always at least had some pain." She closed her eyes and said, "Thank you."

I walked out to give her a moment to be thankful. A tear was in my eye as I walked out seeing her pain free.

I walked down the hall a little farther and noticed a woman standing outside the door crying. I stopped and asked if she was okay. She said the nurses were drawing blood from her little girl. "I can never stay in there and watch," she told me.

I heard the little girl calling her mom to help her; she was afraid. The mother told me her daughter had a problem with her heart. She cried as she told me how she hated to see her daughter have to go through so much.

I put my hand on her shoulder and told her it would be okay. I waited with her, trying to comfort her. "How old is her daughter?" I asked.

"One year old today," she told me.

My heart went out to the little girl and the mom.

A nurse came out told her she could come in. I walked in with her, and the nurses left, saying they were finished. I asked the little girl her name, and, though still crying, she told me it was Jane. I told her that was a pretty name and said I had known a girl name Jane. Her mom put her arms around her and held her. The mother started coughing and asked me if I didn't mind staying with Jane while she went to the restroom.

I stood next to Jane, and her mother explained that I was going to stay with her until she came back from the restroom. She pointed to the door saying she would be right inside there.

I placed my hands on Jane's stomach and rubbed it, telling her, "Mommy will be right back." I began to focus, trying to make the little girl better. It wasn't long before the tingling came into my hands, and I knew she was going to be all better.

When Jane's mom came out of the restroom, I was talking to the little girl and she was smiling and laughing. Her mother smiled, happy to see her daughter laughing, and said, "Thank you."

"No problem," I said. I told Jane she would be okay and said good-bye. I left the room, happy in the knowledge that the little girl really would be better.

I walked downstairs. The next floor of the hospital was the labor and delivery ward. I looked at the babies lying in tiny cribs behind a large window. When I turned to walk down the hall, I heard a woman crying out. I went to her door and knocked. When no one answered, I pushed the door open. A woman, who was clearly in labor and in great pain, was lying on the bed. I walked over beside her bed.

Through the pain, she asked, "Are you ready for me?"

"No, I'm not your nurse," I said quickly. "I was walking by and stopped to check on you. Are you getting ready to have your baby?"

"They are going to take it. He is turned wrong. His feet are facing down." She gasped as another contraction hit her. "I wanted to have a nature birth," she said, sounding defeated, after the contraction had passed.

I stood beside her bed. I could see she was in a lot of pain. I placed my hands on her stomach and told her everything was going to be okay. I began to focus on trying to help her. I knew she wouldn't notice. She was in too much pain. I started to feel the tingle in my hand. I could feel the baby moving inside her. When the tingling stopped, the baby stopped moving too.

"I have to push," she said.

"You need to wait on the doctor," I told her.

"No," she yelled, crying out in pain. "I have to push."

She started pushing. I looked down and saw that the baby's head was coming out. I ran to get the nurse and told her the baby was coming out.

"That's impossible," the nurse said. "She is going in for a C-section."

I told the nurse I had seen the baby's head coming out. The nurse ran into the woman's room. The baby was halfway out. She called for the doctor and then helped the woman delivery the baby.

The doctor came in just as the baby had completely emerged from his mother's womb. "How could this have happened?" she asked. "We were getting the delivery room ready."

I smiled at her and said, "That baby was ready to come, and he came."

The mother was smiling too. She said she was happy that she'd had a natural birth and a healthy baby boy.

I decide to go home for the day. I looked at my phone to check my messages and saw that Steven had called twice. I dialed his number. He answered and asked if I was home. I told him I was just now leaving work.

"Poor baby," he said. "I know you must be tired."

I laughed. "I'm okay," I told him. "I'm going home to relax and do nothing." I said I'd call him back when I get home and hung up as the bus pulled up.

When I got home, I felt happy as I thought about all the people that I'd been able to help. My dad wasn't home yet, as he was working late. I wanted to sit in the garden and wait on my dad to get home; only I was too tired.

I took a shower, lay across my bed, and thought of my mother. I started to focus on her. I closed my eyes. I hadn't talked to her in a long time. As I focused, I could feel my head getting light or something; whatever was going on, I could feel it.

Then suddenly, my mother was standing there. As always, she had a smile on her face. "Hello, baby," she said.

"Hi," I replied. "Dad and I miss you. We need you here with us. There must be some way you can come home. I love my dad, but I need my mother. I need you, and dad needs you. You have this beautiful garden and this beautiful home. And dad had it just for you, only you aren't here." I could feel the tears rolling down my face as I talked to her. I didn't give her a chance to say a word; I just kept talking. "I need you here to help me. I am going through so much. The one person I loved and still love broke up with me because I told him I was different. He just left. Now he's with someone else and afraid to be with me. I'm dating someone else too. I don't want it to be like this. I want it to be as it was. I need you here to talk to me and to tell me if I'm doing things right and making the right choices. Yes, I have my father. But I need my mother. Dad hurts. I am hurting. We need you."

Finally, I stopped talking, and Mom started to speak. "I know you are angry with me for leaving," she said. "I know your dad and you are hurting and that I am the cause of a lot of the pain you've both been through. I never wanted to be away from either of you. If I had known on that day what I know, I would be there with you and not here. I'm hurting too. The pain I go through daily knowing you are hurting and alone because of what I did is terrible. Baby, I know you hurt; only your pain is nowhere close to the pain I feel. You were my baby when I left. Not being able to have you with me when you were small you were my baby and my heart. Yes, I love your dad. But you were my baby; it was so much harder being without you and not knowing if you were okay. Not being able to see you grew each day hurt. I missed you losing your first tooth. I missed so many precious moments. I missed all your good days, as well as your bad ones; your first day of school; all the talks about your first boyfriend and your first kiss. I missed it all. I hurt just as much now as I did back then when that door closed and you weren't there with me. Not having you with me was like having all the life taken out of me. I feel that same pain every day that I am away from your dad and you. I know the pain you're going through being without me. I feel it every day. And I am sorry. I am sorry I missed all the best part of your life. I'm sorry about not being there when you needed me to help you through all your problems or to hold you through all your tears and comfort you. I am so sorry. Please forgive me. Please forgive me, baby."

I could not see Mom through my tears, but I knew tears were falling from her eyes as she talked. "The only piece of joy I get is when I see your face," she said. "I will always love you both. One day, I will return. I hope it won't be too late for us. I hope your dad still has love for me and finds it in his heart to forgive me. I love the two of you more than life itself."

"Dad never chose another woman," I told her.

"Your dad is a good man," she said. "He always has been." She looked around at something I couldn't see before continuing. "Nyah, please never step through the door to come here unless you plan to be here for a long time. Remember that you cannot come and go as you wish. You have to wait until the door opens to return, and you won't know when that will be or how long it will take." She told me that when the door opened again, she would come back. She hoped it would be soon.

I told her how I'd been helping people here get better without them knowing. She said that was good. I told her that I'd helped Grandma and that she was walking now. "Dad knows that I'm different. He loves me the same. He said it is a gift."

"Tell your dad that I love him more than he will ever know. Tell him that one day, I will return to take care of him and you and my garden."

I told her I had to go and promised that I'd come and talk to her more often. After we'd told each other how much we loved each other, I said good night and broke my focus. When I opened my eyes, she was gone—it was that fast. Tears still streamed down my face. I wanted things to be different for us. I wanted my mother here. Even though I couldn't remember her at all, I wanted my dad to be happy and her to be back home with us.

My phone ranged. It was Steven. I wiped away the tears and answered. I needed to talk to someone, and he was a good choice. He would get me in a better mood. He sounded cheerful and happy as he greeted me and told me how much he missed me. I smiled. I felt better already as I listened to him talk. My mood changed quickly, and it wasn't long before I was laughing along with him.

I told him I couldn't wait until Friday's game. I had never liked going to the games before, but I looked forward to them now. Even though I was talking laughing with Steven, my mind always seemed to flash back on Teddy.

I heard my dad come in I told Steven that dad just came home and that I wanted to talk with him. I said I'd call him back.

I walked downstairs. My dad asked how my day was. I told him, "Long but good." I didn't mention what I had done at the hospital. We didn't talk about that part of my life. He didn't ask, and I didn't tell him anything. He told me he was going to change, get comfortable, and watch a movie.

"Yeah, right." I smiled. I knew he would be asleep before the movie had really gotten going.

He laughed and said he got good sleep when he fell asleep in front of the TV.

As soon as the movie started, he was asleep.

The next day when I got home from school, I got a call from Sara. She told me Kaylin had taken ill and had been in and out of the hospital. Mr. and Mrs. Daniels had taken her back to the hospital last night. I was glad to learn that she was at the same hospital where I worked. I told Sara I would go see her today and thanked her for calling.

I called my dad, but he didn't answer. I left him a message and said I'd be at the hospital. I knew I wouldn't be seeing Steven today, as he had football practice. I decided to change my clothes and head over to the hospital. I was off today, so I didn't have to rush.

At the hospital, I found out Kaylin's room number and headed over to see how she was doing and find out what was going on with her. She was asleep when I walked in. I sat down beside her bed. I could tell just by looking at her face that she'd lost a lot of weight. I took her hand. She opened her eyes to look at me. Her eyes looked sunken, and when she talked, I could tell from her voice that she was weak.

"What's wrong?" I asked her.

Her face was painted with sadness even though she was trying hard to smile. I asked her again what was wrong and looked into her eyes as I waited on an answer. The only reply I got was tears that began to flow from her face. I put my arms around her and cried with her. It hurt me so to see her lying here suffering from whatever was going on with her. I had grown up with Kaylin; she was one of the sisters I'd never had. I loved her as if she was my own sister. I held onto her and told her she was going to be okay.

She looked into my eyes. "Yes," she agreed, "I am going to be just fine." I could tell she knew she was not going to be fine. She looked scared.

The nurse came in to check on her patient, and Kaylin said yes when she asked if she needed more pain medication. I stepped back to let the nurse do what she had to do. But as soon as she was gone, I returned to Kaylin's side.

Kaylin looked at me. She smiled and said, "It's good to see you. How is life treating you? I know you are having a good time with your dad."

"Life is great," I told her. "Dad and I are happy and doing well."

She asked about Teddy, and I told her Teddy and I were no longer together. I told her about Steven and then said, "Enough about me. We will talk later about me. What is going on with you?"

Kaylin took her eyes off me. She looked down as she told me she had cancer and that the cancer was in stage four. I took her hand and held on tightly. As we held each other's gazes, tears fell from both of our eyes.

"No matter how bad it looks, no matter what stage you are in, you have to believe, without a doubt in your mind, you are going to get better," I said.

"I have been holding on," Kaylin told me. "This came so suddenly and moved so quickly."

Tears flowed from my eyes as I held tightly to the sister I had taken as one of my own. "You, Sara, and I are sisters," I told her. "Nothing is going to happen to you. You're only going to get better. You hold onto that and believe it from your heart."

Kaylin smiled at me. She told me she was feeling better just from seeing and talking to me. "Don't get angry with Sara or Mr. and Mrs. Daniels. I made them all promise not to worry you. You've been through enough, dealing with all the problems in your life. I didn't want you dealing with mine."

"Remember that we're family," I replied. "We go through things together. Never keep anything from me about you, Sara, or Mr. and Mrs. Daniels. Promise me."

She said she was sorry and promised. I asked how she was feeling, and she said she was fine at the time but that the pain get severe sometimes, mostly at night. "But I'm hanging in there," she added.

I knew what I had to do. I stood up and told her I wanted to do something. I held onto her hand, placed my other hand on her leg, and began to focus on her getting better. I didn't care if she asked questions later. I would deal with that later. I stayed still and focused, holding onto her. I wanted her better. As tears fell from my eyes, I began to feel the tingling. I held on tightly until it was gone. I turned her hands loose and looked into her eyes. They were closed, and tears were falling. She opened her eyes, smiled, and said, "Thank you for the prayer."

I said, "You are welcome," and left it like that.

I told Kaylin, "You will get better. You just have to believe."

As we were talking, Sara, Mr., and Mrs. Daniels walked in. They were glad to see me, and we gave each other hugs. Mrs. Daniels asked how I was doing. She said she knew I loved staying with my dad.

I told her it was great but that I missed them all. She told me how things were different for them now that I was gone. Mr. Daniels was the type of person who said little. But when he talked to Kaylin, you could hear the hurt in his voice, and it was clear that he cared for Kaylin and Sara as if they were his own. I listened to each of them as they talked to Kaylin. Their voices were filled with pain as they asked how she was feeling today.

"You know," Kaylin said. "I am feeling great right now. No pain at all. Maybe it's because we're all here together."

Sara was quiet. I asked her if she was okay.

"Yeah," she said. "I just hate hospitals."

"Hospitals are good," I told her. "They help get you better. I work here."

She asked what I did.

"I transport patients where they need to go in the hospital," I explained. "It's only after school and some weekends, but I work full time during the summer."

The nurse walked back in and asked Kaylin if she needed anything. Kaylin said that she was fine. We had a good time visiting with each other. I stayed there all day, and the time passed quickly. I noticed it was dark outside when the nurse came back in asking Kaylin if she needed any more pain medication.

Kaylin told her again that she was fine.

"No pain medication?" the nurse asked in surprise. "It has been over three hours. Usually, you take it every hour."

"I'm not in any pain," Kaylin told her. "It must be the good company I have."

The nurse smiled and paused on her way out the door. "This is the first time I've seen you smile and in no pain since you've been here," she said. "That is good."

The Danielses soon said they had to leave, as Mrs. Daniels had to cook dinner. Sara gave Kaylin a big hug and then gave me one. The family told Kaylin they would be back tomorrow. I stayed a while longer, feeling good that Kaylin wasn't in any pain and knowing that she was better.

My phone rang. It was my dad asking if I was still at the hospital. I told him I was but that I was getting ready to leave soon. He offered to pick me up. He was on his way home he would wait in front of the hospital. I told him I'd be down in five minutes. I told Kaylin that I would be back tomorrow after school.

"Okay." She smiled. "That would be great."

I hugged her. "Believe," I said as I was leaving.

Chapter 22

*M*y dad was waiting outside for me. He said he knew I hadn't taken time to eat and that he was planning on stopping by this sub place that had the best hoagies. I said that sounded good, and we picked up two hoagies to go.

On our way home, Steven called. I told him I was with my dad and I'd call him later. I wanted to put a smile on my dad's face. I told him I had talked to Mom and that she'd said she would come back somehow and that she would always love him. As soon as I told him, I wished I could take it back. I hated seeing the sadness that crept into his eyes even as he kept a smile on his lips.

"It's strange," he said softly. "I'm not used to how you are able to help people and able to talk to your mom. But I think it's great. I have to admit that I'm confused about all this. But because I know your mother and you are my daughter and because I live with you and love you both, I can accept you. I know I will always love you two with all my heart. I will learn about all this maybe one day. But for now, all I want is my family, who I know and love."

I thought about Steven as Dad and I rode in silence the rest of the way home. I had told Steven I would go to the game. Only now I was going to have to tell him I wouldn't make it. I wanted to be at the hospital with Kaylin.

When we got home, I called Steven to explain what was going on. Steven said he understood and thought I should be there with Kaylin.

I told him how sorry I was, and he said there'd be more games but that he'd miss me. He suggested that we could do something on Saturday if we were both free. I told him that sounded great and we talked and laughed more before getting off the phone.

I told him I would see him tomorrow at school, but I was going to be late. I was going to stop by the hospital first to check on Kaylin. I talked to my dad before going to bed and told him I was going by the hospital to check on Kaylin before school.

My mind stayed on Kaylin that night. I knew she was going to be okay, but she had been through so much. If only I had taken the time to call or even to visit. I'd been busy worrying about my problems. I felt badly that she'd had to go through so much when I could have helped her before her illness got to this point. I closed my eyes, and I was still thinking of Kaylin as I drifted off to sleep.

The next morning, my dad was up early. He asked if I wanted a ride to the hospital, and I said that would be great. Kaylin was sitting up and smiling when I walked into her room. I smiled back and told her she looked so much better.

"I feel so much better," she told me. "I haven't had any pain since yesterday." She told me the nurses could not believe that she no longer needed the pain medication. She was so grateful and she thanked me again.

"Thank you," I said. "For what?"

"For believing with me," she replied. "I feel like getting up and taking a shower myself this morning. What are you doing here and not in school?"

"I wanted to stop by and check on you," I told her. "I'll go to school in a bit."

She told me she couldn't wait for breakfast. She was hungry, and she hadn't eaten any food since she'd been in here. Seeing the changes in her was a relief. I knew that, no matter what the test results showed, she was going to be just fine now.

When Kaylin left to take a shower, I called Steven and told him I'd text him when I get to school. He said he was glad I was coming; he wanted to see me today. I told him I would see him soon and hung up.

Kaylin came out of the bathroom from her shower. She looked fresh. Just then, a nurse came in with her breakfast. When Kaylin told the nurse she was glad to see her with her breakfast, the nurse smiled and said she was glad to see that she had her appetite back.

Kaylin turned to me. "I am doing well now," she said. "You get to school."

"I'll stop by after school," I promised.

She smiled, saying, "Okay."

On the bus for school, I couldn't wait to see Steven. I would get there just in time to spend the first break with him. I texted him to let him know I'd made, and he texted back that he'd see me soon.

After class, I explained to my friends why I wouldn't be going to the game tonight.

"We could go by the hospital and sit with her for a while and have plenty of time before we leave for the game," Sissy pointed out.

That did sound good, and I agreed.

I looked up and saw Steven walking toward us. He was all smiles. "I wonder why he has such a big smile on his face," Sissy teased.

"Do not even think that," I said, glaring playfully.

Steven came up and took my hand. He asked my friends could he borrow me for a while. They all said yes; they were getting used to him borrowing me from them. "Sure, take her," Sissy said.

Steven put his arm around my neck as we both walked off laughing. I was just as happy to see him, as he was to see me. He stopped, turned to me, and gave me a nice, small kiss. I hated that we didn't have long and wished it was lunch break. We walked and talked for just a few moments, and then it was back to class. I realized that I had started to have feelings for this guy. If I could get Teddy completely out of my system, I knew Steven and I had a great chance to have something special between us.

It still hurt when I saw Teddy with his friend, just as I knew it hurt him when he saw me with Steven.

During lunch, Steven and I set under our tree—the same tree Teddy and I had sat under so many times. Being there did bring back memories of Teddy and me. I couldn't help but think of how we used to sit here, laughing and planning our future together.

Steven was good at getting my attention and keeping it from wondering off. As we sat there, we talked about many things. He told me he'd always cared for me, even when I wasn't available. Now that I was his, he was never going to let anyone come close to taking his place.

I looked into his eyes. Somehow, I didn't have the tingling I'd had when Teddy used to look into my eyes like this.

"I know you may think it's too early to say we love each other. But for me, I can say that I love you. I promise, I will take a lifetime showing you if you allow me to."

I asked him how he could say he loved me. He didn't really know me yet. Getting to know a person took time, and even more time was needed before you could tell someone you loved him or her. I thought that maybe I had better keep this moving slowly. Steven was jumping with his words too quickly. Maybe they were coming from his lips and not his heart.

"You might not remember. It's been years," Steven said. "But I still remember the day when I first realized how much I wanted to be with you. You were walking with your friend, talking, laughing, and having, fun not paying attention to where you were going. I was busy carrying on with the guys and not paying attention to where I was going. We bumped into each other and you fell down. As I reached to help you up, you looked into my eyes. At that moment, I saw how beautiful you were. I knew then that I wanted you to be mine. I have cared deeply for you ever since. You were the most beautiful women I had ever bumped into. There you were, reaching for me with your hand out and smiling back at me. It was love at first sight. Only you were with someone else. I've kept my feelings to myself. Once I saw you with your friend how happy you were, I kept quiet. I would never come between that. I always watched you from a distance, though, wishing that one day a chance would come for me. And here we are."

It was scary hearing that coming from Steven. I smiled, not knowing what to say. All I could manage was, "Here we are."

By then, it was time to go back to class. As always, Steven walked me to class. He told me he had practice and said he'd call if he got a chance before the game and, if not, after the game.

After school, Sissy and the crew gave me a ride home. We stopped at my house so I could change before going to the hospital.

When we got there, Kaylin was all smiles and looking better. I introduced her to my friends, and after they'd greeted each other, she told me how good she was doing. The doctor was letting her go home in the morning. The doctors couldn't believe how well she was doing. They'd even run more tests.

I told her how happy I was for her, gave her a big hug, and reminded her to keep believing that she was better. She told me that was what was keeping her going.

My friends jumped right in, talking and laughing with Kaylin as if they'd known her forever, and she was talking and laughing right along with them. Before we knew it, we'd been there over two hours. I told the girls we needed to go and let Kaylin rest before the nurses threw us all out.

I hugged Kaylin and told her I'd call her tomorrow. She thanked my friends and me for coming.

As we left for the game, I was excited. I couldn't wait to see Steven.

When we arrived, Steven's family was already there. They waved at me as I walked in. I walked over to where they were sitting, with my friends following me.

I introduced the crew to Steven's family. Steven's mother said, "You all are welcome to sit here with us if you like."

My friends didn't give me a chance to answer. "Sure, that'll be fine," said Sissy.

The girls settled into the seats just below theirs. I sat next to Steven's mom, and she told me how I was all her son talked about around the house. Mrs. Myers told me her son cared a lot for me. "He only had one other woman in his life that he cared for, and she moved away," she said, adding that he seemed to be starting to care for me the same.

I wondered why she was telling me about another girl Steven had cared for before me.

Mrs. Myers told me how happy she was for the both of us and said she wished us all the happiness.

Soon the team came took the field. We all stood up, cheering them on. Steven saw me and waved. His mother said, "He sure has a big smile on his face tonight, and I know why." She looked at me and smiled.

We all stood throughout the game, cheering our team as they won.

After the game, we made our way onto the field. Steven grabbed me. He hugged me and said how glad he was that I'd made it. Steven then hugged his mother and dad. He asked where his sister was, and his mother said, "She had a toothache. She stayed home."

Mrs. Myers told Steven how good a game the team had played and that she was proud of him and told him they were taking off. Steven stayed with me and my friends talking before he had to leave. He hugged me and even gave me a kiss. He said he'd call me later tonight.

My friends gave me the eyes. "He's hooked," one of them said.

"No I do not think so," was all I said.

My friends talked about Steven and me during the entire ride home. We had fun, laughing and talking about our boyfriends. They dropped me off, and I was glad to get home just to rest. I was tired. I wanted to shower, relax, and wait to talk to Steven that night.

My dad was home. When I walked in, he looked at me and flashed a grin. "By the big smile on your face," he said, "I'd say you all won."

I told him he was right and then sat down to give him the update on Kaylin. Then I told him more about the game. He sat back with a smile, saying how good it was to see me happy and smiling.

I told him he'd have to join me sometime at a game. Dad said that sounded like fun and that he'd love to join us sometime.

Then Dad said, "I've always liked Steven. And I know you'll always do what's right. I am sure Steven has your best interest at heart." I knew this was the birds and bees talk in Dad's kind of way. He told me he knew we were both at the age where we might want to try new things in life. He said, "Just be careful. I would never want to see you get hurt in any way."

I told him, "When the time comes where we might try new things, I'll have that covered."

He looked at me, and I could tell from his big smile that he loved the answer I had given him.

My phone rang. I looked at the phone, looked at my dad, and told him I had to take the call.

Smiling, my dad said, "Tell Steven hello."

I went upstairs to my room. I bragged on how well he and his team had played tonight, and we made plans to go out tomorrow. Finally, that empty feeling inside had begun to be filled.

The next day, Steven came by my house around eleven o'clock. He picked me up as planned so we could spend the day at the beach. We said our good-byes to my dad, and he told us to be careful and to call him when we got there. The drive to the beach would take about an hour. We sang along with the radio as we drove alone the country road, taking in all the beautiful scenery.

We had been driving for almost an hour, and we were still having lots of fun, listening to and singing with the radio, when a strange feeling came over me. This was a feeling I'd never had before. I didn't know what was going on and couldn't explain the feeling, so I just stopped singing. I sat in silence and looked at Steven. He wore a huge smile and continued to sing along with the radio. I was trying very hard to hide the way I was feeling. I thought that maybe it would pass soon. But it didn't; it only got worse. It didn't hurt or anything. It was strange and it had taken over me. I looked at Steven smiling. I could hear him singing, but it was as if his voice was fading away, and then his voice was completely gone. I saw his smile and his lips moving as he sang with the radio, but I couldn't hear him or the radio at all.

I sat there feeling scared. I didn't knowing what was going. Then suddenly, everything started to change. The scenery began to change as if I was somewhere else. I was watching something change right before my eyes. I saw this car driving along the highway. I looked ahead and saw this truck driving along. Things began to get clearer. I could see what was going on. I saw what looked like to be my dad's car. It was my dad's car. My dad was driving his car, and the truck crossed into my dad's lane, heading straight for my dad. I tried to say something, but my voice was gone. I couldn't speak or even move; it was as if I was paralyzed. All I could do was watch.

I could see my dad doing something in the car. When he finally noticed the truck, he hit his brakes. But it was too late. The truck hit him head-on. His car went flying into the air headed toward the woods. His car took down a tree and landed upside down in the woods off the road. I could see my dad in his seat with his seat belt holding him in place. I could see blood everywhere. My dad wasn't moving. I was sure he had passed out. I just couldn't accept the facts—that he might be dead. I looked at the truck. It had flipped on its side on the road. The man who'd been driving the truck lay outside on the ground. I could hear a child inside the car crying. I couldn't see the child, but I could hear him or her crying. I saw many cars and people beginning to stop and help. Some stood by the man lying on the ground, and some stood beside the truck where the child was crying. No one was going to help my dad, since no one knew about his car. I saw the flashing lights coming. The strange feeling I was having and what I was seeing started to fade.

I begin to hear Steven voice. It was getting louder and louder until it became normal again. I heard the radio, and he was still singing. I was able to move again, so I pulled out my cell phone to call my dad. I didn't know whether what I had just seen was real or not.

My dad's phone just rang and rang. I left a message for him to call me as soon as possible. I hung up and dialed his number repeatedly. Still, no answer came. I tried the house phone with the same results—no answer. I left a message, hung up, and called again. Still no answer came. Tears had already begun to fall.

Steven saw that I was crying and stopped singing. "What's wrong?" he asked.

I couldn't answer him. He pulled the truck over and faced me, asking me again what was wrong. He begged me to talk to him, but I couldn't stop the tears from falling. I sat there not knowing what to say or do. Then I opened my mouth. "I'm sorry, but we need to turn around and go back. Please don't ask any questions. Just please turn around and head back." It was all I could say. I did add that I'd had a feeling that something was wrong.

Without asking any questions, Steven turned the truck around and headed back home. He looked at me, and I looked back. I was still crying, but I managed to say, "Thank you."

"Sure, we can go to the beach any time," he said.

I told him I had a bad feeling. I had called my dad, and he wasn't answering his phone. That wasn't like him. I just knew something was wrong. I was scared for my dad, especially if what I'd seen was real. No one knew he was there. I told Steven to take a different route, not telling him why. I knew the route would lead us to where I'd seen the accident.

Steven looked worried but agreed. I was glad he wasn't asking questions and was just going the way I'd told him.

After we'd driven for about an hour, we ran into traffic. I knew then that what I'd seen was real. I started crying harder. I was scared for my dad. I knew I had to get to him. I had to find him. Traffic started to move again. I could see the accident ahead of us. A tow truck was getting ready to load the truck. Ambulances and fire trucks were still there. As we got closer, I told Steven to slow down. I was looking for the tree that was down.

I saw it. I told Steven to pull over, and he did. I jumped out of the truck and started running for the woods. Steven jumped out, running behind me. He was calling out to me to stop, but I had to get to my dad. I made my way into the woods, searching frantically. Tears were flowing, and it was hard to see clearly.

Then there it was—my dad's car, just as I had seen it. He was still hanging upside down with his seat belt holding him in place. I looked at the car and saw how it was smashed in. I looked back and told Steven to get help.

I could hear Steven telling someone another car was back here. I knew he didn't know yet that it was my dad. I ran toward my dad's car, screaming. I tried to open the door, but I couldn't. It was jammed. I ran around to the other side. That door was crushed in and wouldn't open. The windows were all broken out, and the top had smashed in so far I couldn't get into any of them. I ran back to the side my dad was on. I called his name repeatedly. He wasn't responding at all. There was so much blood.

I tried to put my arm through an opening in the window. If only I could touch him. All I needed was to get my hands on him. But I couldn't reach him no matter how hard I tried. I couldn't get to him to help him. I started crying harder, saying, "No. Please, Dad, don't leave me. Please.

Finally, Steven was by my side. When he saw it was my dad, I heard him say, "Oh no. Hurry."

Steven was holding me tight. I was still trying to get to my dad somehow, but I couldn't.

I heard noises coming up behind me and turned to see the firefighters, rescue crew, and police all running to help. They told us to move aside so they could get to him. I moved, only not far. I heard someone order for him to be flown to the hosipital. Then a firefighter said there was no way to get him out without cutting away the top of the car.

I felt terrible. I kept telling Dad to hold on. I didn't know if he could hear me, but I kept talking to him, hoping he was holding on.

When the firefighter began cutting the top of the car, the emergency personnel tried to get me to leave. Steven told them I was the man's daughter, and I told them I was not leaving his side. My dad was just hanging there, not moving, not doing anything.

Then a terrifying thought occurred to me. *What if he is already dead?* I could see that he had lost a lot of blood. It was everywhere—on him and all over the inside of the car. So many people were there trying to help. I knew dad needed my help more.

Steven held on tightly to me, not letting me go. The emergency crew asked us to step aside. I begged them to please hurry and get him out. They assured us they were going to get him out as quickly as they could and told me everything was going to be okay. I knew they were just telling me Dad was going to be okay. It's what they tell everyone when things looked bad.

Steven tried to pull me away. I told him that, even though it looked bad, I wasn't leaving until Dad was out of the car and on his way to the hospital."

I closed my eyes in Steven's arms. As he held onto me, I started praying aloud. Steven joined with me as I prayed that my dad would make it. I had helped many people. Now I could do nothing to help my dad. All I could do was pray that he was alive still.

The firefighter had finished cutting through the car. I tried to run over to my dad, but someone pulled me back, saying he had to get dad out and take care of him. I was helpless. As the team pulled Dad from the car and started to work on him, I saw again, how much blood there was. Four of the men lifted him carefully onto a stretcher, and then they were running with him from the woods. Out in the open, they were still working on him when I heard the plane touch down.

I tried repeatedly to break loose from Steven to get to my dad. Only Steven held me tighter. I told Steven I could help my dad if he would just help me get to him. Steven didn't understand what I was talking about. He said we had to stay out of the emergency crew's way to let them help my dad.

As the four men loaded Dad into the plane, someone else told us what hospital they were taking him. We jumped into the truck, and Steven started for the hospital. All I could do was cry. Steven kept telling me Dad was safe now and that everything would be okay. He pulled out his phone to call his parents and let them know what had happen and that we were on our way to the hospital. I called my grandma to tell her what had happened. Only I was crying so much, I couldn't get it out. Steven took the phone and told Grandma what had happened, which hospital Dad would be at, and that we were on our way there. My grandma must have asked about me because I heard Steven say that he would be there with me. After saying good-bye, Steven handed me the phone. He drove fast, and we made it to the hospital quickly.

As soon as he parked, we ran in.

Chapter 23

I asked the nurse at the front desk where Nathan Tompkins was, telling her I was his daughter. She told me the doctor on call had taken him to surgery already.

"For what?" I asked.

She told me she didn't have that information. I would have to speak with the doctor when he came out. All I could do was cry. Steven walked me to the waiting room. Just as we sat down, my grandma and aunt walked in. They asked how Dad was, and I told them he was already in surgery when we arrived. I explained that we didn't know anything and all we could do was wait on the doctor.

I introduced Steven to them, and they thanked him for being here with me. He told them he wouldn't be any other place. My grandma had her walker. She hardly needed it anymore. More often than not, she was walking well on her own. Grandma sat next to me. She put her arm around me and told me everything was going to be okay. I cried. I knew that if Dad just made it through the surgery, I could get a chance to help him, and everything would be okay. Grandma told me to believe. She said she had prayed and that Dad was in God's hands.

I kept looking at the clock on the wall. It seemed as though its hands were barley moving. My phone rang. I'd forgotten to take the ringer off. I didn't feel like talking, so I handed the phone to Steven. He told me it was Sissy and then walked away to answer. I could tell he was telling Sissy what was going on, and I knew she would pass the word to the rest of my friends. Steven put the phone in his pocket and came back to sit next to me.

We had been there for hours, and we hadn't heard anything. I was starting to worry. Why was it taking them this long? Had something gone wrong?

Finally, the doctor walked into the waiting room and asked if we were the Tompkins family. He told us Dad had lost a lot of blood and was bleeding internally from his broken ribs. They'd had to operate to stop the bleeding. Dad had also broken his leg in two places, and they had to place a pin in one part of his leg. He still wasn't responding, but he was stable for now. All they could do now was watch him and wait. He said Dad was very lucky. "I know you all want to see him," he added, "but it is crucial that he rest."

I asked if we could see him for just a minute.

"Just for a few moments. But please," he cautioned. "He needs rest."

I jumped up with Steven behind me. Grandma smiled and told me to go first. "We'll wait," she said.

Steven hesitated. "You can go," he told my grandma and aunt. "I'll wait."

"No," Grandma said. "You go with her. She needs you."

We followed doctor through double doors, and he led us to the intensive care unit. At Dad's door, he reminded us to take only a minute or so.

I stood there frozen as I looked in at my dad. He looked so helpless. Tubes were running into him from every direction. I put my hands to my mouth and cried silently. I had to help him. I knew I had to. I looked at Steven. "I have to go in," I told him. "You stay here. I am going in only for a second."

"Okay," he said.

I opened the door and walked to my dad's bedside. Crying I placed both hands on him. "Dad, I love you," I said.

As I cried, I began to focus on making my dad better. I started to feel the tingling in my hands. I cried more as I realized he was going to be better. I held on to my dad tightly until every bit of the tingling had stopped. I took my hands off my dad, looked down at him, and told him he would be okay now. Then I kissed him, turned, and walked out of the room.

Steven put his arm around me. He didn't ask any questions. I was glad. Maybe he thought I'd had my hands on my dad for comfort.

Steven and I walked back to the waiting room, and I told my grandma and aunt they could go see my dad. Steven and I sat down. We weren't waiting long before Grandma and my aunt came back. Tears were streaming down both their faces. We all hugged each other. Grandma told us to go get a good night's rest. There was nothing more we could do but wait.

Tomorrow was Sunday. I knew I was going to be here at the hospital early. I told Grandma I wouldn't be at church tomorrow and that I was coming back here early.

She smiled. "I knew you would," she said.

Steven said, "I will be here with her."

Grandma said, "As soon as I get out of church, I will be here."

Grandma told the doctor to give us a call if anything changed at all. The doctor said someone would be in touch. Grandma asked if I wanted to stay with her.

"No," I said. "I'll be okay at home."

She told me to call if I needed anything, we hugged, and they left Steven and me sitting there.

I looked at Steven and said, "Thank you."

"For what?" he asked.

"For everything," I told him, "Most of all, for trusting me and staying here by my side."

"How did you know?" he asked.

"I just felt like something was wrong," I told him. "My dad always answers his phone when I call, or if not, he always calls back soon."

Steven didn't ask many questions, and I was glad about that. I didn't want to have to give him answers.

I thanked him again in the parking lot. I was glad we were outside in the dark so he couldn't see my tears falling again. Only this time, they were happy tears. I knew my dad was going to be okay.

Steven took me home. He told me he didn't want to leave me alone and asked if it was okay if he stayed with me. He said he'd be glad to sleep on the couch.

I said sure. I was sure he knew nothing was going to happen between us. He called his parents to let them know he was staying here tonight and going back to the hospital in the morning with me. Then he told me he was going home to pick up some clothes and said he'd be back. I told him I'd call Sissy and update her.

He held me and kissed my forehead before he left. Every time he kissed my forehead, it reminded me of Teddy.

I went upstairs, took a shower, and put on some shorts and a T-shirt. I didn't want to wear pajamas. I called all my friends and let them knew how my dad was doing. Sissy offered to stay over with me. When I told her Steven had offered to stay tonight, she started to tease me about what might go on. I told her that wasn't what was happening. "We will be good," I said. "He's taking me to the hospital early in the morning. I told her I was going to fix something to eat and that I'd talk to her tomorrow and hung up.

My phone ranged. It was Steven telling me he was in the driveway. I walked downstairs opened the door, and found him standing there with a bag in each hand. He smiled. "We haven't eaten anything, and my mother cooked spaghetti. She had plenty, so she sent us some."

"Sounds good," I said. "I'll warm it up."

He had changed clothes. He looked good in his shorts with his big legs. I smiled, got the plates and set the table, and fixed us drinks while the food warmed. His mom had fixed some cheese bread to go with the spaghetti. After we ate, we cleaned the kitchen up, and I told him to thank his mother the dinner was good.

I went upstairs to get a pillow and blanket and brought them back downstairs. Steven had turned on the TV. I showed him the bathroom, and we sat on the couch, lay back on the pillow, and watched TV. He pulled me into his arms and told me everything was going to be fine. I knew my dad was going to be better, and I felt hugely relieved.

It was late. I wasn't planning on staying with him on the couch. But lying in his arms felt so good. I didn't want to move, so I just lay there. He kissed my forehead and pulled the blanket over us. My eyes were getting heavy, and I soon drifted off to sleep.

The next morning, I woke up still lying in Steven's arms. He was still asleep. I lay there not moving and trying not to wake him. I didn't know what time he'd gone to sleep. I knew his arm had to be hurting from me lying on it all night. It was good to have him here with me.

He soon moved and opened his eyes. When he looked down at me, I smiled and said, "Good morning. Is your arm hurting?"

He smiled, saying he'd slept well with a beautiful woman in his arms all night. I got off him, giving his poor arm a break and asked if he drank coffee.

"No," he said, "but some juice would be good"

I went into the kitchen, poured him a glass, and brought it to him. I told him it is only six o'clock. He could relax more. I knew he hadn't slept well with me on his shoulder all night. He smiled, saying it was the first time he'd had a woman sleeping on him all night and that it had been great. I told him to rest. I was going upstairs to shower and get dressed, but we needn't hurry. I told him I was going to call the hospital to check on Dad.

I knew he was going to be okay, but I still worried. This was my dad.

When I talked to the nurse, she told me he'd had a good night. He was stable and he'd woken up doing much better. My heart jumped with joy. She told me the doctor would talk to me more when I get there. I ran back downstairs smiling. As I told Steven the good news, I saw a smile of relief cross his face.

I called Sissy to share the good news. I forgot it was still early. She sounded half-asleep when she said, "Good." Then she added, "I am sure you are up and all happy and bright-eyed. You have your man there. Go bother him and have fun."

"Go back to sleep," I said, "and don't start talking your trash."

I went downstairs. Steven was watching the news. It did feel good to have him around. I walked by him, smiling. His eyes stayed on me until I was in the kitchen. After I'd poured myself some juice, I went back into the living room to join him. He told me how beautiful I looked. I smiled and said, "Thanks."

I sat next to him and watched TV. He pulled me closer to him, saying he loved it when I was wearing his arm out. He kissed me. I knew I did not need to be here in his arms like this, but it felt so good and I didn't want to get up. I lay there, and we kissed more. We both knew that, if we kept on, things would get out of our hands. I pulled away, finally coming up for air.

He said, "I think I'd better get up and get dressed so we can leave for the hospital."

After a few more long kisses, he did get up. Once he was dressed, we left for the hospital.

Dad was sitting up in his bed. His leg was in a cast, and he was covered in bandages from all the glass cuts he'd received. But most of the tubes were gone. I smiled and asked how he was feeling.

"Great, now that you are here," he said.

Dad greeted Steven, and I walked over and gave him a big, tight hug and a kiss. "Are you in any pain?" I asked.

"No pain at all," he said.

Dad said that, when he'd first woken up, he hadn't known where he was or that he had been in an accident. I told him I'd never been that scared but once in my life. Steven said he was glad to see my dad doing much better.

We all sat down, talking and even laughing at times. The time flew by.

After a while, Steven told us he had some errands he needed to take care of. I told him I would walk him to the elevator. I thanked him for everything, and he pulled me close, kissed my forehead, and said he'd call me later.

I walked back to my dad's room. We talked, and I told him how I'd seen his accident happen, how his car had been thrown off into the woods, and how I'd known no one knew he was there. I told him about directing Steven to turn around and take the route that would lead us to the accident. "I ran through the woods and found your car," I told him, catching my breath at the pain of the memory. "It was lying just as I'd seen it. I tried to get to you to help, but I couldn't get to you no matter how hard I tried. They had to cut you out."

Dad said he knew it was bad but hadn't known it was that bad. He thanked me with tears in his eyes for being that special person, his daughter.

The nurse came in and asked Dad how he was doing. She asked if he was in any pain or needed any pain medication. He told her he was in no pain.

I stretched the recliner out, and we were watching TV when the doctor walked in and told my dad how lucky he was. He explained that they'd had to put a pin his leg and perform emergency surgery to stop the bleeding inside from the broken ribs. "The good news," he said, "is all the test results have come back good. The doctor told Dad he should be fine with plenty of rest.

Dad asked the doctor if he could go home today.

"Not so fast," the doctor said. "You're a doctor. You know how it goes." He told Dad he wanted to keep him another night to make sure everything stayed normal and said that, if that was the case, Dad could go home tomorrow.

No matter how hard my dad tried to get out today, the doctor would not give in. I told Dad it would be okay. "I'll be here with you, and Grandma's coming over with the others after church."

After the doctor left, Dad and I watched TV. Soon, I'd fallen asleep. I dreamed of Teddy and me. We were together and happy again; it was as if we'd never been apart.

I woke from my beautiful dream to realize it was only a dream when Grandma and my aunt walked in. They were glad to see Dad doing better and to hear that he might be able to go home tomorrow.

Grandma handed me a big bag. I could smell the delicious aroma coming from the bag and knew she'd brought some of her home cooking. I was hungry. I hadn't eaten anything yet. I smiled and dove straight into the bag. I found a large plate with a little of everything—from collard greens to potato salad to mac and cheese. She even had chocolate cake for dessert. I did not waste any time. The food was delicious, and I was starving. Grandma sure did know how to cook. I always licked my fingers instead of using a paper towel when I ate her cooking.

I was full once I'd finished the food, but I couldn't stop until I'd had some of the chocolate cake.

Dad wasn't hungry for his plate. He had eaten already and said the nurses had him eating special foods. I was glad. I would definitely eat his food tonight. I assured my grandma it wouldn't go to waste with me around.

My dad looked at me and smiled, saying he was sure about that. I smiled and thanked Grandma and told her how good everything was. I was so full; all I wanted to do was take a long nap. The chair I was in wasn't the kind that would let you get that comfortable. So I sat up, watched TV, and listened to everyone talk.

My phone rang. I walked out of the room and looked to see who was calling. I was shocked. I had just dreamed of Teddy, and now he was calling.

He said he'd heard about my father and told me how sorry he was. Teddy asked how my dad was. I told him Dad was doing well and might be going home tomorrow. He asked if he could stop by the house tomorrow if Dad went home. Before I gave the request any thought, I'd said yes.

He said okay, said he'd see us tomorrow, and hung up. I had a strange feeling inside—the same feeling I used to get when I was around him. I walked back into the room. I decided I'd wait until everyone left to tell Dad that Teddy would be stopping by. I sat down and listened to my grandma and aunt laugh and talk. They were happy that Dad was okay.

Grandma said they had to leave and promised they'd come by the house tomorrow.

After they left, I told dad Teddy had called and said he was planning to stop by tomorrow to see him. Dad said that was good. I was excited as I told Dad what Teddy had said, but I tried not to show my excitement. Still, I think Dad somehow knew it was there. But he didn't say anything.

Dad was quiet. When I looked over at him, I saw that he had drifted off to sleep. I pulled a blanket over me and lay there in silence, lost in thoughts of Teddy.

My phone vibrated. It was Sissy. I got up quietly, walked to the waiting room, and called her back. She wanted to come to the hospital. I told her that wasn't necessary. Dad was doing well and going home tomorrow. He was sleeping now and needed to rest.

She said she'd call me tomorrow. I told her I wouldn't be in school, as I was going to stay with my dad. She told me she had some juicy gossip. Teddy had broken it off with his supposed girlfriend. I asked Sissy how she found out everything that goes on. I told her Teddy had called and wanted to stop by the house to see Dad tomorrow.

"Yeah right," she said. "He wants to see you."

I told her I had to go. I wanted to get back to Dad. We'd talk tomorrow.

I called Alice, my supervisor at work, to let her know I would not be coming in tomorrow after school. I told her my dad was coming home, and she told me to take the time I needed to take care of my dad and just keep her updated.

I knew my dad was asleep. I sat in the waiting room thinking. I decided to take a walk. I was walking along the hall in the opposite direction of my dad's room. I noticed this old man lying in his bed. I couldn't help but notice him. His door was opened. He had a cast from his leg to his hip and a brace on his neck that kept his neck from moving. The old man said something. Only no one was in his room but him.

I stopped, walked in, and asked if he needed anything.

"Could you please give me a drink?" he asked.

I took his cup, put the straw to his mouth, and held it as he drank.

He stopped. "Thank you," he said.

I couldn't help but ask him what had happen. He said he was on his roof trying to fix a leak when he fell from the roof. When I asked him if he was in any pain, he said, "Please do not say that word. I stay in pain. But the nurse just gave me my pain meds to ease it some. I'm fine for now."

I asked if he had family here with him. He said it was just him and his son, who was in the military. His sweet wife had passed away three years ago. He said she was the sweetest thing a man could ask for. He'd married her straight out of high school. He told me he knew God loved her to death because she was the sweetest woman. He was eighty-four years old and still tended his own farm and land. He never slowed down for anything. His wife used to tell him to slow down, but he never did. He said his wife used to tell him God had a way to slow you down. "Now I see what she was talking about," he said. "Look at me—flat on my back and can't do anything but lay here."

Before I knew it, I was sitting beside him and we were laughing as I listened to him talk. He told me he'd broken his neck and leg. "I've never had anything happen to me all my life until now," he lamented. He told me about all his animals. I asked how he managed all that work by himself. He said he'd hired two young men to help him said and they'd both been with him over ten years. They were taking care of the farm for him now. "I wish I could be there helping them instead of lying here doing nothing," he said wistfully.

"You have to get better," I told him.

"Yeah, I know," he said. "I banged myself up pretty bad. But this is hard for me, and the pain is bad at times."

I stood beside his bed and placed my hands on his legs. He was busy talking and didn't notice when I began to focus on him getting better. As I focused, I could hear him talking in the background. The tingling moved through my hands, and I knew he was going to be better. When I removed my hands, he grew quiet. I thought something was wrong. "Are you okay?" I asked.

He said, "Baby, I don't know what is going on. I feel good. I feel like a new person."

I smiled and asked if he needed anything else before I left.

"Yes," he said. "Tell that nurse to come in here. Nice talking to you."

I told him to take care. After telling the nurse he needed her, I walked farther down the hallway.

I heard crying coming from a room and I went to the door. I didn't know if I should go in. The door was halfway open, and I could see a woman sitting beside the bed holding an older woman's hand. The older woman's eyes were closed. I pushed the door open a little more and asked if everything was okay.

"Yes," she said.

I walked in, took a tissue, and handed it to her.

"Thanks," she said. She nodded at the bed and told me that was her mother. Tears rolled down her face as she told me her mother had a bad heart. The doctor had said she was too old and weak to make it through surgery. "There is nothing else to do," she said sadly. "She won't live long like this."

I looked at the old woman as she lay there helplessly. I thought of my grandma and how I'd feel if it was her lying there. Her daughter cried as she told me this was the fourth day her mother had lay there doing nothing, not opening her eyes or responding to her.

Her phone rang. "Excuse me," she said. "I have to step out."

I told her I would stay with her mother until she came back.

I walked to the woman's bedside. When her daughter was out the room, I placed my hands on her legs and began to focus. It didn't take long for the tingling sensation to move through my hands. After the tingling stopped, I stood there looking down at her. I noticed her hand move a little. Then it moved again. This time, she brought her hand to her face and wiped her eye.

Her daughter walked in at that moment and burst into tears as she ran to her mother's side. I stepped back, watching as she picked up her mother's hand, calling her name. Her mother opened her eyes and answered her. I walked out and left them to their happy moment.

On the way back to my dad's room, I heard a little boy laughing. As I walked by, he saw me and waved. "Do you want to play?" he asked.

I walked into his room. His mother sat beside his bed. "Excuse us," she said. "He does that all the time with the nurses."

The little boy asked me again if I wanted to play.

"What game?" I asked.

"Find the marble," he answered.

"Yes," I told him.

He held out both hands and asked, "Which one?"

I pointed to one hand. He opened it, saying, "You were wrong."

He hid his hands behind his back and then asked me again. I pointed to the same hand. This time I was right. "You get a surprise," he said, beaming. He looked at his mother and said, "Give her a surprise."

His mother handed me a piece of candy.

"Thanks," I said. "I love playing games with you, and I love that I get candy when I win."

He smiled at me and told me to sit down. He wanted to tell me a story. I sat down. His mother told him I might not have time to hear a story. "It's okay," I said. "I have time."

The little boy started telling me his story. It was about how he could do magic. "You have to hold my hand for one minute," he said.

"Okay," I replied.

I took his hand. I didn't know what was wrong with him, but I focused as he talked. I could feel the tingling go through my hand. I knew that, whatever was going on with this little boy, he was going to be okay. He turned my hand loose just as the tingling stopped and told me, "Now you can do magic."

I thanked him for letting me play and told him I had to go.

"Thank you," his mother said as I walked out.

I went back to my dad's room. He was still asleep. I stretched out in the chair to watch TV, feeling good as I ate the rest of my chocolate cake. I stayed the night with my dad.

The next morning, his doctor came in. He said everything looked good, and he could go home. I called my aunt to see if she could come pick us up. I didn't want to call Steven. I knew he had school today. My aunt said she would be there soon.

"Thanks," I told her. "We'll be down as soon as they release him."

It took a while for Dad to be released. But finally, we were on our way home. I was glad to have him coming home.

My aunt stayed with us. She fixed us all lunch while she was there and helped get my dad settled in. She said my grandma wanted to come sit with my dad and that'd she go pick her up and then return.

Dad was doing well. He did have the cast on his leg still. Soon, my aunt was back with my grandma. They both had overnight bags with them and planned to stay until Dad was up and moving around again. I was glad they both were going to be here with us for a while. I figured that, since they were here with Dad, I could go to school.

My grandma was happy to be here. She was already talking about getting dinner started. She loved to cook. Dad called his office to get an update on things and give instructions on what needed to be done with some of his patients. He told his colleagues he'd be back soon and to keep him updated.

It felt good to have my grandma and aunt staying here with us. Grandma told me, "You do what you usually do. Let us worry about taking care of your dad and the house."

I smiled, knowing they were going to do everything anyway.

I went to my room to get started on my homework. My phone rang. It was Teddy calling to see if it was a good time for him to stop by. I told him yes.

Teddy must have been close by because the doorbell rang soon after. My aunt called to me that I had company. I walked downstairs, and Teddy was standing in the entry. I took one look at him and felt that feeling in my stomach—the same one I used to get whenever I saw Teddy. I tried to shake it, but the feeling wouldn't go. It only got stronger the closer I got to him. Teddy watched me as I walked to the bottom of the stairs. He had that smile on his face that he always used to give me when he was happy to see me.

"Hello," I said. I smiled back at him and led him into the living room where my aunt and grandma were sitting.

"I remember you," Grandma said. "I remember Nyah talking about you." She smiled and added, "All good stuff."

"Teddy came to visit Dad, so I will show him up to Dad's room," I told Grandma.

I led Teddy upstairs to Dad's room. Dad looked at us and smiled as we walked in. Teddy asked Dad how he was doing, and Dad answered, "A lot better." He told Teddy to have a seat and said it was good to see him. I stood there for a little while, hating to leave the room. I wanted to stay but told Dad that I would let Teddy visit and walked out.

Chapter 24

I went to my room and tried to pull myself together. I was trying to be in control of myself; only my feelings were running the show, letting me know who was in charge. I opened my book to get started with my homework. There was no need for me to hang around with Teddy, I told myself. We were not together anymore.

Teddy had been in there talking to Dad for about thirty minutes. I couldn't take it any longer. My book was open, but I hadn't answered a single question. I closed the book. I had to see what was going on with Dad and Teddy.

I stood in the doorway and asked my dad if he needed anything. Dad looked at me and said no and then asked Teddy if he wanted anything. Teddy said a drink would be nice. I turned to get it for him.

As soon as I got to the step, Teddy's voice called to me. I turned, and he was behind me. I stopped, and he said, "I'll walk with you." I went downstairs and into the kitchen with Teddy behind me. I asked him what he wanted to drink.

My grandma was walking out of the kitchen. She told Teddy to try the chocolate cake she had brought over with her.

"Sure," Teddy said. "I would love a slice of cake and milk."

I poured him milk and cut him a slice of cake. He asked me to join him, saying he knew chocolate cake was my favorite.

I couldn't help but smile. I sure wanted a slice. Teddy was right. It was my favorite. I cut myself a slice and got out two forks. I handed one to him, and we both began to eat the cake. Teddy said how good the cake was as he reached over and rubbed chocolate from my lip with his finger, taking it straight to his mouth.

I could not take this. My feelings were going crazy, and I was trying not to let him see that. "Thank you," I said.

I was about to get up to pour myself a glass of milk when Teddy picked up his glass and put it to my lips, saying, "I know you want something to drink."

I opened my mouth as he held the glass to my mouth to drink, just like old times. He removed the glass again, and I said, "Thank you."

Teddy looked into my eyes and said, "I love you, and you have that look. I have seen it too many times. You still love me deeply. It shows on your face."

I took my eyes off him and looked at the floor. I wasn't quick to speak. I knew I wanted him back. I loved him still with all my heart. But I was with Steven now, and I didn't want to hurt Steven. "Teddy, you know me well," I finally said. "Yes, I love you still. But we went our separate ways. We have other people in our lives. I won't see anyone hurt, especially not Steven." I told Teddy I was sorry.

Teddy told me that he and his friend had gone their separate ways. He didn't love her and couldn't lead her on any longer when he knew they would be friends and nothing more. I looked at Teddy. As badly as I hated to say it, I said, "I am with Steven. I cannot hurt him."

Teddy stood and held my face in his hands. "My feelings and the love I have for you have always been with me, no matter how hard I tried to push them out," he said. "They stayed and are just as strong for you now as ever before." He leaned over and kissed me on the lips like never before.

I couldn't move. I just stood there looking at him. He said he would always love me and that, one day, I would be his again. He kissed me again, turned my face loose, and said he was going to say good-bye to my dad and he was leaving.

I didn't walk him back to my dad's room. I couldn't. I did not want my dad to see the expression I knew had come over me. I stayed in the kitchen, putting away our dishes in the sink. When he came back to the kitchen to say good-bye, I turned to Teddy and said, "I'll walk you out."

Teddy said good-bye to my aunt and grandma and thanked her for the delicious cake. I walked him out to his car and thanked him for coming to see my dad. I looked at him and asked, "Why'd you have to mess up what we had?"

His eyes met mine. "I'm sorry," he said. "And I will get back what we had. That's a promise."

He said he'd call to check on Dad later, waved good-bye, and drove off.

My heart was sad when Teddy left. I knew I still cared for Teddy deeply, and I wanted to be back with him. I knew I was with Steven, but Teddy still had hold of my heart.

I went back into the house. My grandma was in the kitchen starting to cook. Grandma told me she could see in Teddy's face that he cared deeply for me still and that she could see the hurt that was there also. She said she knew I was with someone else but told me, "Always follow where your heart leads you."

A tear fell from my eye. I knew what she was referring. I told her I was going to check on Dad and went upstairs. Dad was quiet, and the

TV was on. I thought he was asleep. I had turned to walk out when he called my name. "Teddy still loves you," he told me. "He regrets what he did. We had a long talk. Teddy made a big mistake. He asked me to forgive him and said that one day he'll win you back. He was talking from his heart. It is a big deal when a man sits in front of another man in tears asking for forgiveness." Dad said he knew I would do what was right.

I smiled at Dad but didn't respond. I asked if he needed anything. He said no; he was good and going to get some sleep. I told him okay and walked out. I needed to try to get my homework done since I was going to school tomorrow.

Steven called later on that day. He wanted to stop by, but I told him Dad was sleeping and that my grandma and aunt were here. I told him I would see him at school tomorrow. I couldn't deal with having him over today.

The next day at school, Steven and I sat in the same place during lunch and talked. He tried to cheer me up. He said he could tell something was wrong. Steven said he knew I was worried about my dad. In truth, my mind was on Teddy. I hadn't seen him once today, which was good. I saw the girl Teddy had been with, but I hadn't seen Teddy with her.

I was at my locker before my last class, and when I turned around, the girl who used to be with Teddy was standing there. She spoke softly, saying, "Hello."

I looked at her and saw that tears were falling down her face. She told me how much Teddy cared for me and said the two of them had never had a relationship. She told me it wasn't that she hadn't wanted a relationship. But Teddy had told her he loved me and she could never be me. She told me she cared for Teddy and could easily love him. It was just that she knew his heart was with me. She said she knew I was talking to someone else but that, if I had any love for Teddy in my heart, I should work it out with him. "You still hold his heart," she said.

I thanked her for the talk and said I was sorry that things hadn't been going well for her and Teddy. I told her I had to go. As soon as I left, I felt the tears forming in my eyes. I brushed them away. I had to get through my last class before the school day would end.

Steven had practice after school, so he wasn't taking me home. Sissy offered me a ride, but I told her no; I wanted to ride the bus today.

She looked surprised but said, "Okay."

I had a lot on my mind. I was all mixed up and had to get my feelings together. I didn't go to work. I wanted to spend time with my dad when I got home.

My grandma and aunt were there, and I was glad to see them. I loved to be around them. I went upstairs to see my dad. He was asleep, and I didn't wake him. I went to my room and called Kaylin to check on her.

Kaylin told me she was great. Her doctor had given her some good news. He'd run test after test and hadn't been able to find a trace of cancer. I told her I was glad to hear that. Tears of joy filled my eyes. I was so glad she was better. I told her to keep believing.

Kaylin said she would, and after I'd told her everything that was going on with Dad, she said to wish him a good recovery. I told her to tell the rest of the family hello for me and promised I'd call back soon.

I stayed in my room and did all my homework. Then I looked in on my dad. He was awake. I walked in and asked how he was feeling.

"Great," he said. He wanted to get up and move around. He said he knew his leg was better—that he hadn't felt any pain from it. He said he wanted to take the cast off. Dad said he would give it a little more time so no questions would be asked.

I looked at him and smiled.

Dad knew something was bothering me. "Should I ask?"

I looked at him. "Teddy," I said. "Ever since he was here, some of those feeling are back that I thought were gone."

Dad looked at me and smiled. "Maybe those feelings have been there all the time," he suggested. "Take time to find yourself and your feelings and go from there."

"I don't want to see anyone hurt," I told him.

"You have to be happy," Dad said. "You have to choose your feelings that make you happy."

I had a lot of thinking to do. I was sure I knew what I wanted. It was just that I really didn't want to hurt anyone.

I stayed with, Steven trying hard to keep my feelings for Teddy under control. I was good as long as I didn't run into Teddy. I thought everything would work out on its own. I went back to work, and that kept my mind from thinking so much. Dad was doing much better. He was up and moving around. My aunt and grandma went back home, and it was dad and me again.

He stayed on the phone a lot with his office, making sure things was running right. I know Dad was not used to staying home so much doing nothing.

He finally cut his cast off at home. When the two pieces split apart, the two pins were inside the cast. He picked them up, looked at me, and asked, "How?"

"I don't know," I said.

Dad stood up and walked on his leg. He said it had healed completely. He didn't know how I did it. He thanked me, saying he could get back to work.

Life was getting back to normal.

Teddy called again. He said he was checking on my dad. But he and I stayed on the phone talking for hours. We laughed about old times. Then he asked, "How long are you going to keep us apart?" He told me how much he loved me and said he'd wait on me for as long as it took.

I told him I had to do something to get off the phone. Only I forgot I was talking to Teddy and not Steven. Teddy knew me. "You do not have to do anything," he said. "You can't answer the question, so you want to get off the phone."

Teddy knew he was right. But I still wasn't answering his question. I told him I did have to go and told him to take care. "Good-bye," I said.

The next day at school, Steven wasn't there. He hadn't called and said he wasn't coming. I wondered if he was okay. During the first break, I called his phone. It rang and rang. Just as I was about to hang up, a woman's voice said, "Hello."

I asked if I could speak to Steven.

"He's busy," the woman responded and asked if she could she take a message.

I asked whom I was speaking to.

"April, a friend of Steven's."

"Yes, April," I said. "Tell him Nyah called."

"Okay," she said and hung the phone up.

Steven had never told me about any friend named April. I didn't think the worst just because the girl had answered his phone, but I did wonder what was going on. Why was he with this April and not in school? And why hadn't he called me? I didn't try to call back until lunchtime, since he had not returned my call.

I called Steven's phone again, and this time, there was no answer. I didn't bother to leave a message. Five minutes later, he called me back. He said he was sorry he hadn't called.

I asked him who April was.

Steven was quiet.

"Hello," I said. "Are you still there?"

"You talked to April?" he asked.

"Yes," I said. "She answered your phone. Is anything wrong?"

"No," he said, "but we need to talk."

Steven said he'd pick me up after school.

I said, "Okay."

"Okay, see you then," he said, and hung up. That was not like Steven. I didn't know what was going on, but I had a feeling something was wrong.

The end of the school day came, and I walked out with my friends. Steven was there waiting in his car for me. I told my friends good-bye and got into the car with Steven.

We exchanged hellos like usual. But for some reason, something felt different with him. I asked him if he was okay.

He said, "Yes."

"I was worried when you didn't come to school and didn't call," I told him.

Steven said he was sorry. He had something going on that he had to take care of.

"You had your friend April with you," I pointed out.

Steven looked at me and said that was why he wanted to talk to me.

When he said that, a bad feeling went through me. I listened as he talked. Steven started out by saying that April was the girl he used to date. He had fallen in love with her. Only her family had moved away." I remembered the girl Steven's mom had told me about at the game that night. Steven said, "April has been gone for five years, but she kept in touch. She didn't call often, but she stayed in touch. April wrote and told me her family was planning on moving back home; only she didn't tell me when.

"Last night, April showed up here. Her family has moved back, and she came by my house last night to surprise me. She just said she was back, but we didn't get a chance to talk last night. She came back over early this morning and asked if we could go somewhere to talk. So I agreed. We talked over breakfast, and then we went to the park. It was just like two friends catching up."

I looked at Steven. "Were you so busy catching up that you couldn't take a little time out to call and let me know you were okay?" I asked.

Steven just said how sorry he was.

"I called you several times," I said, "but you were too busy to answer my calls, only getting back to me when it was a good time for you. I want to ask you one question. Please, Steven, be honest. Do you still love her?"

He didn't answer me right off. Then he said he didn't know, but he told me they'd never ended things between the two of them before April moved away.

"You say you don't know if you love April. But you were so occupied with her that you didn't take time to answer my calls. You must still have some feelings for her." I could tell there was more to it than he was telling me. I said, "Something happened." I was thinking the worst but only asked if he'd kissed her.

Steven looked at me with sadness in his eyes. "Yes," he admitted.

"More than once?" I asked.

"Yes," he said again. "And I'm sorry, but I wanted to be honest. April said she wants to get back together. But I told her I was with someone else." She said she respected that.

I asked Steven, "How did you feel when April asked if you wanted to get back with her?"

He paused for a moment. "I love you," he said, "but I still have feelings for April." Steven pulled into my driveway.

I looked at him. "Steven, I of all people know how it is to hurt," I said. "I would never want you to stay with me while you wanted to be back with April. If you and April want to take up where you left off, please don't stay with me. I don't want to be with you if your heart is still with her. You will never be happy with me if you're in love with April. I care for you, yes. But I never want you to be with me and be unhappy.

If you and April still have some flames that burn between the two of you, please go where your heart is. I will be okay. I promise."

Steven just looked at me. "You so understand," he finally said.

"Let's just say we will always be friends," I told him. "Your girl is back for her man, and I would never want to come between true loves."

Steven bent over to kiss my forehead and said, "We will always be friends, and if you ever need me, remember I am here. Thank you."

I hugged him and got out the car. "Thanks for being my friend and thanks for the ride home," I said. "You take care."

Chapter 25

I walked away from Steven feeling nothing. I thought to myself, *now I am back with no one.*

However, I did have someone in mind. This may have worked out for the best.

I went into the house. Dad was sitting in the chair. I sat next to him and told him Steven and I had just ended whatever it was we had between us. "We're just friends," I told him.

Dad said he was sure there was some lucky fellow out there waiting. I hugged him and told him how much I loved him.

Steven's girlfriend, April, started coming to school. It was odd to see them together, but there was no hurt. Everyone would be happy. My friends were upset, but I told them it was okay; everything would be just fine. They got over it.

Soon, things were back to normal, and I spent some time hanging out with my friends. I had my job after school to keep me busy. Working and helping all the patients who needed my help felt good. After I'd clocked out, I would often go around the hospital helping anyone I could.

One Friday at school during lunch, I was under my tree reading a book when someone asked, "Could I join you?"

Without looking up, I knew it was Teddy. I looked up, smiled, and asked, "What took you so long?"

Teddy sat there with me. He took my hand and asked me, "Would you give me the pleasure of having one more chance? I accept you as you are. I know that I love you more than anything and never want to spend another day without you."

I looked into Teddy's eyes and told him, "Even though you were not here with me, you were always here with me. You stayed in my heart. I loved you."

He took me into his arms and kissed me, just as my friends walked up. They all clapped for us. Teddy and I were back together. Life was happy again. After a while, you couldn't tell that we'd ever split up. We stayed close together.

We talked all the time. We asked each other questions about the time we'd spent with our other friends. He asked me how far I'd gone with Steven. I knew what he was referring to but acted, as I didn't.

He asked, "Did you do what we had planned to do together on our special day?"

I looked at Teddy and smiled. "No," I said. "I have not had sex yet."

He smiled, hugged me, and said, "Thanks. And I am the same as you left me."

We looked at each other and laughed. Teddy walked me to my locker and then to class. He thanked me again for giving him another chance and told me how much he loved me. Before turning and walking off, he kissed me there in front of the class as though he was never going to stop. For once, I was happy to be back with the one I truly loved.

That night when I went to bed, I had a strange dream. I dreamed I was in the park again in the woods were the old woman and I had stayed. I saw myself walking in the park, looking as though I were looking for something. I woke up feeling strange.

That Saturday morning, I decided to go to the park. I hadn't been there for years. I got dressed, caught the bus to the park, and walked slowly to the park's perimeter. As I entered the park, it was as if I was seeing my whole life in front of me as it had happened when I was there. I remembered it all. I walked into the woods where we'd stayed and found the bridge we'd put our tent under. The woods had grown up, and the trees were thicker now. Some of the things the old woman had left behind were still there. I looked over all the things as they lay in place, covered with dirt and grass but still as she had left them. I could feel nothing but love for her as I looked at everything.

I walked on and saw what used to be the tent. It lay on the ground, now under some broken branches. I found the toilet seat where our bathroom had been. I smiled, and tears begin to fall down my cheeks. This was where it had all started when I'd woken up that night. So much love was in my heart for this place that was nothing but meant the world to me. This place was full of loving memories of me and the old woman who had taken care of me the best she could and shown me so much love.

I went back to the bridge and sat down in the same spot where the old woman and I had sat and eaten together so many times. I thought of the night I'd woken up scared and how the old woman had taken me in her arms and held me, humming that beautiful tune until I fell back to sleep.

I lay back on the bare ground and cried. All of a sudden, I heard this loud, roaring, like a train coming. It grew louder and louder. I stood, trying to see where the noise was coming from. But I couldn't see anything. The noise grew louder and louder. I covered my ears. Then back among the trees, I saw a light. It was daytime, but I could see this ball of light coming from the deeper part of the woods. I watched it as it came closer and closer, my hands still over my ears. The light was so bright it was hurting my eyes. I closed them.

When I opened my eyes again, there in front of me, I saw this giant ball of light turning around and around and growing larger and larger. The noise was still there, but it was calmer. My vision started focus. I could see something on the other side of the ball of light. It looked like a different place was back there. But I knew all that was behind the ball was the woods. I had stayed here. I knew these woods well, and I knew that what I was looking at was a different place.

I walked up to the ball of light and watched it as it turned. I was looking at a different place inside it. I put my hand out to touch it, and my hand went through it. I wanted so much to go through just to see the other side. I didn't try though. I was too scared.

I just stood there, and as I watched, the opening started to grow smaller. I noticed something moving. I squinted and saw a person standing in the distance on the other side. She came closer and closer. I could see the person up close now, but she was still standing on the other side of the ball of light. It was a woman.

The opening on the ball of light now looked like a big door. The woman stepped through. I couldn't move. As soon as she was through the door, it snapped shut, and the ball backed away and faded off into the distance, moving deeper and deeper into the woods. The light was bright again as it left. I closed my eyes, and when I opened them again, I couldn't see clearly.

The woman stood there looking at me. My vision was starting to come back into focus. I watched the woman walk toward me, and I could see her better now. As I studied her, I realized it was the woman in all my dreams. This was my mother.

At that very moment, I saw my childhood before me, and I could remember it all. My dad—I remembered him and all the fun times we had. I was his sunshine. I remember my family from my own memories, not just from someone telling me who they were. My mother—I remembered how she looked and talked. But most of all, I remembered how she loved me.

I ran to her, and she ran to me. We both stood there in each other's arms, crying and holding each other tightly. "I am home, baby, I am home," my mother whispered in my ear.

We walked through the park, and I took Mom on a tour of Isabella's and my former home. I couldn't hold back the tears, as I looked around at all the special memories of this place. All that had happened here meant the world to me. I showed her the little tent we'd sleep in and the bathroom I'd used plenty of times. I showed her where and how we'd gotten our drinking water. I took Mother to the bridge where Isabella and I had sat so many days and nights.

Mother and I sat in the same spot, holding each other and crying. I told her all about Isabella and how she'd taken such good care of me. Mother said she wanted to meet her to thank her. Mother told me this was the same place the door had opened and taken her away. "Here we are together again," she said. The door had opened, bringing her back to the exact same spot.

We both stood and walked out of the park together. I turned and let the tears flow, looking back at the place I'd once called home. This would always be Isabella's and my home away from home.

When we got to our street, Mom stopped. She looked at the house and cried. We walked to our house, and I opened the door. Dad was sitting in the living room watching TV. Mom and I walked in.

Dad looked up at us, and he looked like he was seeing a ghost. He stood but did not move. Mom ran to him, crying. Dad still couldn't say a word, but the tears told me he was happy. I ran and joined them. We all embraced and shed more tears.

Dad finally spoke. "My family," he said.

I knew then who I was. I knew that, no matter what I was, I was a person who cared, a person who took time out to stop and listen, to talk to and help anyone in any way I could. No matter what world I was part of, I was Nyah, and I was here for a reason—even if it was only to help.

A day would come for all of us when we would need someone's help. You never know. That stranger stopping to lend you a hand, sharing a friendly conversation with you, or even just a hand shack may be more than just a stranger passing by.

To all readers,

I hope you've enjoyed reading *Who Am I?* As much as I have enjoyed writing it. I hope that you will follow along on the next adventure with me in my next book, *Lost Love*.

Happy reading to all, Thanks Denita Christful